TIME OUT!

KEVIN CREAGER

Black Rose Writing | Texas

ISBN: 978-1-68433-774-3
PUBLISHED BY BLACK ROSE WRITING
www.blackrosewriting.com

Printed in the United States of America
Suggested Retail Price (SRP) $19.95

Time Out is printed in Sabon

*As a planet-friendly publisher, Black Rose Writing does its best to eliminate unnecessary waste to reduce paper usage and energy costs, while never compromising the reading experience. As a result, the final word count vs. page count may not meet common expectations.

Dedicated to my wife, Sue, and my grandchildren, Colette, Emily, Alanna, and Riley, so that they have something of their grandfather's to show their children.

Special acknowledgements to the Springfield Writers' Club, Carl Ahlm, Ruth George, Jim Arter, Nancy Flinchbaugh for their assistance in reviewing and critiquing this book. Special thanks to Canfield High School, the University of Cincinnati, and Miami University for providing the memories to drive this story.

TIME OUT!

CHAPTER 1

Wally Stephens stood for a moment in front of Ye Olde Bookshelf bookstore and found himself sighing. Which surprised him a bit. Then he realized that very little surprised him and that realization made him sigh again. It was, apparently, a morning of surprising revelations and deep sighs.

Though he enjoyed his job as manager of the bookstore, it hit him that he was only twenty-seven years old and already feeling like he was in a rut. He had no life outside of the bookstore -- well, very little -- and nothing he could call exciting. He needed something different to happen, but he also needed this job, so he sighed once more, no surprise this time, and opened the door.

He glanced down at Ye Olde Bookshelf mailbox, otherwise known as ye olde basket under ye olde mail slot next to ye olde front door. Wally almost remembered when he used to get excited about getting mail. Physical paper mail, rare as that concept may be to many people now. Mail that you could pick up, and hold in your hands, and take with you into another room. Set somewhere so you could look at it anytime without having to log on to a separate device, and enter passwords, and scroll through unwanted messages that you should probably have deleted or answered long ago. That was the problem with email. You could ignore it and ignore it, ... and ignore it, even stuff you wanted to read, but just not right now. Just scroll right past it, until later, when you had more time, which you never really did. But paper mail, in an envelope, almost demanded that you do something with it right now, either open it or throw it away. It's in your hand, in front of your eyes, saying, "I'm still going to be here. You can't just open another program or go do something else. It's easier to open me than to find a drawer, pull it open, put me in it, and close that drawer back up. I'm not going to be out-of-sight, out-of-mind. Open me. Now."

And besides, it had a stamp, proving that somebody cared enough about you to pay for sending you a message.

Yeah, mail used to be exciting. Back when people took time to write complete letters, and send cards, and the mail was at least personally significant to you. But not much of that kind of writing anymore. Just some kind of quick inane note online to tell you about what was happening during that brief inane moment, to be immediately forgotten by the next more or less inane moment. Wally had very little appreciation for texting.

This morning's mail, though, proved to be different. Among the ads and the requests for money (the Retired Bookbinders' Association?), he found two envelopes specifically addressed to him. Setting aside the obviously business or junk mail, he first picked the one with a personal return address. Maria Sharper sounded familiar.

"*Hi, Wally,*" Pretty casual beginning, he thought.

"*This is Maria Sharper from your high school class.*" Oh yeah, perky cheerleader type, though he wasn't sure if she had actually been a cheerleader or not. But definitely perky. Not really his crowd in high school. As if he had a crowd. "*I'm now Maria Carpenter, but I didn't think you might know me by my married name.*" No, he didn't think he'd been invited to that wedding. "*Believe it or not, it's time for our tenth-year high school reunion. Yea!!!*"

Yea.

The letter went on to give a date and time. And asked for him to RSVP ASAP with his plus 1.

A plus 1. It had been a while since there had been a plus 1. He briefly wondered if his girlfriend from high school, Sheila McClain, was going, and if she was going by herself. Wally shook his head. It didn't really matter because renewing that relationship was not a good idea. It was a terrible idea. And she would have emphatically agreed to that notion.

Oh well, he thought to himself and put the invitation aside. The girl that always came to mind from high school, the prettiest girl in class, the most popular girl in class, the one he never dared approach or dream of talking to, was Cindy Connor. She still outshone anybody else he could think of asking. Wally sighed, once more if he was still counting. If she was at the reunion, he wouldn't pay attention to his plus 1 anyway. Maybe he just wouldn't go and would merely dream of what life would be like if he had only known then in high school what he knew now. He'd have been so much more polished and sophisticated and confident and ... whatever else he hadn't been then. Much more of something so that he could have at least spoken out loud to Cindy, something that wasn't a mumble.

The other envelope came from a Dr. Vernon Sheffield in the Alphabet Building, downtown Oldsfield. Not too far away, but he wasn't familiar with that building. Possibly named after Jebediah Alphabet or something, probably one of the original businessmen of Oldsfield. They had strange names then.

"*Mr. Stephens*,". Okay, a little bit more formal, but it didn't seem like a form letter.

"*Have you ever wished that you knew then what you know now?*"

He stopped reading and glanced back at the first envelope.

Cindy.

CHAPTER 2

Wally Stephens pulled out the letter one last time to check the address and to review the heading. *Have you ever wished that you knew then what you know now? Time travel could be the answer. What have you got to lose? You've already been there.*

He rolled his eyes at the ridiculous concept of time travel, but it certainly was an intriguing possibility. No, real time travel wasn't possible, but what did this mysterious Dr. Sheffield mean by that reference? A mental regression, maybe through hypnosis? Go back into your memories, but live them differently? Why not, he thought. Why the hell not? There certainly are some things I wished I had done differently. I'm not going anywhere the way life is now. I know time travel can't really happen, but … what if? What if I really did know then what I know now?

Wally straightened his shoulders and marched up the walk to the front of the Alphabet Building, took a deep breath, smiled confidently, opened the door, and stepped inside.

The smile disappeared as soon as the door clicked shut behind him.

He stopped and glanced back at the closed exit. "What am I getting myself into?" he mumbled audibly.

He was startled when his words echoed back from the dark halls of the lobby. It was almost seven o'clock in the evening and the ground floor of the building appeared to be empty. Only a few dim lights were on and there was no one in sight.

"Hello?" he called out tentatively.

"*Hello-lo-lo-lo…*" His voice carried back to him, resounding off the walls lost in shadow.

"Is someone there? –meone there? –meone there?…"

"*Someone's here –meone's here –meone's here…*"

"Where are you? –are you? –are you?…"

"*Right here –here –here…*"

"Shit –it –it –it …"

"Tsk, tsk, tsk."

Wally whirled around to find a shorter, balding man with a slight moustache standing just behind him.

The man pushed a small button on the wall and the echoes stopped. "You shouldn't use words like that. Someone might hear you."

Wally looked at the man, then at the button, then at the man again. "Are you Dr. Sheffield?"

"Yes, I am," Sheffield extended his hand to shake Wally's. "Vernon Sheffield. And you are Wally Stephens. I apologize for the noise." He gestured down the hall. "We were experimenting with the resonating field earlier and I couldn't resist the opportunity to play just one more game."

As Wally looked back down the hall, Sheffield must have touched the button again.

"Boo –*boo –boo –boo* …"

Wally jumped. Sheffield laughed, then turned the field off once more.

"Come on. My office is right over here. Walk this way."

Sheffield, crouching, took a few waddling steps, with his feet pointing out to the side. Wally stayed standing in the same place, staring at him. The doctor straightened up as far as he could go, still well short of Wally's average height, and sighed audibly, muttering, "No sense of humor. Why did it have to be him?"

Once Sheffield began walking normally, Wally shook himself, and decided that, despite the doctor's odd behaviors, he was already pretty much committed to listening to whatever Sheffield had to say. He followed the doctor down the hall passing through an open door. They continued through a rather nondescript typical office area with a couple of chairs and a desk, but nothing appearing to be personal, to a door in the back wall. Sheffield opened it and they entered another room. This was a fairly large room, as large rooms go, full of impressive looking machinery, with computer screens and wires and dials and knobs and switches and noises and …whatever else is needed to make a large room look impressive. In the middle of the room sat a single wooden chair, not impressive at all, actually appearing rather uncomfortable. A young dark-haired woman wearing glasses stood off to one side waiting for them. She smiled and nodded to Sheffield.

Sheffield walked over to one of the machines and gave it a kick. It started making even more whirring and clicking sounds.

"There. That's better."

He turned back to Wally. "Now, Wally -- may I call you Wally? Good, I'll call you Wally. If I call you Mr. Stephens, I'll get confused over who's running this show." He ran a hand through his nonexistent hair. "Now, Wally, you're here because you received a letter asking if you had an interest in time travel. Traveling in time, theoretically speaking, of course. And that we were looking for some volunteer assistance with our research. Is that right?"

"Y-yes, that's what the letter said." Wally looked over at the young woman, trying to telepathically ask if Dr. Sheffield knew what he was talking about. She smiled back. It was a pretty smile, but it didn't tell him anything. "I, uh, thought it was an interesting topic. And, to tell you the truth, I'm at a point in my life where I could use doing something different. I go to work, which I like – I manage a small bookstore, but then I come back to my smaller apartment and I have nothing else going on. And I mean nothing. I don't know what help you need, but, what the hell, it's got to be better than doing nothing."

"And that's where we come in." He spread his arms. "Take a seat, any seat."

After glancing around, and discovering it was the only place to sit, Wally sat down on the wooden chair.

Sheffield picked up three small rubber balls from a table and began juggling. Wally looked at the woman again. She laughed. It was a pretty laugh, but it still didn't tell him anything.

"Look over here please," Sheffield interrupted. "I can't do this forever."

Wally frowned, hoping this was going somewhere. Maybe he should have guessed from the topic that this whole idea was ludicrous, that time travel existed only in science fiction. But he had been hoping, wildly hoping that there was just the slightest possibility that he could finally …

"Now, some people have theorized that time is circular." Sheffield began juggling the balls in a circle. "And that there is no way to go from one point on the circle to another without following the prescribed pattern. However, if we could somehow learn to take shortcuts, jump from one point on the circle across to another…"

He tried to change the pattern of his juggling, but dropped one of the balls. He bent down to pick it up and dropped another one. This ball rolled under one of the machines. Sheffield put the remaining two on the floor and lay flat, attempting to reach the missing one. He shifted and accidentally kicked the others. They rolled under another machine.

The young woman covered her mouth, trying in vain to suppress a louder laugh, and looked the other way.

Wally knelt on the floor to help the doctor and received a kick in the knee for his troubles.

"Ow," Wally stood back up, rubbing his knee painfully. "Dr. Sheffield, I think I get the picture."

Sheffield, having finally reached the ball, withdrew his arm and looked up. "You do? Really? That's funny. The board of directors had no idea what I was talking about. And I'd gotten even further into my speech before I dropped any." He looked at the ball in his hand. "Well, I don't need this anymore," and rolled it back under the machine.

He stood up and dusted off his knees. "Sit down. Sit down again, please. Well, what do you think of the idea? Does it make any sense to you?"

Wally shrugged. "I don't know." He really had no idea what sort of shape to ascribe to time, if any. He knew it was considered a dimension, but didn't think that meant it had to have a shape.

To Wally's surprise, Sheffield laughed. "Good for you. Neither does anyone else, including me. I have no idea if time is circular, or if you can jump from one point to another, or if it's a square or a triangle or simply a straight line going on forever." He demonstrated the shapes with his hands as he spoke. "But it's the only thing I can think of." He picked up a pencil that Wally realized had never been sharpened and started twirling it with his fingers. "All we really know is that we have a machine that will take you through time and that you are the one that has to do it, and you have to do it now."

"What? What do you mean, I'm the one that has to do it?"

"Because you already did."

"Wait a minute, I've never done anything – I didn't go anywhere." Wally raised his hands in surprise. This was news to him.

Sheffield sat down on one of the machines, his rear end accidentally pushing several buttons, flicking a couple of switches. The machine coughed and began vibrating.

"We already know that on this date, you go back in time. You become a part of history. You're there."

Wally looked around the room. "Where?"

"Well, this is where it gets a little complicated. I know where you're going, but apparently you have to make the decision now where to go. Because that's what you did then, er, are going to do, uh … oh, forget it. Where do you want to go?"

"This is where it gets complicated?" Wally shook his head. "You mean, I go back in time, and where I went in history is something I decide right now?"

"Right," Sheffield nodded. "Well?"

Wally looked for the young lady for help, but found she had left the room. He wasn't sure if that told him anything or not.

"Um … how about the signing of the Declaration of Independence? That would be worth going back for."

"No."

"No?"

"You didn't go there. Not that I know of anyway. Try something more personal."

"How about … when my parents met?"

Sheffield stood up. The machine stopped vibrating, but a dial began spinning wildly.

"That's what they do in all the books and movies. Think, man, think. Somewhere else. Or is it some*when* else?"

"Why don't you just tell me? You obviously know, so why don't we just skip all this guessing?" Wally was beginning to let his frustration with the vagueness of Sheffield's responses slip through. He stood up, wanting to leave, but still holding out a smidgin of hope that there was something to this whole idea.

"Because I can't. You see, you also have to have an idea of why you're going there and what you hope to accomplish – and that has to come from you." Sheffield waved him to sit back down.

"Look, you were interested enough in the idea of time travel to come here. Surely you must have thought of something you'd want to do if you could travel through time. Everyone has. What is your secret?"

"Well," Wally glanced at the closed door through which the young lady had apparently disappeared. "There is something ... but it's silly."

"Tell me."

Wally leaned back in his chair and pretended to inspect his fingernails.

"It's ... it's really silly. But ... my high school reunion is coming up next week. I had a crush on a girl in my high school, Cindy Connor, but I was too shy to do anything about it. We did work on one project together in biology and she was always nice to me. I've never had the same feelings about anybody else and I've found out that she's still single. I've often thought since then that if I'd been more mature and that if I knew then what I know now ..."

"You want to go back and seduce a high school girl?" Sheffield interrupted. "You could get arrested for that. And I'm not too sure where I would stand as an accessory, either morally or legally."

"No, no. I was thinking more along the lines of when she was a college senior. I would have to use a different name, because it wouldn't make sense to her for the same person that she knew in high school to be so much older. I guess my fantasy is that she would fall in love with me then, and now, when I show up at the reunion after having disappeared for so many years, she would fall in love with me again. I told you it was silly."

"You have thought this out, haven't you? Where did she go to college?"

"Bradford State."

"You're right, it's silly … but that's it."

Wally's mouth fell open, or gaped open, or something. "You mean that's where I actually go, er, went?" He really hadn't thought that was going to be the answer. It couldn't be.

"Yep."

Wally gestured around the room. "Do you mean to tell me that this is one of the major scientific achievements of all time and you're going to use it to send me somewhere because of a crush? For some romance and maybe, er, sex?"

"Well, the romance and, er, sex is up to you. But you're going to Bradford State, about six years ago. So that would seem to be what you're wanting to go there for."

"Wait a minute," Wally stood up again and walked over to one of the still whining and clicking machines. "I still haven't said I would go. I mean, I don't know anything about how this works, or how safe it is." He punched a button, expecting Sheffield to stop him. Sheffield didn't move. A blue light on the control panel started flashing. He pulled a knob. A candy bar slid out of a slot.

"What the …?"

"That's if you get hungry," Sheffield picked it up. "You want it? It's got nuts."

Wally shook his head. Sheffield shrugged and unwrapped it. He took a bite.

"We know it works and that you'll be alright. As I said before, you were there. If it didn't work, you wouldn't have been there. That's what resolves the so-called time paradox. If you were already there then you can't change anything by going back, you see what I mean?"

"Has anyone else ever gone back, or to the future?"

Sheffield shrugged again. He was getting quite good at it. "I don't know. You're the only one I know about."

"No one has ever done this before?"

"Yes, you did. Say, this is a good candy bar. Sure you don't want a bite?"

Wally shook his head. Again. "I haven't done this before. Or at least I haven't done it yet…"

"You will."

"This is getting quite confusing. I don't even know what term to use anymore." Wally sat down again and gestured to the humming, blinking, clicking machines.

"This is all crazy. Tell me a little about these. What do these machines actually do? If I'm supposed to do this, I better know what is going to happen to me physically." He shifted uncomfortably in his seat, as if he could feel the electricity running through his body. "What are all the buttons for?"

"Good question."

When Sheffield didn't continue, Wally prompted him, "Well?"

"Oh." Sheffield started. "You want me to tell you." He pointed to the candy bar machine. "You've already seen the candy bar machine. This one turns on a green light and goes 'whirr'. This one turns on a blue light and goes 'whizz'. The one behind you is for playing video games. This one…" He pushed a purple button.

"Wait a minute, wait a minute. I mean, how do they make you travel in time?"

Sheffield pushed the button again to turn off the cartoon that had just come on one screen. "Oh, they've got nothing to do with your time travel. They just give me something to do during the day. And they looked good to the board of directors."

"They've got nothing to do with my time travel?"

"No. I could have sworn I just said that."

"Then where's the time machine?"

"You're sitting on it."

Wally jumped up and looked at the chair. "That? But that's just a chair. A hard chair at that."

"I assume comfort must come with a later design. Look underneath."

Wally got down on his knees and peered beneath the seat.

"See that small box attached to the bottom of the seat? Don't touch it! It's already set for the right time, so please don't mess with it."

"That's all there is to it?" Wally stood up and dusted off his knees again. He briefly wondered when someone had last swept. "How does it work?"

"I haven't the foggiest. I didn't invent time travel, I'm just the one that has the means to do it."

"You haven't the foggiest?"

"Did I not turn off the resonating machine? You seem to be having trouble understanding what I'm saying."

Wally ignored that. "You don't know how this works. But I am going to sit on this chair and I am going to go back in time."

"See how simple it is?" Sheffield pushed him gently back into the chair. "And they said you were as dumb as a doorknob."

"Wha-...?"

"Now, relax. In just a few moments you will be going back six years to Bradford, old BSU. But first we're going to give you something to take with you."

As if on cue (it probably was), the young woman reentered the room, carrying a large suitcase and a briefcase. She set them down, glanced briefly at Wally, smiled what was apparently intended to be a confidence-building smile, then backed up. Wally had given up trying to figure out whether it really meant anything or not.

"The suitcase." Sheffield snapped his fingers to regain Wally's attention. "The suitcase, Mr. Stephens, contains several changes of clothing that are appropriate for being a poor graduate student, and a lot of money, in bills dated from before that year. May I have your wallet, please?"

Wally took it out and handed it to him. It didn't occur to him until too late that most people don't willingly hand their wallets over to someone they just met.

"Oh, and your watch. They didn't have these communication watches six years ago. They have existed for only the last two years. It would be a dead giveaway."

Wally took it off and, a little more reluctantly, gave it to Sheffield.

"Thank you. Now, in the briefcase, you will find another wallet. Money and new identification are in it. Actually, old identification, but new to you, I think. You will be Andrew Wright, a graduate student in psychology."

"But I don't know anything about psychology."

"That's no problem. Neither does anyone else really. That's what one of my degrees is in, just so you know. You can say anything you want to and no one will know the difference. It seems to have worked for years for quite a few psychologists."

Wally himself shrugged this time. Making sense of it all was beyond him at this point.

Sheffield pulled a slim slightly older looking laptop computer out of the briefcase.

"This is the most important item you will have with you. Turn it on and read it as soon as you get there. Follow the instructions completely. You can not deviate at all."

"Can't I look at it now?" Wally put out his hand. "I need to know something about what I'm getting into. Anything."

"No." It went back in the case. "Absolutely not. The laptop itself is from that time period, but it has a special more up-to-date program installed on it, called MyFate. One that will sometimes keep you up on what you need to be doing and when. It has to be done at the right time and in the right order. And no one else can see it. Well, almost no one. You'll find out what I mean later."

"How do I get back? Is there a reverse switch? Can I do something if I need to return immediately? What if I can't get back and I'm stuck there?" His voice rose a few octaves as that reality occurred to him.

Sheffield grimaced and spread his hands. "Hopefully there's instructions on that. Just don't miss the opportunity when it comes up. Now, are you ready?"

"No!"

"Good. Here, hold these."

Sheffield set the cases on Wally's lap. With his hands occupied, Wally could not stop the doctor from reaching under his chair and apparently pushing a button or flicking a switch or something ....

CHAPTER 3

One moment the doctor was there. The next, he was not. There was no blurring of the senses, no whirling sound, no black, incomprehensible vortex. It was simply one instant there, the next somewhere else.

Wally set the cases carefully down on the floor. He was in what appeared to be the larger room of a small two-room (three, probably counting the bathroom) apartment. Sunlight was coming in the window, so he decided it was day. His mind seemed to be working very slowly at the moment.

He stood up. He sat down. He stood up. He sat down again. He didn't feel different but nothing seemed to be processing.

It took more time than it probably should have for Wally to recall that he was supposed to do something immediately. It was now too late to do it immediately, but at least as soon as possible.

Pulling the laptop out of the briefcase, he pushed the button to turn it on. The screen instantly came up with a message.

Get out of this building. Now. Right away. Leave. Do not go to another screen or touch anything else. Read the next message when you are outside. GO.

Wally started to close it when a notice in bolder black print at the bottom of the page caught his eye.

Wait a minute.

Push the chair over into a corner — you can't carry it, that would look odd -- and take the two cases with you. Now go. Hurry.

Wally couldn't find a corner (they were all filled with something) but he pushed the chair against a wall. Grabbing the cases, he walked quickly to a door and opened it, finding the bathroom. The next door he tried led to a small landing at the head of a staircase overlooking a hallway. Except for the muted sounds of traffic from outside, he did not hear anything.

He started down the stairs, as quietly as he could. The first step creaked. The second step moaned. The third step creaked and moaned.

"Oh, hell," he muttered and ran down the rest of the stairs. None of the other steps made any noise.

As Wally reached for the front doorknob, he heard footsteps coming up the walk on the other side of the door. He looked to the right. A closed door. He looked to the left. Another closed door. But also a row of mailboxes built into the wall. He turned left just as the door opened, set the cases down, and pretended to be trying to get into one of the mailboxes. Sweating profusely, Wally prayed that he hadn't picked this person's mailbox.

Footsteps. A door opened, more footsteps. A door closed.

Slowly, Wally turned around. Breathing a sigh of relief, he reached again for the front door. Again, it started to open from the other side.

Facing the mailboxes once more, he felt the sting of the sweat return.

Footsteps. This time they ran up the stairs. Another door opened and closed.

Not even glancing up the stairs, Wally picked up the cases, pulled open the front door, tripped on a step, caught himself with a railing, and hurried down the front walk. He turned right at the sidewalk and passed a number of (who was really counting?) buildings before he stopped and leaned against a tree to try to control his shaking.

He realized he was facing a college campus. It appeared to be Bradford State.

CHAPTER 4

Wally had visited Bradford State once, when he had been considering graduate school. His first thought was it hadn't changed.

His second thought was, of course it hasn't changed, you fool. I've gone back in time.

His third thought was, good God, I've gone back in time.

He looked back along the sidewalk, half expecting to see someone, anyone, come running after him. Why he half expected that he didn't know, but he did. Almost to his surprise, there was no one there.

Crossing the street, he walked onto the campus, searching for a bench or at least a grassy spot to sit down. Students were passing, but no one paid him any attention. He thought back to his own undergraduate days and could only remember young women in the spring. College students hurrying across a campus were apparently as self-involved as anyone else in a big city.

The suitcase was beginning to get heavy (it certainly was full of something) and he wanted to look at the laptop again. It was also starting to get chilly now that he had stopped sweating as much. He hadn't been dressed for cold weather and, with leaves on the trees starting to edge with red and yellow instead of all bright green, he guessed it was fall.

After about five minutes of wandering, Wally managed to find an empty bench. Opening the suitcase, he pulled out a sweatshirt with the words, "Property of Western Oshawa University" across the front. He moaned. It was his alma mater, but it was also Bradford State's bitterest rival.

But he was cold and the sweatshirt was warm and the whole situation was crazy. After pulling it on, he took the laptop out of the smaller briefcase and opened it up.

You almost didn't make it out, did you?

Wally nearly dropped it, but caught it in time.

Well, now, you get to go back. Forgot that you left the chair there? You need an apartment and that one's available. If you get back there now, before somebody else rents it. Only this time you can knock at the door.

Once you get back to the apartment, you can read the next message at your leisure. If you don't get that apartment, you may lose that chair, and if you lose the chair, you may never get back to your own time.

I hope you remember your way back to that house. You really didn't have to go this far. You could have just stopped at the sidewalk.

Now that it was important to return to the house, Wally wasn't sure if he could find his way back. He'd been so anxious to leave (as he had been instructed, he thought with a brief touch of irritation) that he hadn't paid much attention to what the building looked like and he had gone as far away as he could.

It took him twenty minutes to retrace his steps to where he thought he had leaned against the tree. He'd considered asking someone for directions, but didn't know what he'd say. "Excuse me, could you please tell me how to get to a building that has an apartment for rent? And this is a very particular apartment because it has a time traveling chair."

He walked slowly back along the street, trying to recall anything about the house. He had tripped coming out of the building, so there must have been steps, and he had grabbed at something to right himself, so there must have been a railing. But that was about it.

The seventh house had the steps and railing, and looked vaguely familiar. Vaguely was going to have to be good enough at this point.

The door was opened by a young, pretty, dark-haired student. (He assumed she was a student. In his memory, all female college students were young and pretty). There was a sense of having somehow met her before, but he couldn't place it.

"May I help you?" She sounded sincere. She sounded so sincere that, for an instant, Wally wished he had several reasons to need help.

"Um, yes. Do you happen to know if there's an apartment for rent here?"

She laughed. "Good try. Not necessarily the most original line, but not a bad try."

"I beg your pardon?" Wally was trying to remember if that phrase had meant something more six years ago when he was in college.

"Look, whoever you are, do those letters over the door mean anything to you?" She pointed to a sign over the doorframe.

He backed up to get a better look at it.

"I'm afraid not." He tried a smile. "It's all Greek to me."

She laughed again and flashed an even more sincere smile. "Look, I don't know if you're for real or not. But if you are looking for a place to stay, try next door." She pointed to the next building down. "This is a sorority. You do know what a sorority is, don't you?"

"Yes, yes, I know." Wally stammered in embarrassment. "I'm sorry. I just…I just, …uh, thank you. I'll go next door."

He backed away, turned, and tripped on these steps, grabbing this railing to steady himself. (Yes, now that he had tried the 'trip' method, it was a different house).

When he got to the sidewalk, he looked back because she had been nice to him, despite his awkwardness. She was still standing in the doorway, watching him. She waved and yelled, "Y'all come back now, y'hear?"

For some reason a television theme song from the 1960's began running through his mind.

At the next house, Wally searched diligently all around the doorway and stoop for any letters or signs. He was rewarded by a small notice stuck in one of the door's windowpanes.

Apartment for Rent, Maybe

Just to make sure, he turned and tripped himself going down the step. However, he missed the railing and fell flat on his face. As he was still lying there, the door opened.

"Hello."

He looked up to see a short, older, gray-haired woman standing there, wiping her hands on her apron.

"May I help you? Or have you found what you're looking for down there?"

Wally stood up and dusted himself off (he'd been doing a fair amount of that lately). She came down to help him.

"I, er, was just checking to see if this was, um, the right, er, place." He hesitantly said.

"Well, I certainly hope it isn't a wrong place."

"No, that isn't, um ...." Wally tried to peer past her through the doorway. "Look, I know this sounds strange, but could I please look inside your doorway, for just a second?"

"Certainly. If that's what you need to do." She raised her eyebrows, but helped him up the steps then dusted off his bottom (he really didn't think it had been that much in need of cleaning).

He stuck his head in the door. There were the mailboxes. He pulled his head back out.

"Exactly six seconds." Wally was surprised to see her holding a stopwatch. He started to smile, then realized she wasn't joking, then realized she was still smiling, then realized he didn't know what to do. His mind still seemed overwhelmed.

"I'm sorry."

"It's nice to meet you, Mr. Sorry. I'm Mrs. Weidenbach." She extended her hand, which Wally shook timidly. "Did you find what you wanted in there?"

"No ..."

"No?"

"No, I'm sorry. I'm not Sorry." Wally was apologetic, but was losing track of the conversation.

"No, you're sorry and you're not sorry?"

"No, no, no. My name is not Sorry."

"Well, I'm glad to hear that you don't have a sorry name. What is it?"

"What is it?" For the life of him, Wally could not think of the name he was supposed to be using. He searched his mind desperately, both for the name and for some way to change the subject. "Um, do you have an apartment for rent?"

"Yes, as a matter of fact, I do." Mrs. Weidenbach just stood there and continued to smile.

"Uh, could I have it?"

"Well, you'd have to pay for it. I'm afraid I'm not just giving them away."

Wally paused for a moment, not sure how to take that comment, but knew he needed to get that apartment. "Yes, yes, I understand. I mean I want to rent it."

"Would you like to see it first? Most people do."

Wally started to say he'd already seen it, but stopped and a sudden vision of there being more than one apartment available flashed through his brain.

"Yes, that's a good idea. I'm sorry."

"I thought you said you weren't?"

"Please, show me the apartment." Wally was beginning to perspire again even though it wasn't really that warm in the hallway. The theme from another television show from long ago started playing somewhere, probably only in his head. He recognized this one as The Twilight Zone.

Halfway up the stairs, Wally blurted out, "Wright."

"Well, it's to the left, actually."

"No, I'm sor-. My name is Wright. Andrew Wright."

Mrs. Weidenbach stopped.

"Are you sure you're right this time?"

"Yes, I'm Wright."

"You're not wrong?"

"To the left, did you say?" Wally started up the stairs again and silently cursed Dr. Sheffield for giving him that name, as well as for a host of other things.

Mrs. Weidenbach opened the door and, for a moment, Wally panicked. He could not see the chair. Then she pushed the door all the way open and he sighed in relief. It had been hidden from view on the other side of the door.

He set his cases down in front of the chair hoping to sort of block her from taking a good look at it and realizing it didn't belong.

"It looks fine. I'll take it."

"I haven't shown you the bedroom or the bathroom yet."

"That's okay. This looks fine. I'm sure the rest is fine. Everything's fine."

"That's nice."

"Um, do you have a contract for me to sign? We might as well do that now. I'd like to move in right away if that's okay."

"Certainly. Let's go back downstairs to my rooms and we'll take care of that."

On their way down, Mrs. Weidenbach spoke over her shoulder, "By the way, that silly-looking chair you put your suitcase next to isn't supposed to be in that living room."

Wally stopped suddenly.

She continued from several steps below him.

"I don't know how it got there. It wasn't there this morning."

"What do you mean?" He hurried to catch up (or down, really).

"Well, we'll have to move it. It doesn't belong there."

"It's fine. I like it. Can't I just keep it there?" His heart was beating, his pulse was racing, everything was moving except his thought processes.

"Is that what you really want?"

"Yes, I'm sure."

Well, if that's what you want." She reached the bottom and opened the door to her apartment. "But it really should go in the bedroom."

It didn't occur to Wally until much later that, in that small a space, the living room and the bedroom were really still the same room.

When they had reached the point of signing the contract and handing over the rent money Wally suddenly realized that his new wallet was still upstairs in the briefcase, along with what was supposed to be enough money to pay for this. He excused himself to get it, but when he returned, he was struck by a few changes.

For one thing, Mrs. Weidenbach had removed her apron and unbuttoned the top of her blouse. For another her carefully combed hair had gone awry. And for a third, she was smoking a cigar.

"Mrs. Weidenbach?"

"Yeah," she removed the cigar and spat into a bowl on the table. It didn't sound empty. "What the hell you gaping at?"

"Uh, nothing."

"Good. Keep it that way. You got the money?"

"Yes, right here." He counted it out.

"Cash? I never get paid in cash."

"I'm afraid I haven't had a chance to go to the bank yet." Though he might not have been prepared for anything else that had happened, he had been expecting that question.

"That's okay. You don't have to explain it to me. I don't give a damn where or how you got the money. Just so long as I get paid."

She took the money and stuffed it down the front of her blouse. Wally was glad he didn't have to ask for change.

As he started up the stairs, the front doorbell rang. He heard Mrs. Weidenbach answer and then a man's voice ask if there was a room for rent. He turned to look but, from his vantage point halfway up the steps, all he could see were the legs, and the hiking boots the man was wearing. The landlady told him the room had just been rented and she firmly shut the door on the man's, "But, I …" It was a good thing Wally had hurried back to get the apartment just in time.

Back in the room, Wally was caught between an immediate desire to open the laptop again and an urgent need to go to the bathroom. The urgent need won.

He washed himself, and picked up the computer. He started to sit down in the time-chair, thought better of it, and lay down on the bed. Turning it on, he read,

Well, you should now be in the apartment. If not, you're in deep trouble. If you're in deep trouble, go immediately to Appendix A.

Wally flipped to the link and found Appendix A. It was instructions on how to break into a house. Possibly of practical value, but not right now. He turned back.

If you are in the right apartment, keep reading.

By now, you are probably wondering what kind of site this is. In fact, I know you are wondering that.

This is your diary, sort of. Only it's already been written out for you. By you.

You see, I am you. This journal is a collection of advice, information, directions, whatever you need to survive here. Don't ask me when you wrote this (as if you could ask me about it). I don't know. And, if you think about it too much, your brain will hurt. All I know is that you have to do certain things and behave in certain ways in order to not change the future. And this journal is a day by day, or maybe week by week, listing of those things.

DON'T TRY TO LOOK AHEAD.

That's the number one rule. Events have to occur in the proper sequence. Don't try to change it.

As an example, if you were to look ahead, say, three weeks, and find out that you were going to have sex with the girl of your dreams then (don't count on it), you might just sit back and say, hey, I don't have to worry about it, it's going to happen anyway. But, if you haven't worried about it and didn't work at it, it might not happen. And then the whole fabric of time, and the universe, and everything would collapse and it would all be your fault. Well, probably not the destruction of everything, but, sometimes, things happen simply because you didn't expect them to.

Understand? No? Take my, um, your word for it.

At the bottom of each page, there is a date that tells you when you may read the next page.

Wally glanced down at the bottom. It had today's date. He looked back up.

Yes. You can go to the next page now. Just don't read any further than today's date. Seriously, I mean it. Actually, you can't anyway. These messages are programmed to only appear when you need them.

Wally was tempted to try to peek ahead a few days anyway, but on the off chance that it might say "You get beat up today by six football players who don't like your sweatshirt", he didn't. He scrolled to the next page.

One thing that you should be aware of is that this program does not tell you every little thing that you will do nor will you find an entry for every day. It will inform you of places where you may have to be (such as this apartment), or activities that you may have to do (such as leaving when you first got here) in order to end up where you have to end up (such as on your bed reading this book).

Okay, for the rest of today, you're pretty much on your own. You can put most of your money in a bank (Beggar's National will do, but it's not imperative), buy some groceries, get to know the campus. Whatever. Now, you're not supposed to run into Cindy Connor (be still my heart) yet, so you probably won't accomplish much by trying to look for her. You have to get yourself used to this time and life first.

Tomorrow is another story. You're going to be very busy and you're going to have to do it just right.

Tomorrow morning at 10:00 (get there at 9:30 to be early in line, otherwise the wait is terrible) you will register for the following classes at Burgess Hall:

Advanced Psychological Theory
Introduction to Theoretical Research Applications
Irrelevant Research Practicum I
Practicing Theory and Research

As you have not really enrolled in the university, you need to go to the registrar's office, and the registrar will try to keep you from registering. You will explain that you did enroll and that you did send in a check and you can't help it if their computer fouled up. They will understand (after all this is graduate school, these things happen ... a lot) and will permit you to sign up for the classes with the understanding that you will not receive any grade if they haven't found your payment by the end of the term. That's okay – you will be gone by then anyway (I hope).

At 1:00, you will go to the Psychology Department, 2nd floor at Burgett Hall and interview with Dr. Samuel McElroy to be his graduate assistant. You will get the job. Don't worry. He'll hire anybody that applies. The rest of the Psychology department thinks he's crazy (he sort of is) and won't assign him an assistant. So he has to hire his own. Your advantage is that all the legitimate students know about him and won't work with him either.

You will need this job for two very important reasons. One, you need to earn money (where do you think the money you have now came from?). Later I will tell you what to do with your new money so that you will be able to get the other money before you come back in time. Understand? Never mind, I'll explain it again later.

Second, this will give you the opportunity to meet Cindy. She will be in one of Dr. McElroy's classes.

CHAPTER 5

A few minutes before 1:00, Wally found himself sitting on a chair outside Dr. Samuel McElroy's office waiting for the good doctor to return from lunch ... or breakfast. The secretary, a Mrs. Fochs, hadn't been quite sure when he had left. She hadn't seemed too concerned about it either.

The MyFate had been right about the registering. It had been time consuming and a pain, but he had gotten on the class lists. And he wasn't nearly as upset as the ninety-two other students whose names had really been lost by the computer. (It briefly crossed his mind to wonder if they were all from the future, too, but the resultant scenario caused his brain to ache).

At that moment, the door opened and a man stuck his head out.

"Mrs. Fochs, have you seen my watch?"

The secretary, startled, looked up. "Dr. McElroy, I thought you had left."

"Did you see me come in?"

"No."

"Then why would you think I had left?" He turned to Wally. "Did I ask her something? Or did she ask me something?"

"You wanted to know if she had seen your watch." Wally noticed that Dr. McElroy did not appear to be much older than he himself. His clothes looked like they had been slept in. Come to think of it, the rest of him looked like it had been slept in, too.

"That's right. I last saw it about 9:00." He held up his wrist to look at the watch there. "That was about four hours ago."

"Isn't that your watch?" Wally asked.

"Huh?" Dr. McElroy looked back at his wrist. "Could be. It looks something like it. A little older, maybe." He turned his head towards the secretary, who was pointedly ignoring him. "Well, she still hasn't seen it, has she?" and pulled back into his office.

The door was left open. Wally looked over at Mrs. Fochs, who was looking in his direction again. She shrugged her shoulders and waved for him to follow McElroy in.

The place could have been called a mess, but actually it looked more used. Books and papers were everywhere, but stacked as if they meant something. Space was certainly not being wasted. McElroy was behind his desk, just about to pick up a book.

He looked up and saw Wally standing there. "Who are you?"

"My name is Andrew Wright," Wally remembered it this time, "and I'd…"

"Andrew?" McElroy interrupted. "Do they really call you Andrew?"

"Uh, some of them do." Wally hadn't thought of that, but decided he didn't really want to be that formal. "But I prefer being called Drew." That had just suddenly come to him.

"Drew, huh? Well, they call me Dr. McElroy. Unless it's my wife. Sometimes she'll call me Sam, or Mac, or Elroy … sometimes she'll call me Dr. McElroy, too. But I usually don't want to hear that from her. That always means trouble." He put his book down. "Did you want to see me about something? And sit down, will you? I'm not the head of the department."

Only one chair. Wally bent down to look underneath, but there was no little black box. He had decided that he couldn't be too careful when he was dealing with "doctors". He sat down, but ready to spring back up in an instant.

McElroy raised one eyebrow, but didn't say anything. He looked under his own chair though, too.

"I, uh, understand you're, um, looking for a graduate assistant," Wally started.

"You're kidding. Did someone send you here? This is a joke, right?"

"Uh, no."

"Who told you about this?"

"A ... a friend." He couldn't say "himself". Wally was beginning to wonder if he had made a mistake somewhere. Actually, he had made several mistakes, starting with entering the Alphabet Building.

"You didn't read it on a bathroom wall?"

"On a bathroom wall?" This mistake could be serious.

"Don't think I don't know about the graffiti in the bathrooms. 'Dr. McElroy is looking for some grad ass.' I have to tinkle occasionally. I've seen it. Actually, come to think of it, I've seen it about most of the rest of the staff, too -- sometimes with phone numbers. I wonder if that works for them."

"Do you need a graduate assistant?" Wally interrupted.

"Certainly I do. I've needed one for years. But for some reason, the department won't assign me any. They act like I'd lose one or something. I don't think I would. There are worse things than that anyway. Do you know of someone who'd like to apply?"

"I'd like to apply." Wally thought he had implied that somewhere along the way. But, to be honest, he'd lost track of the conversation a while ago.

"Are you a student?"

"Yes."

"Here?"

"Yes."

"Now?"

"Yes."

"Fine," McElroy reached across the desk to shake his hand. "You're hired."

"Great."

The professor picked up his book and began to read. Wally sat waiting. McElroy looked up. "Yes, what can I do for you?"

"Um, what do I do?"

"Oh." He laid the book down and leaned back. "Good Lord, I've forgotten what graduate assistants are supposed to do. It's been so long." He looked around the room. "I don't suppose you do windows."

"No, I don't think so."

"A shame. I could use another one." He swiveled back. "Do you know anything about parapsychology?"

"Parapsychology? You mean, like ESP and that stuff?"

"ESP, spiritualism, precognition, time travel, anything like that, that most people don't believe exists. But I draw the line at Bigfoot. Looks too much like my wife's cousin."

Wally's ears picked up at the mention of 'time travel'. "I'm afraid not, but I'd like to learn."

"Well, that's one of the classes I teach." The professor tilted his head to one side and squinted at Wally. "One more time, how did you come to be here?"

Wally at first thought he meant how did he come to be at Bradford State and didn't know what to say, but he realized he better make the assumption that McElroy was referring to his office.

"I needed a job and someone said you needed an assistant."

"There you go," McElroy slammed his palm on the table. "Some people would have said that was coincidence, but I think there's more at work here than that. I need an assistant, you need a job, and, wham, it works out. There are forces beyond our ken, you can count on that."

He reached into the drawer beside him and pulled out a small rubber ball.

"Look at this."

He rolled the ball across his desk. To Wally's amazement, it rolled halfway, then stopped and rolled back into McElroy's hand.

"Was that magic? Was it physics? Was it telekinesis – mind over matter? Or was it this almost invisible string that I have attached to the ball? Who knows?" He put the ball back in the drawer and withdrew his hand. The ball came back out, dangling from a finger. He grabbed the ball and yanked, pulling the now almost visible string away from his finger. He dropped it in his drawer and shut it.

"What will you be wanting me to do?" Wally asked, hoping it wasn't going to be tricks like that one.

"I'm doing some research that I could use your help with." McElroy was still picking at his fingertip. "And I'll also need you to help with grading tests and maybe even some class discussions, particularly in my

Beginning Issues of Paramount Unimportance Lab. That class is tomorrow at nine. Can you make it?"

"Yes, I think so." In scheduling, Wally had left his early mornings open to sleep in. So much for that.

"Fine. Give Mrs. Fochs out there a copy of your classes and times and we'll work out a schedule. She'll also go over the paperwork for your job." He opened a drawer and shuffled some papers. "Now, if only I can find my watch."

CHAPTER 6

MyFate

A few tips about visiting the past – in case you hadn't considered them:

1) Personal computers, cell phones, televisions, almost everything electronic or dealing with communication are not as advanced or are considered as cool as in your time period -- keep that in mind;

2) Don't say you've already seen a movie before its premiere, particularly several years before it's premiere;

3) Don't tell everyone who will win the World Series (make a few bets if you want – what the hell);

4) Remember what year this is – it's not a big deal to write down a year that's past, but people notice if you put down a year that hasn't happened yet.

CHAPTER 7

Wally arrived twenty minutes early for Dr. McElroy's class, but he found the professor there before him. On the stage (Beginning Issues of Paramount Unimportance was a popular class and was held in an auditorium). Asleep. With his coat balled up for a pillow.

At first, not knowing whether McElroy wanted to be awakened or not (he did appear to be breathing), Wally came up quietly to him. Upon hearing a light snoring, he backed away so as not to wake him and knocked over a chair. The noise made the decision.

McElroy sat up and stretched. "Is the class over yet?"

"N-no. They're just starting to come in now."

Wally pointed to a few students wandering in who weren't paying the slightest bit of attention to the two of them.

"Good." McElroy got to his feet, shook out the coat and put it on. "It works every time. I came in this morning, and wanted a quick nap. I told my body to wake up before class started, and," he snapped his fingers, "there you go."

"I'm afraid," Wally interrupted, "I knocked the chair over."

"Right. I knew that. My subconscious must have known you were going to do that." He ran his fingers through his hair as if combing it out. It all fell back exactly the way it had been but he seemed satisfied.

"How much time do we have till class starts, Wright?" He looked at his watch.

Wally saw that the professor had glanced at his own watch and assumed that it was a rhetorical question. It took him a few seconds to realize that the "Wright" had been a reference to his name and that McElroy was waiting for an answer. He checked his own watch.

"We've got about ten minutes, sir."

"Fine, fine. Like my new watch?" He held it out for Wally to inspect.

"Yes, sir. It looks like the same one you had on yesterday."

"Nonsense. It can't be the same one. I've got this one on today. I had that one on yesterday."

McElroy looked out at the half-filled seats.

"What the hell. Let's get started. If they're late, they're late. It's not important."

Wally stared at him, but McElroy had already stepped to the front of the stage.

"Ladies and gentlemen, boys and girls, students and ... other students." The noise faded a little. "I am Dr. Sam McElroy and I am in charge of this class for the rest of this term. Probably for the term after that, too, but, unless you do not pass, that is of no importance. To you.

"Which brings me to the title of this class. Beginning Issues of Paramount Unimportance. For years you have been taking notes, and memorizing facts, and studying for exams on issues that somebody else has been saying are critical for your growth and development as a student and a person. Questions such as, who won the battle of Wyatt's Fat Farm? How many bones are really connected to the hip bone? Was it really 'that time of the month' for Mary Shelley when she wrote Frankenstein? How many bushels of apples must be picked by three Ukrainians so that Peter can reach Tucson by 2:30 in order to rotate his tires and bisect a rhomboid?

"And what was your response to these questions?" McElroy held up his arms.

"Who cares?" the class shouted back at him.

"Boy, this is a live one," he whispered to Wally. "I've got them right in the palm of one of these hands."

He turned back to the class. "Believe it or not, there are probably very sound reasons for you having to learn that information. But" he paused and shook his finger at them, "that's not important here.

"In this class, you will decide what you want to learn about. This is your opportunity to pick something, anything that piques your curiosity. I will spend my time up here discussing matters of great unimportance, but of interest to me.

"For example, I may do a study on developing the dexterity of the ring finger. I've always been curious about that, but does anyone else care?"

"No!" yelled the class on cue. There were a few scattered "yeses", but the professor didn't seem to consider them important.

"Whether you attend class or not doesn't matter to me. But if you don't come and watch what I do, you may not know what you're supposed to do when it comes time for you to present.

"That's right. There are only two criteria for this class. One, you have to pick a topic that is unimportant to anybody else here. If anyone comes up with a solution to the world food shortage, they fail. However, if you want to talk about how to harvest lima beans faster, that's okay with me. I couldn't care less about lima beans.

"The second criteria is that you have to present your subject to the class. You get to come up here and tell us about what you learned. I don't particularly care why you wanted to learn about it, just that you did. My assistant here, Mr. Wright ... take a bow." He pointed to Wally, who did not take a bow. "Mr. Wright will set up a schedule for the presentations. He will also, from his limitless experience and wisdom, answer any questions you may have about the process."

Wally wasn't too sure about that.

McElroy continued, "How well you do in this class is of no importance to me. I don't give a fig for what kind of grades you get. But, if you do, you'll make sure you work hard. Just remember, don't worry about what I think of your project. It's not important.

"I do recognize, and you will learn to recognize, that there is very likely nothing scientific or truly meaningful about how you do your study. What I want you to get out of this class is the idea of pursuing something that is of interest to you and only you, and to figure out a way to look at it. Actual research techniques – validity, reliability, statistical analysis, that sort of thing – can be learned in another class, if you really want to. They are important if you want to make your research matter to the rest of the world. But keep in mind that is not the point of this class. Got it?

"Now," he went to his briefcase and pulled out a few large colored squares of cardboard. "I want to talk to you today on McElroy's Theory of Color Perceptivity."

He held up a card and pointed to a young woman in the front row. "Tell me, what color is this?"

"Blue."

"And you, sir?" pointing to another student.

"Blue."

"How about you?"

"Blue."

"Is there anyone here who doesn't think this is blue? Those of you in the back row or color-blind don't count."

Of course, some joker yelled out "Red!"

"Those of you with the brains of a snail-infested sea urchin don't count either. Okay, I think we agree that those of us with any real color sense perceive this as blue. This card," holding up another one, "Mr. Sea Urchin, is red. Is that okay with everyone?" McElroy took a few steps to his right, continuing to hold up the cards.

"But, are we all seeing the same blue and the same red? We call this blue, but 'blue' after all is just the label that we give what we perceive is this color. The color is still there, whether we call it 'blue' or not. Most of us were taught to think 'blue' when we saw this color as little children. Some of you, such as our snail-infested friend, took a little longer to learn this. As a matter of fact, may have grasped the concept only very recently.

"But, what if you and your neighbor are actually seeing different colors up here? What if what he sees as 'blue' is what you would see as 'red'? You both see this color, you both call it 'blue'. How would you ever know that you're actually perceiving different colors?

"Well," he put the cards back in his briefcase. "Isn't that interesting? Isn't that fascinating? But is it important? Of course not. It makes no difference whatsoever. Just something to mull over, to ponder in the late evenings, to argue drunkenly about in a bar.

"Have a nice day, and see you in the next class – that is if we both have the same perceptions of what a nice day is or when the next class starts. Just remember, that my perception is the one that matters here."

CHAPTER 8

Wally approached his first class as a student with some understandable anxiety, and also with a great deal of irrational apprehension. After all, it had been a long time since he had actually attended school. And, he recalled that he had approached all those classes with more than some anxiety too.

He sat down in about the middle of the room, middle row back and same distance from both sides, and looked around. There were about a dozen students in the class and most were several years younger than he was. The one next to him, a little closer in age, leaned over and stuck out his hand.

"Hi, I'm Derek Trueblood. What's your name?"

Wally shook his hand. "Drew Wright. Nice to meet you."

"I heard this class is a bitch. But then, I heard that from someone who hates my guts and will do anything to irritate me, so who knows. You coming back to school after working for a few years?"

"Um, yeah," Wally said. "I was managing a bookstore, but decided I needed a change. How about you?"

"Nah, I got my degree in medieval metaphysics last spring, but I'm not ready to go out and fight the madding crowd yet. So, grad school looked like a good delaying tactic."

"You went from metaphysics to psychology?"

Derek shrugged. "What else am I going to do with a degree in metaphysics, except manage a fast food restaurant?"

"Gentlemen." Unbeknownst to them, the professor had arrived and was now addressing them. He spoke in a heavy eastern European (Wally guessed) accent. "Would you like to teach, or do you wish me to?"

"Oh, you go ahead and teach." Derek smiled. "You get paid for it, we don't." Wally stared at him. He didn't remember too many students talking to their instructors like that. And certainly not before class had even started.

"A Mr. smart-mouth one, eh?" The professor apparently didn't appreciate it very much, either. "And who would you be?"

"Drew Wright." Wally, startled, stared at him again.

The professor checked his class list to make sure it was a real name. "Andrew Wright, I suppose. Well, Mr. Smart-Mouth Wright, I will remember your name. I hope you do not give me too many occasions to use it."

He turned to go back up front. Wally whispered to Derek, "Why did you do that?"

The professor caught that comment too and came back. "And what is your name, Mr. Smart-Mouth Wright's talking friend?"

"Uh, Derek Trueblood."

The professor this time looked down his list as if he was sure this one was not a real name, but was surprised when he found it. He checked it again, shook his head, raised his hand as if beseeching the heavens for patience, then strode back to the podium.

Derek winked at Wally and mouthed, much more silently this time, "Okay, we're even."

The teacher did not even want to look in their direction any more.

"I am Dr. Askovarik. It is on the board. Spell it wrong at your own considerable risk. This class is Theoretical Research Applications; dedicated to the philosophy that you can theoretically apply research to anything you want to. If you are in the wrong class, please leave now." He looked pointedly in Derek and Wally's direction, but without any real hope. "You can take notes, you can record me, you can use a photographic memory if you wish, but you will remember what I tell you or you will not pass."

Wally had brought a notebook and pen to look good, but did not spend much time following the lecture. He took a few notes, but doodled for most of the hour. He didn't really know what parts he was supposed to take notes on.

At the end of class, Derek approached him.

"You must understand this stuff pretty well. You didn't take very many notes. How about if we get together when we need to study?"

Wally had never thought much about the idea of passing or even studying. He didn't plan on being there when grades were handed out. But he figured Derek didn't need to know that.

"Well, okay, though I don't think I can really help much. But I'll have to let you know when I can. I'm working for Dr. McElroy and I don't know yet how much time that's going to take."

Derek shrugged, "Whenever." He held up his watch. "Do you have Irrelevant Research Practicum I now? With Dr. Bluebaugh? She's really supposed to be something. And then how about something to eat afterwards?"

Wally took more notes in Dr. Bluebaugh's class, which amused Derek as he took less. As he explained to Wally in the Bradford Union Cafe, he had been too busy trying to figure out if she had been wearing underwear. He still wasn't sure.

"It's a little game I play – to see if I can match certain observable personality traits with the wearing, or not wearing, of certain undergarments. I'm thinking of doing my thesis on it. Want to help me with the research?"

Wally took a bite of something called the Bradford Club sandwich, lifted the top of the bun to take a closer look at the secret sauce, frowned, and redirected his attention to Derek.

"It sounds like the type of research that would go well in McElroy's class. So, did you come up with any conclusions regarding Dr. Bluebaugh?" Derek shrugged his shoulders. "And, do you do the same thing with the male professors?"

Derek looked at him in surprise. "That never occurred to me." He set his Bradford Burger (with a different, or maybe the same, secret sauce) down. "I never thought of that. Does that make me a sexist or something?"

"Or something." Wally picked at his Bradford Fries. "Now, when Askovarik catches you staring at his rear, you have a good explanation."

He looked at his watch. "I have to get going. I'm supposed to have open office hours for McElroy's class later this afternoon and I have to pick up something from my apartment first."

"I'm just going to get a refill on my Bradford Cola," Derek held up his cup, "then I've got to get to the next class. Wyatt is doing a class on the Psychological Value of Weight. By the way, where is your apartment?"

"Oh, ... I can't think of the house number offhand. It's right next to the Sayita Ainta Soa sorority, something like that. Do you know where that is?"

"Yeah, I know where all the sororities are."

Wally picked up the last of his lunch. "Do you want any of my Bradford Brownie?"

"That? That's just a regular brownie. There's nothing special about it. The Bradford Brownies are browner."

CHAPTER 9

Dr. McElroy had told Wally not to expect too many students the first day, or even the first week, maybe not even the first month. After all, they hadn't had any time or motivation to come up with any questions yet. And, he admitted to himself, he didn't have any answers anyway.

To while away the time, Wally had brought both The Laptop (he now thought of it in capital letters) and one of his textbooks. Putting aside the textbook (someday he ought to open it, just in case he actually had to answer a question), he opened The Laptop and it came up on the day's date.

Not much going on yet. But I'm sure you just wanted some reassurance.

Believe it or not, Derek is a good friend to have. However, don't get too caught up in his freewheeling lifestyle. He's probably going into his family's insurance business – he just doesn't want to go there yet.

Do pay attention to the people you meet. Some may lead you to Cindy. Some may lead you home. You will have to rely on both.

Wally looked at his watch. He now had only one hour and fifty-three minutes left of his two-hour office time. Sighing deeply, he picked up the textbook (*Psychology – You and the You That You Don't Want Anyone Else to Know*) and turned to page one.

After he returned from getting a drink of water for the eleventh time, he resettled himself and heard a knock at the door. He looked up and saw a tall fellow with the most perfect white teeth and waviest blonde hair, leaning against the door frame.

"Can I help you?"

"Yeah, I'm in Dr. McElroy's class." He turned to his left and spoke to someone just outside the door, "I'll be just a minute," then entered the room and took a seat across the table from Wally.

"My name is Darryl Thomas." Wally shook the offered hand and responded with, "Drew Wright."

"Look, I'm not one of you psych guys." Wally almost laughed out loud. "I'm in sports management and I just needed some general hours. But, is Dr. McElroy for real? I mean, what's with all this 'not important' crap? I've got to figure out what I need to work on and set my study time based on what I need to get by. I can't afford to fail anything, or even to drop anything more."

Wally started to laugh, but realized that Darryl was very serious. "I'll be honest, I don't really know yet what he's looking for. I just met the guy myself. My suggestion is, don't worry about it until you've seen him lecture a few times, like he said. I get to set up the presentations, so talk with me a couple of times and watch what others do before we schedule yours. Probably the biggest thing now is simply to think of some topic, something you would just be interested in learning more about."

Darryl's smile returned.

"All I'm interested in learning is how much money am I going to be able to make throwing a football..."

Wally sat back. Oh, this was that Darryl Thomas. Yeah, he was set to make a lot of money playing pro football, but that was in the future that he wasn't supposed to know about yet.

"Oh." Here Darryl leaned in and whispered, "and how many girlfriends will I have before I graduate." He glanced back at the door, as if worrying he might have been overheard. "You know what I mean?"

"Yes, probably." Wally was anxious to change the subject. He really didn't want to hear about Darryl's legendary conquests. "Look, I don't think any of those things is what Dr. McElroy is talking about. Is there anything you've ever been curious about, just for the heck of it? It could have to do with your major, or with football, or even just with you. Anything at all?"

"Well." Darryl drummed his fingers on the table. "There is something I've often wondered about." He again looked at the door. Wally wondered just who was out there, then prepared himself for the worst in listening to Darryl's proposal. "You know, I'm good-looking." He ran his fingers through his hair. "Damn good-looking. I know that. Everyone knows that. I just wonder sometimes if I even need to say anything to get what I want, to get people to do stuff for me. Usually I can get what I want with a smile." He demonstrated.

Wally sighed. He supposed it could have been worse. "Alright, I know that's something that I could care less about." He scratched his head. "For the lack of anything better to do, how would you be able to keep track of something like that?"

"I don't know. I told you, I just wondered, I never thought to really check it out."

Wally pulled out a pen and ripped a piece of paper out of the back of his notebook.

"Tell you what. Let's try this to start with. Carry a notebook or at least some paper with you and note when you talk with someone, who talked first and whether it was positive or negative. Whether it was a good thing or a bad thing." Darryl looked puzzled, as if he wasn't quite sure what that meant. "Whether it made you feel better or worse, or not anything different. Mark down whether they are asking you for something or if they are offering to do something for you or to give you something." As he was talking, Wally was quickly sketching out columns with headings. "See how that works."

"Yeah, I suppose I could do that. Might not be too hard if I just have to check something. Thanks. Maybe I could be more specific as I go."

"One can only hope so." Wally handed him the paper with the several columns outlined on it.

"I've got to go, I've got somebody waiting for me and the afternoon is short, if you know what I mean. Thanks for helping to set this up." Darryl winked, stood up, and extended his hand again. He did have charm going for him.

Wally also rose and shook the proffered hand, again, realizing as he did so that many sports fans of the future would have given a lot to be in his place.

"Good luck, Darryl. If you need anything, just let me know. I'm not going anywhere … just yet."

As Darryl went out the door, he spoke to the mysterious other person in that room, "Okay, Cindy, I told you it wouldn't take long. I've got an idea now for a project and you can help me with it."

It took Wally a moment to catch the significance of that "Cindy". He came around his desk and arrived at the doorway just as the outer door to the waiting area closed. He started across the room, but pulled up at the sound of a "Mr. Wright?" He paused, recognizing that those words were supposed to mean something to him, then caught on that they actually meant him personally.

A young woman stood up from her seat and was smiling at him. There was something familiar, very familiar, about that smile and, as a matter of fact, about the rest of her.

"Yes?"

"I thought it was you. I wasn't sure when you were standing on the stage next to Dr. McElroy, but I thought it might be you."

The voice was on the tip of his tongue, too, so to speak.

"Well, you were right. It is me."

Then she laughed, which was even more familiar.

"Did you ever find the right house, with an apartment for rent?"

"Oh. Oh! You were the girl at the sorority!" He shook his head. "I'm sorry, I was sort of flustered then and walked up to the wrong door. Yes, I did find the apartment, right next door as a matter of fact."

He stopped, not sure what to say next. Now that he was paying attention, she was kind of pretty, in a pretty attractive way. Really.

"I'm Lori Gibbons."

Wally continued to look at her.

"And you're Mr. Wright."

"Uh, Drew, call me Drew." He started to wake up. "I'm still a student here, too. So, you're in Dr. McElroy's class?" Which, he vaguely realized, she had already said.

"Yes, I'm majoring in psychology, so I wanted to meet you. Maybe get some ideas from you, on deciding what to do with it. What are you planning to do with your degree?"

"What degree?"

"Your graduate degree." When he didn't respond, Lori continued, "When you finish your graduate program." Still no reaction. "From here. In psychology. What kind of a job are you going to have? What do you want to do?"

Wally had no idea what to say, but decided he'd better become more involved in the conversation. Looking at the outer door for a long, regretful moment, he remembered The Laptop's comment about paying attention to the people he'd meet. He pointed back to his tiny office. "Come on in."

Sitting down, Lori noticed The Laptop on his table, and, before he could stop her, she pulled it to her.

"Is this what you're working on? Can I see it?"

Noting nothing on the screen and not waiting for a reply, she pushed the Return button.

Wally sat in stunned silence (it does get very silent when you're stunned), waiting for her to say, or do, or … something.

Lori looked up at him. Her silence was also stunning.

Wally leaned in and looked down at the page, trying to read it upside down.

Lori. Please stop reading. This is none of your business at this moment. Please do not be offended. Drew will share with you at an appropriate time. Believe me. But that time is not now. Please close this page.

"Um," he began. And ended.

She looked down at it once more to make sure she had read it correctly, then slowly shut the computer. She pushed it over to the side of the table.

"At least it's not porn. Maybe. Some day, I hope you will tell me what that is about."

Wally breathed out for the first time in a long minute (or two).

"Some day, I hope I can, too."

***

Darryl and Lori were the only two students that had come in. Thankfully, Lori had gathered up her things without any more questions.

"Well, I guess I'll be seeing you .... At least that's what it," she pointed at The Laptop, "sort of said, anyway."

"Yeah, it sort of did say that."

She walked out before he could think of anything else to add. Then he just sat through the rest of his time, staring at The Laptop, almost afraid to touch it.

He did have to touch it eventually, to carry back to his apartment. Mrs. Weidenbach was waiting for him inside the front door.

"Hello, Mr. Wright. Did you have a good day?" Without waiting for a reply, she added, "Would you do me a big favor, please? I need some help with something in my kitchen."

Wally hesitated. "Can I just put these upstairs and come right back down?" He wanted to put his computer in his room, out of sight.

"Oh, it will take only a second ... unless you want it to take longer."

She turned and walked away, leaving Wally with nothing to do but follow, slowly.

She gestured to the kitchen table. "Just put your things there. I dropped something behind the refrigerator and I was just wondering if you could just pull it out a little bit so I can reach behind and get it."

"What did you drop?" There really didn't appear to be enough space between the fridge and the wall for anything to fit.

"Oh, just ... something."

Wally set his belongings down, making sure The Laptop was on the bottom. He took a deep breath and grasped the refrigerator, working it back and forth to edge away from the wall.

"Ah. I just love it when a man shows off his muscles."

Wally paused, but decided not to turn around just then. Maybe never turn around.

"That's it, just a little more." Mrs. Weidenbach stepped into view, starting to bend down to reach behind the fridge. Wally noticed with a start that somehow another button on her shirt had come undone. Just then, a phone rang in another room.

"Oh, damn, I'll be right back."

As she left the room, Wally hurriedly pulled the refrigerator out further, far enough to uncover anything that could have fallen there. He looked down, but didn't see anything. As he turned to get his books and leave, Mrs. Weidenbach returned. That was quick. And her shirt was buttoned back up.

"Uh, I didn't see anything down there." He thought better of what he had just said and quickly pointed to the floor.

"Well, why would you, Mr. Wright? There isn't anything down there," she pointed to the floor, too, "to see. Would you please push the refrigerator back against the wall?"

"Okay." He started to push and saw that she had gone over to the sink and wasn't even looking in his direction. When he had finished, he finally did pick up his books.

"I'll see you later, Mrs. Weidenbach."

She smiled at him and said, "I'm sure you will. Have a nice day, Mr. Wright."

CHAPTER 10

Time went by. Slowly it seemed, but then Wally checked the calendar and realized two weeks had passed.

Classes had come and gone and Wally found himself actually taking notes because some of the stuff really was interesting, believe it or not. Other students had appeared during his open hours, but not Lori, or Darryl, ... or Cindy.

He and Derek went to the Homecoming football game, but he didn't see much of the game. He was continuously looking for Cindy. If she was dating the star quarterback, of course she had to be there. Somewhere. Twice he saw what he thought might have been her in the distance, but he was too far away to be sure and definitely too far to make a "fancy-just-running-into-you-even-though-we-haven't-met-yet" appear natural.

Getting a hot dog, he stood in line behind a man who seemed a bit too old to be a student, even older than Wally. He was wearing long pants and hiking boots, when most of the students were wearing shorts and either tennis shoes or flip-flops. And he was also wearing a sports coat, definitely too hot for the game. Wally thought he looked out of place and just didn't have the professor-type look, but he promptly forgot the man when it came time to make his decisions regarding what to put on that hot dog.

However, he did run into Lori at the end of the game. And she still had a dazzling smile.

"Hi, did your computer program say if you could talk to me yet?"

Derek looked puzzled.

"Uh, no, I mean, yes," Wally stuttered. "Yes, I mean, I can talk to you. Just not about … what it said … to talk to you … about … later."

Derek now looked even more confused. "You have a computer program that tells you when to talk with attractive women? And when not to?"

"Uh, no. It was about something else."

"Your program told you not to talk to her about something else?"

"It's, never mind … Derek, this is Lori. Lori, Derek."

"Nice to meet you," they said in unison, then chuckled. Lori's chuckle was prettier.

Wanting to make sure they moved on to a different topic, Wally asked, "Enjoy the game?"

Lori shrugged, "I'm not much into football. I like the atmosphere, but there are a lot of people here. And a lot of drunk people here. I think it's just an excuse for them to party."

Three male students walked by with no shirts on, but with jersey numbers painted on their chests to protect them from any potential cold. Apparently the numbers were insulated because the students didn't seem to be feeling a thing. So far, even though he and Derek had been looking, no females appeared to trust just the numbers for warmth.

"I come to the games because my Dad would get upset with me if I didn't." Lori continued. "And because my roommate, Peggy, thinks the players' butts look sexy in their tight pants. Especially the quarterback, Darryl Thomas." Another young woman, but a redhead this time, came up to them. "Don't you, Peggy?"

Peggy didn't have any idea what they were talking about, but she was in a good mood because she had gotten to see a lot of athletic butts, so she just nodded and smiled.

"Yeah, I think he gets that a lot," Wally reluctantly agreed.

Lori nodded. "Probably, but, personally, I don't get it. I see him in class and he's always surrounded by a group of other students. He seems so into himself, do you know what I mean?"

"It's interesting that you would say that," Wally started to say, but then realized he probably shouldn't be talking about Darryl's project for class. Maybe there was some sort of confidentiality issue involved -- he didn't know if there was a code for graduate assistants or not. Lori waited for him to continue. "It's just interesting that you would ... notice that."

They suddenly realized that they were standing alone. Derek and Peggy had moved a few steps away and were simply smiling at each other.

"Did they just make a connection?" Wally asked.

"And she's not even looking at his butt," Lori commented.

"Look," Wally said. "Do you and ... Peggy want to go get something to eat with us? With Derek and me?"

Lori flashed her smile again. "Sure, we were just going to go back to the sorority and open a can of soup. But," and she looked at the two others. "I do think she can be talked into doing something else for a meal."

"Well, how about soup and a sandwich? Derek and I were just going to stop in at Salvatore's. The after-game soup and sandwich special is a grilled bacon and swiss cheese, and the Bradford Chili. And its secret ingredient. Which I hear is vanilla."

"Vanilla? Really?"

Wally held his hands up. "That's what they say. But the chili is so spicy, I don't think you can taste anything else. They probably add it just so they can say it has a secret ingredient."

"Peggy. Peggy Mishkavitz." She called to her roommate. "We're going to Salvatore's with Drew and Derek."

Peggy turned her head slightly, but kept her eyes on Derek's. "Okay. Whatever."

Overall, the meal went well. They had to stand in line with the after-the-game crowd for thirty minutes to get to the counter to order. Halfway through, a table opened up and Lori claimed it for them. Peggy wasn't ready to leave Derek's side.

The sandwich was tasty until they took a spoonful of the chili. Beyond that point they couldn't taste anything. Peggy didn't seem to care. She kept eating the soup without reacting while the others went through several drinks to keep from being burned. Lori took only a couple of bites of the chili, but Wally and Derek manfully consumed their entire bowls, while inwardly regretting it.

The conversation went in general getting-to-know-you paths. Lori and Peggy were juniors, Lori majoring in psychology, Peggy in philosophy. Both degrees were going to require more legitimate later career decisions. Derek expounded on medieval metaphysics, which Peggy found fascinating, but the others regarded as pretty much gibberish. Peggy did not have a current boyfriend — that she would admit to, and Lori was sort of seeing someone from her hometown that she only saw on holidays and it wasn't serious. Wally told himself he was glad she was seeing someone else, and that he was here to find Cindy, but he was only half-convincing.

He shared very little about himself. He didn't know what he could say. Make up something about his fake identity? Or try to stay close to his real background and risk Cindy hearing about it? It suddenly occurred to him that, at some point, with luck, he was going to have to come up with a personal history that would make sense to Cindy.

MyFate

Yes. It is about time you thought of that. Remember that you're supposed to be a couple of years older than Cindy so it's not like she would be expected to know you from high school. However, it's probably a good idea to not be from the same town as she may think you should know the same people or have siblings the same age, that sort of thing. Maybe a town close by, how about Liggettsville? That way you can still have some landmarks in common – parks, museums, ball teams -- without being expected to know everything. You are now Drew Wright from Liggettsville who graduated about six years before her and you have been working at ... lets keep the same job – managing a bookstore, you can talk about that without it meaning anything to her, and you decided you needed to change careers. Any other history can just be what I, you have been doing for the last six years.

And you can probably say the same things to Derek and Lori.

CHAPTER 11

Two days later, Wally was back monitoring another one of Dr. McElroy's classes. One of the compulsive students who wanted to get her project over and done with was going to be presenting. Not too many were ready to go at this point, but this girl, Emily Pressman, could get this class completed and then spend more time studying for what she considered was the real work in her other classes. After introducing her, Wally went to the back of the auditorium with a microphone. If somebody had a question, then he could rush over to him or her. Dr. McElroy sat in an empty seat in the front row, trying to stay awake.

"I picked something that I knew I could really care less about." She paused. "Social dynamics inside the boy's, or men's, if you prefer, bathroom."

All of a sudden a lot of students sat straighter in their seats. Even Dr. McElroy cocked his head as if listening more intently, but also ready to interrupt if needed.

"I was focusing on urinal usage. I had been informed that there was a male student bathroom in Burgett Hall with six urinals and one in Burgell Hall with seven urinals. It doesn't matter how I know."

Though she had consulted with him about having to enter the male bathroom prior to beginning the project, reassuring him that it was purely academic and not voyeuristic, Wally did not know all the details of her research and found that he wanted to know where she was going with this. Well, he knew where she had apparently actually gone, but he meant, what was the point?

"I theorized that boys, or young men I should say, in putting the facility to its proper use, would likely select a urinal a distance away from one already being used, either two down or three up or maybe even at the far end. I'm assuming that social interaction among males is not the goal of being in the bathroom. But where would they go if they couldn't pick one at least a distance of two urinals apart? Would being further away from the door be the deciding factor? Or the size of the guy already using one?" There were probably several different interpretations of what was meant by "size" going through the heads of the listeners. "Or some other factor?

"With two different bathrooms, I had two choices as to the number of urinals that could conceivably be comfortably used. In Burgell Hall, males could, standing every other one, at the most use four urinals at a time -- 1, 3, 5, and 7. In Burgett Hall they would be limited to, at the most only three at a time, 1, 3, 5, or 2, 4, 6. But, if the first one into the room in Burgell picked Urinal 2, that would limit the choices for the next users."

By now everybody was spellbound. It is true that most were chuckling, but they were listening. And would have a story to tell their friends later.

"I created a chart for keeping track of this usage." She pressed a button on her handheld tablet and a chart came up on the screen behind her, displaying several rows of seven urinals, apparently Burgell Hall. For some reason they were all colored pink. "I also did one for Burgett, but for the purposes of this presentation, I will just use Burgell.

"At the top of the page is a space to note the time period of the observation. For each row the observer marked a 'one' for who came first or was already there when the observation started. A 'two' was marked for who came next and so on. They stayed on this row until somebody left then started another row when others came in to replace the first ones. In other words, if we got up to three guys using them before the first one left, that would be one row. First one leaves, another guy comes in, we started the second row marking who was already there. And so on. We did this over three days for about two hours each time."

Dr. McElroy, who had his own microphone, spoke into it and his voice boomed throughout the auditorium.

"Miss Pressman, you have several times used the word 'we'. I take it that means there was more than one of you involved in this. So did this matter to other people too?"

"Mr. Wright, your graduate assistant, signed a paper for me stating that I could go into the boy's bathroom for the purposes of academic research." She was starting to blush slightly. "The first time I tried it, someone called security because a female was sitting in the corner taking notes. The security officers didn't look happy but they rolled their eyes and reluctantly said 'okay' when I showed them the signed document. They gave me a badge that said 'Bathroom Monitor'. However, I discovered that, usually, once a guy saw that I was sitting there, he went into a stall. Or turned around and left. The ones that didn't do one of those things sometimes smiled at me and sort of creeped me out. So I recruited several male students I knew to help me out – Josh Smith, Josh Jones, and Owen Carmichael. They took turns charting and pretending to use the facilities in order to set up certain scenarios." She turned toward the rest of the class. "Could you please raise your hands so the rest of the students can acknowledge your willingness to watch guys go to the bathroom?"

One hand tentatively started to go up, then went quickly back down when he realized no one else was going to admit to participating. But a voice did come from the other side of the room.

"I can tell you positively that we had absolutely no interest in the results of this study. None whatsoever."

There was a big laugh and Emily's face became redder. A hand shot up near the back and Wally hurried over to offer the microphone. A young woman stood.

"I have a question."

Emily nodded. "Go ahead."

"Did you offer them any incentives, any pay, to assist you? I wanted to know if that's expected in case I need some help with my project."

"We ... worked something out.'

That brought a few smiles from some males and mostly puzzled looks from the females. Dr. McElroy quickly stood back up.

"Miss Pressman, can you share the results of your study with us?"

She took a deep breath.

"Certainly, Dr. McElroy. It came out pretty much as I had theorized." She pushed a button again and a chart appeared on the screen, filled with columns and numbers and categories and percentages – a typical psychological graph. Of very little interest to anyone except the presenter.

"The guys tended to use a urinal as far away as possible from another user and only filled in the gaps by necessity. If someone was at number one, they usually went to five, six, or seven, trying to leave at least three in between them. Then the next male would go to the urinal as in-between as possible, with at least a gap of one. If it was busy, which happened most often at class changes or just before lunch, and there were no urinals available except right next to someone, they used it fifty percent of the time and the other fifty percent they went into a stall." She flashed through several pictures displaying stick figures standing in front of urinals. Some of the students appeared disappointed that there weren't actual photographs.

Dr. McElroy spoke once again.

"Thank you, Miss Pressman. I am sure if anyone wishes to know any more specifics, they can see you at a later time. I have seen as much as I care to. This was obviously a project that took some time and effort and too much thought into how to go about doing it, but ..."

"I have a question."

A hand went up from the middle of a row halfway back. Wally went to the aisle and waited for this young woman to make her way to him. As she got nearer, he realized she looked familiar. It was Cindy. A few years older than when he had last seen her and probably much wiser.

"Here you are, Miss ...?" He had more trouble getting the words out than he had expected.

"Cindy," She looked at him for the first time with a slight start of recognition, but a great deal of uncertainty. "Cindy Connor." It was obvious she was trying to work out why she should know him.

"Here you go." He handed her the microphone.

"Uh, thank you." She turned hesitantly toward the stage, giving him one more glance on the way. "Um, Emily, can I, can I ask you, what made you think to do this? I mean, why go into the boy's room? Why not do a study like this on the girls using stalls, or using the sink? I understand that the stalls may not be as … open as the urinals, but we still want a sense of space."

Emily reddened as much as she possibly could, then shrugged, figuring there wasn't much more to get embarrassed about.

"I guess I just wanted an excuse to go into the boy's bathroom."

There were a couple of low, and some not so low, comments about "I could have helped you with that…"

Dr. McElroy took charge once more.

"Thank you again, Miss Pressman. If there are no more questions? No?" Without looking around or waiting for a reply, he went on. "Miss Pressman, I have to let you know that I was concerned about the unimportance of your topic because I can conceivably see someone in architecture or building construction being interested in the value of knowing just how many urinals to install in a public bathroom for customer convenience. I was considering the possibility of knocking a few points off your grade. However," as Emily began to frown, "however, once you have explained your motivation, I feel comfortable in acknowledging that you had no intent in having your study fulfill any useful purpose. Thus your grade will be restored. Class dismissed."

Cindy turned to Wally and opened her mouth as if to say something, but students started filing out and she closed it again with a little shake of her head. Somebody called her name and they both saw her seatmate holding up her books and gesturing that she would bring them out to her.

"Say," Wally started, but Dr. McElroy called to him from the stage.

"Mr. Wright."

Wally looked in his direction.

"Could you come see me for a moment, please?"

Wally turned back to Cindy, but she had already moved toward the door and was starting to get lost in the crowd. In frustration he walked to the front, where Dr. McElroy was waiting.

"Yes, sir?"

"Could you tell me what time it is? I seem to have misplaced my watch again." He was holding up his right wrist, looking at it in consternation. Wally glanced at the left wrist, which held the watch, as usual.

Sighing, he held up his own wrist.

"It's fifteen minutes to ten, sir. You let the class go early." Maybe he should buy him another watch for the other wrist. And one for his pocket. He noted there were also two clocks on the walls, clearly visible to anyone who bothered to look.

"Thank you. Now, if only I can remember where I put my office."

"It's out that door, sir. And to the right." Wally pointed and Dr. McElroy moved in that direction.

Wally looked to the back doors, but the last of the students had left. He went that way anyway. With any luck, maybe Cindy had stopped to get a drink or to talk to someone.

CHAPTER 12

Wally paused as he exited the auditorium to get his bearings and to decide which direction would be the best to pursue. There were still a few students in the hall, but none of them were Cindy. He started walking, glancing into open doors as he passed them, but not having any luck. He did catch one couple in an intimate embrace, but moved on when the young woman glared meaningfully at him.

Pushing through the doors at the end of the hall, he thought he caught a glimpse of what could have been Cindy, maybe, possibly, turning past the corner of a building. Not seeing any other options he ran in that direction, but slowed, then stopped as he got to that corner.

He peeked around. Yep, he was pretty sure it was her. But now what?

In the auditorium, he could probably have said something about her having a good question or did she want to ask him anything regarding her project. But …

But running up to her out here to say those things was going to seem more stalkerish. Or more like a sixteen-year-old boy. Which would have been defeating the purpose of coming back here now, when he wasn't supposed to be a sixteen-year-old boy anymore. He was supposed to seem more mature, more assured, more … something that wasn't going to come across as tongue-tied and awkward.

So Wally decided to just follow her, but not like a stalker at all. Maybe something would come to him.

This following her was probably still going to fall somewhere in the questionable category, but she didn't have to know that. After all he didn't know how to find her outside the one class, so he did have a reason to find out where else she went. Or so he told himself.

Cindy appeared to know exactly where she was going. She stopped once, to briefly watch some shirtless male students playing Frisbee. Wally stopped far enough back to be out of her line of sight and stepped behind a tree just in case. She didn't seem to be the only one watching the playing. An older man in a sports coat and hiking boots stood on the other side of the players. There was something familiar about the man, but Wally was more concerned with Cindy not spotting him. She soon resumed her pace without seeming to look back.

Within a few minutes she reached the end of the campus, and unconcernedly crossed the street without appearing to even check the traffic. By the time Wally reached the crosswalk, there were naturally several cars speeding by and he had to wait for a moment before he could hurry across.

She was further ahead but still in sight. She suddenly turned left up a walk, went up the few steps, and entered a building.

It wasn't until then that Wally realized the area looked familiar. Very, very familiar.

She had gone into his building, the one where he now lived.

It stopped him briefly, but he suddenly realized, oh crap, now I have an excuse to talk to her, and ran up the walk, hoping he was not too late and that she had not already disappeared into her room. Wherever that was.

He yanked the door open and almost collided with her backside. She had stopped right inside the door and was talking with Mrs. Weidenbach. Cindy turned and smiled at him, apparently not surprised in the least.

"Hi. In case you forgot, I'm Cindy Connor. I thought you were going to get here soon."

"Uh, hi," he was trying to catch his breath. "I, uh, didn't know you were living here. I'm Drew Wright. Uh, hi."

"You already said that." She gestured toward the older woman. "I was just telling Mrs. Weidenbach about our class today."

Cindy turned toward her. "Drew, here, is our grad ass."

"Did you say 'grab ass'?" Mrs. Weidenbach asked. Her shirt was buttoned all the way up to her neck and she was smiling sweetly.

"No, graduate assistant, grad ass for short. Though ..." She leaned back to look at his rear.

"My, the way you college students talk nowadays." She winked at Cindy. "But I know what you mean." Then she cocked her head. "Excuse me for just a moment. I think I hear my phone ringing."

Wally thought to himself as Mrs. Weidenbach walked away, *her hearing must be better than I would have imagined. I didn't hear a thing.*

Cindy read his thoughts, "I didn't hear anything. I think she was just leaving us alone for a minute. Well, maybe for more than a minute. Uh-oh ..."

Mrs. Weidenbach came back out of her room. She hadn't been gone long enough to answer a phone. Unless it was just long enough to pick up the receiver and put it back down again. But, somehow she had found time to undo the top three buttons of her blouse and mess her hair up. And she was definitely checking his rear out this time.

"Hello you two. Miss Connor, and Mr., uh, Sorry. I thought I heard somebody come in."

"Wright," Wally said automatically, as he was thinking, *we just talked to you, less than a minute ago. Not long ago enough.*

"Yes, thank you, Mr. Sorry. That's what I thought it was."

"No, my name is Wright."

"Right. I got it."

Cindy had covered her mouth, but her body was shaking with laughter.

"Miss Connor." He glared at her, but she didn't seem to mind.

"Oh, I seem to have interrupted a moment here." Mrs. Weidenbach winked at Cindy with her left eye and at Wally with her right eye. Which looked even more disturbing than it sounds. "Don't mind me."

But she didn't go anywhere. She appeared to be waiting for something to happen right in front of her.

Wally couldn't think of anything to say, so Cindy said, "I live in the first apartment on the right at the top of the stairs. Which one is yours?"

"I'm, I'm at the first one on the left."

"Oh, the one that is haunted."

"What?" Wally was startled. "I hadn't heard anything about it being haunted!"

Cindy laughed again. "No, I was kidding. But I do know they wouldn't let me have that one. They wouldn't even show it to me."

"Really? It was the only one I looked at."

Mrs. Weidenbach leered at him. At least it looked too much like a leer to Wally. "We were saving it for someone. Someone more the right … type." Okay, so it probably was a leer.

Cindy started up the stairs, then looked back at him.

"Drew, Mr. Sorry? Are you coming up?"

He nodded to Mrs. Weidenbach. "Have a good day," then took the first steps.

"My name is Wright," he muttered to Cindy.

"I know, but I don't think Mrs. Weidenbach is ever going to get it right, I mean correct." She laughed once more and hurried up the rest of the stairs.

When they got to their landing, she looked down the hall at his door and said, "This is going to sound funny and don't take it the wrong way, yet, but could I see your room? I'm just curious about what's so special about that apartment. That they wouldn't show it to me, but let you have it."

"Yeah, sure." Wally was thinking, *I'm not having to do anything*.

As he was unlocking the door, she said, "You know, you remind me of someone I went to high school with, only he was really skinny. You're older and more filled out. I don't mean heavy, just more solid. He was really skinny."

"Oh, is that all you remember about him?"

"He was a nice guy. I liked him but we never went out or anything. He was kind of shy. I waited through our freshman year for him to ask me out, but he never did. I hinted enough but I don't think he ever picked up on any of it."

Wally inwardly grimaced. "Yeah, well I was kind of an idiot in high school. Too," he quickly added. "Didn't do much dating. I had no idea which girls liked me so I was always asking the wrong ones, I guess."

"And now?" She looked him straight in the eyes.

He laughed self-consciously. "I hope I'm better now. But still not much dating. Of course, I haven't been here long and haven't really gotten to know any of the girls in my department."

"Girls? Maybe that's your problem. You should be thinking of them as women now."

"Yeah, you're right. Women." He paused. "Like you."

She laughed. "A little bit slow, still a little bit awkward, but you're getting there."

Cindy went over to the hard wooden chair and sat down. "I don't have any of these chairs, and mine has two bedrooms since I have a roommate, but the rest of the apartment looks the same." She smiled at him. "What have you been doing with your life? You obviously have been doing something else besides school."

Wally sat down on the bed, but didn't let his mind go there. "Well, I got my undergraduate degree from …. " His sweatshirt's logo prompted him. "Western Oshawa, in literature. Which doesn't lead to many jobs. I'm working as a manager at a bookstore." All of that was accurate, so far.

"You're working? You're doing that and coming to school fulltime?"

"Um, was working." Wally momentarily wondered if that was going to be true when he returned. If he returned. That job was a lifetime ago. "I decided I wanted more out of life, so I'm sort of on leave. See if something comes of this psych degree."

"Oh, what do you want to do?" Cindy leaned forward. "I'm in education, but I'm not sure if I want to go straight into teaching or go on to get a more advanced degree, say in special education or administration."

Wally realized he hadn't thought of anything like that. He had viewed his taking classes as a very temporary situation with no real goal. He had just expected to go back to his old life, with no drastic differences. But maybe, just maybe he could at least talk about making some changes.

"I don't know," he honestly answered, the most honest comment he had made since arriving in this time and place. "I guess I'll see where this takes me. I've never thought about private practice, so I'd probably have to work for somebody else or some sort of organization."

"Do you want to go into counseling, research? Hospitals, schools, a mental health clinic?"

"I think, maybe, counseling. Despite working with Dr. McElroy, research, whether relevant or not, doesn't really appeal to me. So maybe a clinic or a group practice. I don't want to do the business end of setting myself up. We will have some opportunities for fieldwork, so that will give me a better idea." Wally didn't feel it was necessary to tell her he wasn't planning on doing any of the fieldwork. He changed the subject.

"What about you? You mentioned your high school friend. Where did you go to school?"

"Summerfield High School, in Summerfield."

Wally nodded. "I know where that is. I'm from … Liggettsville." He had to quickly recall what he had told himself.

"That's right next door! I work at the Menninger's Family Restaurant there in the summers. Do you know it?"

"Yeah, I've eaten there."

"I probably served you at some time."

"Maybe." Wally didn't tell her he thought it was now closed. That was in his current lifeline, not hers.

"So what made you choose education?" He figured he knew the answer. Both of her parents were in the field, but he wasn't supposed to know that. Yet.

"Both of my parents are in the field." Now he was supposed to know that. "My mom is a school psychologist and my dad is a kindergarten teacher. So that's pretty much what I know."

"Did you ever think of anything else?"

Cindy paused for a moment. "Now you sound like a psychologist." She pointed at him. "Maybe you should become a school psychologist. Then maybe we could work together."

Wally didn't know what to say, but before he could think of something to keep the notion of them doing anything together in the future going, she shook her head.

"No, I think that graduate program is through the school of education. You'd probably have to switch – reapply and everything."

Wally finally got his tongue working. "But it's something to think about." Which he was now planning on doing. But then he internally shook his head. It was not something to think about – he wasn't going to finish a psychology degree. He was going to leave before any thoughts of a career would have a chance to take shape. That's not why he was here.

But, just as he was reorienting himself as to why he was here, Cindy stood up.

"I better get going. It's cool that you're right across the hall. You can help me with my project in McElroy's class. That is, if you can?"

"Uh, yeah, sure."

"I know. If you're not doing anything, why don't you come over for supper tomorrow night and we can talk about it?"

Wally knew that if he had been planning on doing something else the next night, he was no longer doing it. "Yeah, that sounds good. What, what time?"

"How about 5:30? Then we can spend time talking about the class, and whatever."

It wasn't until she was gone that the "whatever" hit his consciousness. And wouldn't leave.

CHAPTER 13

MyFate

Now you have officially met. And can actually talk with her.

I know, you're yelling right now, "Why didn't you tell me she lived right across the hall? I've been looking all over campus for her and she was thirty feet away!" Just don't yell too loudly or she will hear you.

I told you before, this relationship has to progress in its own way. There's no hurrying it, there's no shortcutting it.

Go to dinner and enjoy the evening. But don't get your expectations up regarding that "whatever". Remember, in her mind, you have just met for the very first time.

CHAPTER 14

The next morning, his mind still buzzing and flying and crackling from the events of the day before, Wally met with Dr. McElroy in his office. This was their weekly discussion of how things were going, and how things were going to go, and how maybe they shouldn't go. He never knew just what was about to happen in these meetings.

And apparently neither did Sam McElroy.

"So, Mr. Wright, what have you got for me? Anything new, exciting, boring even? How's your love life?"

That was a new question, and considering the timing, somewhat startling. "Um, I don't think you're supposed to ask me that."

"Oh, about your love life? Probably not. But if I only asked what I'm supposed to ask, neither of us would ever learn anything, would we?"

"No, you can ask me about other things. You're just not supposed to ask me personal questions, about things like sex."

"Sex? I don't remember asking you about sex. I only asked about your love life, the boring parts. I hope sex doesn't have anything to do with it. I'm not going to tell you anything about sex. You'll have to read my memoirs when I retire."

"Excuse me." Wally shook his head. "Do you have anything you wanted to talk about with me?"

McElroy opened one of the pocket agenda/calendars that he always carried with him.

"Let's see. Let's see. No, we don't have enough time to talk about that. No, we'll wait till the last minute for that one. How about … ? No, that's just for my wife."

Wally had wondered about the wife, but had never met her. He supposed that Dr. McElroy needed somebody, but he couldn't imagine who would be able to actually live with him.

"Oh, yes." McElroy looked up from the calendar. "How are you coming with your doctoral thesis?"

"My … what?" Wally had never ever once considered a thesis. That would take more thought and work than he wanted to put into this program.

"Your dissertation. Your specific study. Which will get published and make your name immortal. Like mine. Somebody is supposed to advise you on it and help you form a committee to assist you and accept it in the end. Yesterday, the faculty reviewed all the students and somebody, I think it was Dr. Askovarik, pointed at me and said that I should get 'Mr. Smarty-Mouth Wright.' Do you know what he meant by that?"

"I think he, he has me confused with somebody else. Another student got in trouble in class and used my name as a joke."

"Oh, hah! Good joke. Saying your name is 'Smarty-Mouth Wright'. I'll have to remember that one." McElroy wrote it down. He looked back at Wally. "So, your dissertation. Any ideas? I could give you some. I'm full of them. At least they tell me I'm full of something."

"No, that's all right." Wally was familiar with some of Dr. McElroy's ideas. "I'll think of something and let you know. I've got a few possibilities myself and I just want to sort them out." He had no ideas, no clue, but he didn't think he should say that.

"Okay, well I'm your advisor on it, so come to me when you want to be advised. Now back to something that really matters then. My research."

Wally had been dreading this. Dr. McElroy had mentioned during their first meeting that Wally was to assist him with his "research", but it had not come up since then. He remembered the professed interest in parapsychology, so it could be anything.

"Did I tell you about any of this yet? No? Well, I want to look into the concept of time travel."

Crap.

Or maybe not crap. Maybe this is where Wally's adventures really started.

"Specifically," McElroy stood up and began walking around the small room, which consisted of two steps that way, then two steps back again, then two steps that way, then …. "Specifically, how does time travel? How do we get from this moment to the next? How did we get from last Tuesday to here?"

Okay, back to crap.

"Me, personally, I have never liked living my life in order, going from today to tomorrow. I was just getting used to yesterday. How do I learn from the past when it's gone as soon at happens? Let me spend a few hours frozen in this moment and I may actually get something from it."

He stopped and held up both arms, with watches now on both wrists.

"Time passing is man's, and woman's to be fair, bugaboo. We can't undo time. But can we stop it? Or at least pause it?"

"You mean like can we go back in time and visit it again?" Wally interrupted.

McElroy looked at him for a moment. "No, that's crazy. Why would you think we could go back in time? I'm talking about making time go slower. Appreciating the moments, giving us more time to reflect before we act or say something stupid. Maybe having a 'time out'. That would be good, for everybody to have a chance to call 'time out' when they need it. To give themselves a chance to regroup, like they do in athletic events. Do you know what I mean?"

Wally didn't really know what he meant, but he pushed on. "So how would you do that? How would you research a 'time out', or do a study?"

As soon as he asked the question, Wally wished he hadn't. He wanted to take his own moment to actually think about this, to consider why Dr. McElroy needed to find out how to slow time, to give himself time to reflect. Maybe this was a real need for the professor based on his own inability to keep himself focused from one second to the next, his jumping all around. His own difficulties in handling time. Then Wally considered, *I don't really want to think about this. This doesn't make sense. Manipulating time is impossible ... except ....*

McElroy wasn't going to give him that time right now anyway. He held up both wrists again.

"You see these two watches? You think they're identical, right?" Actually no, one had a bright blue band, the other one was bright black. "Well, they're not. This one," he held up the left hand higher, "is set five minutes ahead of the other one. Or the other one," he frowned and raised his right hand even higher, "is five minutes behind the first one. One or the other. Which one do you think I'm going to use to tell me the time?"

Wally shrugged hopefully. "The one that tells the correct time?" But even as he said it, he knew it wasn't going to be the right answer.

"The one that I need to use of course." He brought his arms down. "If I do something that I don't think is the right thing to have done, I will go to the one that is five minutes behind and give myself that five minutes over again. To correct myself, to hopefully do it better the second time."

"I'm not sure that's how time ...", Wally started.

"And if it still doesn't work, then," McElroy pulled a pocket watch out of his vest pocket, "this one is set another five minutes behind. And I can do it again. I can redo that five minutes several times. And, if that works, I will set them ten minutes back."

"But ..." Wally stopped himself this time. It didn't make sense in the grand scheme of things, but, maybe, for Dr. McElroy, it might work, giving himself extra time.

"Now -- hah, as if there really is a now, now did that make sense, or do I need to go back five minutes and explain it all over again?"

Wally didn't think it was ever going to make better sense. "No, I understand what you're trying to do. But how are you going to tell if it works?"

McElroy pulled out a small recorder from another vest pocket.

"This is the genius of it, Wright. I'm going to record my conversations with students and other faculty, and my class presentations. My wife won't let me record our personal interactions, I don't know why, I'm sure other people would love to hear them. Then, you are going to transcribe the times I went back five minutes, and we will see what I did differently and what the reaction was. As I said, genius, right?"

It took a second for Wally to realize he had been asked a question and not just called by name. "Uh, yes, right." He didn't know when he was going to find the time to be doing this. Maybe during the time he was supposed to be working on his dissertation. "Why don't you just transfer it straight to ..." Uh-oh, maybe that technology wasn't available yet. "Never mind, I'll work on that."

"Good." McElroy sat down. "Now." He picked up his calendar. "Did we talk about your dissertation? I forget if I went back to do that right or not."

"We're okay, Dr. McElroy. We talked about that already." Wally stood up, ready to leave. "I think we've talked about enough for right now. Definitely for right now. At this time, so to speak."

CHAPTER 15

Wally sat with Derek and ate a late lunch in the student union. He stayed away from the Bradford Burgers and Bradford Fries, and instead tried the Bradford Chicken Salad, which, surprisingly, tasted like the Bradford Burger. And the Bradford Fish Sandwich. And the Bradford BLT. It must have been the Bradford Secret Seasoning. Which could stay a secret as far as he was concerned. He didn't think it was vanilla.

"Derek, what are you doing your doctoral thesis on?"

Derek put down his Bradford Peanut Butter and Wasabi Jelly, which didn't seem to need any extra seasoning.

"I thought you'd never ask. I'm going to send out a questionnaire to practicing clinical psychologists throughout the state, asking how much time they spend on paperwork, like scheduling and writing reports and billing and completing graduate surveys. What percentage of the time is spent on not seeing actual clients."

"Really?"

"Yep. My advisor, and the prof I'm a grad ass for, is Dr. McCulligan. She does that evening seminar – Covering Your Behind – on legal and financial documentation. Paperwork is the love of her life. Her ideal would be twenty percent clients and eighty percent paperwork. And then gradually moving that client work away."

"What happened to your idea on matching personality types to the wearing or not wearing of underwear? You seemed pretty gung-ho about that."

"McCulligan didn't think it was a good idea. If you ask me, she doesn't wear anything under her pantsuit and didn't want me drawing any conclusions from that. Or it's old granny panties and that could mean something too. Anyway, this is an easy way to get the thesis done. I don't have to set up a lab or arrange for subjects. I just send out a survey and collect the data from whatever I get back. My hypothesis is that the more time they spend on keeping the paperwork up to date, the more money they collect. And I can blame any scarcity of data on the ones that didn't respond. And then conclude something. With McCulligan, it will probably be that practicing psychologists should spend more time practicing paperwork. What about you? What are you doing?"

Wally stalled by taking a drink from his Bradford Lemonade, which tasted like the Bradford Root Beer. He figured there were different names on the dispensers but bet that the drinks probably all came from the same tank.

"I'm not sure."

"Huh, that's different. Most of the grad students that have come back after being out of school for a while, seem to know exactly what they want to study. I figured it would have something to do with books, like the optimal arrangement of books by subject in a bookstore, whether pornography should be in the front or the back, the classics easy to get to or hard to find, that sort of thing. Just because that's what you did – ran a bookstore. Maybe you can send out a survey to bookstore owners asking how they think psychology could help their sales."

Wally shrugged. "Maybe." He wasn't planning on doing anything, but he should probably be acting as if he was.

Derek continued. "You know, if it matters where the check-out counter is, the type of signage that might help, reading areas or not, the amount of browsing space. Personally, I like a used bookshop that has some clutter, some mess to it -- that is a little bit over-crowded. It makes me feel like, if I spend time searching. I may find something that was overlooked, something rare that was misfiled."

"That's not how bookstores work. Everything is organized, we know where everything is. Then we can find it when a customer asks for it."

"Yes, but is that how book buyers want it to work? I bet for half of them, the search is the fun part. I never go into a bookstore knowing what I am going to walk out with." He scratched an itchy nose. "Unless it's a gift for my Aunt Matilda and she has said this is the book she wants. In that case, there's no looking for the same type of book. I'm not taking any chances on getting her something that's not exactly what she asked for.

"But, otherwise, I like to browse. Find something that catches my eye. That's the fun part of a bookstore."

Wally leaned back. "I think you've got a point. I knew regular customers that would spend hours just looking and walk out with only one or two books. Even the ones that are looking for something particular, it's not a specific book, but a genre or a topic. And then they'll still spend time wandering."

He wrapped up the rest of his sandwich. You had to know when enough was enough.

Derek had finished off his meal, including the slice of Bradford Apple Pie, which may or may not have had any apples, and may or may not have been a pie. "Of course, you still have the people that just want the latest Nathan Straw or Alec MacArris and that's all they want."

Wally cocked his head. "Nathan Straw? He just writes children books. Is that what you read?"

"What? I read them as a kid. Everybody did. They were good. As a matter of fact, they still are." Derek started to clean up what was left in his area. "I think it's time to go. But, if I were you, I'd think about doing something in the area of book sales or a bookstore. Go with what you already know."

CHAPTER 16

Wally was as nervous as a teenager.

Come on, he told himself, *this is what you're not supposed to be like. This is what is supposed to be different. You're twenty-seven and you're beyond this. You're a grown man, you know more than you did ten years ago. You're more comfortable with yourself. Now tell that to your sweat glands.*

He knocked on the door. Then feeling it had been more the knock of a timid teenager, he went to knock again harder. Just as the door opened and his momentum took him half a step over the threshold.

"Well, hello." Cindy almost had to catch him. "You seem anxious."

"Oh, sorry, I didn't mean to do that. I didn't know if you heard my first knock, so I, uh, was going to do it again. Just to make sure you heard it. You know." God, if that didn't sound like a nervous teenager.

"Well, come in, or the rest of the way in, anyway." Cindy turned around and led him into what didn't look much like his place, and looked definitely much more feminine. That didn't mean it was girly or frilly, just that it looked like someone had tried to make it personal and homey. His place had none of that. He had not had the opportunity to bring anything personal with him and had not added anything to the room. His idea of home décor was a few pens and a couple of old used paperbacks, just because he needed a few books around him somewhere.

Here was a kitchen table set for two, a couch and a rocking chair facing an old television set, and several bookshelves. There were even a few photographs on the walls. And this was just the front room. The kitchen area looked a little larger than his and he realized there were several doors leading off the living room.

"Your place is bigger than mine."

"Yeah, I was originally looking for a place for two, so I guess yours wouldn't have been right anyway. I technically have a roommate, Sarah, but she's never here anymore. She's really living with her boyfriend. But she still pays half the rent, or her parents do, and she still has enough stuff here for when her parents visit, and want to believe that she's using what they're paying for. But, for the most part, it's just mine."

Cindy entered the kitchen, which was providing a spicy aroma of curry and cooking apples.

"I hope you like Mulligatawny."

"Like what?" It was a new word to Wally.

"Mulligatawny. It's sort of an Indian curry stew with chicken and rice and apples and corn. I don't make it too spicy, but I do like the curry. Oh, no, now I'm thinking it may not have been the best thing for a first meal together. Maybe you won't like it. I make a lot of soups or stews because they're cheaper than other meals and they last me for a few days."

Wally hadn't heard anything past the "first meal together".

"I like curry. I just hadn't heard of ... that kind of stew before. It actually sounds kind of good. And it smells great."

"Well, good. I have a couple of boxes of muffin mixes. How about the apple-cinnamon one? I think that will go well with this meal. I usually like some kind of bread with my soups. Could you mix it up while I finish the stew?"

Wally happily stirred the mix, buttered the muffin tins, and filled them. This was one of the advantages of being older -- he had been doing this stuff for years. Once he had put them in the oven and set a timer, he turned to find Cindy offering a spoon of the stew to taste. It was very good, but he almost couldn't swallow it because he was smiling so much. This had become very domestic very quickly.

Dinner went well. He dribbled very little on his chin (that was always a problem with soups), but he never caught her dribbling at all. How do girls, women, do that? They are always so much neater.

He helped her do the dishes and they managed to brush up against each other a few times, just arm contact, but it felt good. He wished he had Dr. McElroy's frozen moment in time to make this particular moment last longer.

They went back to the living room where he thought they might both sit on the couch, but she told him to wait a minute, then brought a folder from her bedroom and flopped on the rocking chair.

"Now that I have bought your time with dinner, could you help me a little in figuring out what I am going to research for this Unimportant Issues class? To be honest, I am completely at a loss as to what we are supposed to do."

Wally laughed, trying to make it a more mature, adult laugh. "As near as I can determine from Dr. McElroy and his convoluted expectations, that seems to be the point. You're to figure out how can you discover something that no one else has, or at least that you don't know about yet? It's to expand your thinking and to get yourself invested in something personal that is not set by someone else. It is not to follow any prescribed research protocols."

"Great." She sighed. "That doesn't help. I'm used to there being a point to what we're supposed to do. Something specific to be learned that we can use later. After all, when we get out in the real world, there is always a purpose for our actions, at least when we're working. Isn't there?"

"Good question. I suppose even politicians have a purpose. Or think they do."

It was her turn to laugh, a much more pleasing sound than his had been. "Well, maybe not specifically that we can recognize, but I suppose what they do is usually to benefit somebody, even it's only themselves."

"Let me ask you, why did you sign up for this class? I'm finding out that, besides the lure of an easy grade, most of the other students had something in mind that they wanted to find out, something that was usually too silly to do anywhere else. You heard the one Emily Pressman did, and it was just to get into the boys' bathroom." In his mind he heard, *and someone wanted to go back in time just to impress a certain female.* "And I had another one where this guy wanted to know whether people would agree with him or do things for him just because of who he was."

"Yeah." Cindy nodded. "Darryl told me about that. Then he pulled out a notebook and waited for me to agree with him, that it was a good project to do. He didn't seem to like it when I told him it was stupid, but I noticed that, when he made a mark, it was the only one in that column."

Wally frowned. Darryl Thomas was the last thing he had wanted to bring up this evening. "I probably shouldn't have said anything. I forgot you knew each other."

Cindy started to nod again but stopped and looked at Wally. "How did you know we knew each other?"

Wally was flustered for a moment. He had to stop and think. Did he know it through his computer program, or had he followed Darryl at some point?

"Oh, uh, he must have said your name, as he was leaving our meeting. He said you were waiting for him. Yeah, that has to be where I heard it." It was true but unconvincing. "And maybe I saw him with you one time." Not true, but a little more believable, maybe. Sort of true – he did notice them sitting together in class one time.

"And you remembered my name from then?"

She had a point. He only remembered the name because he was specifically attuned to it, but he shrugged and said, "I guess."

"Huh." She pondered that for a second. "Good memory."

She pulled her legs up under her on the chair. "Well, you helped Darryl come up with a plan. Now how about me?"

Wally was happy to move on from the football star. "I think what you're supposed to learn from this project is that you can find answers to questions, even if nobody else cares about it. There's nothing so unimportant that it's not worth knowing more about whatever it is. If you want to." Wally was surprised at how insightful he was suddenly sounding. Almost as if he knew what he was talking about. "So, let's get back to my original question. Why did you sign up for this class?"

"Because Darryl wanted to. Easy A." Back to Darryl. This was not working.

"Alright. Is there anything you are curious about? That you want to know just for the heck of it?" Wally paused. "Did you want the easy A?"

"Well, that doesn't hurt. But, no, I don't usually sign up for courses based on how easy they appear to be."

"Simply to be with ... Darryl?" Wally hated to ask it.

"No. It was a time for us to be together, but, as a matter of fact, he cuts out half the time, especially since he has his project now. Oh, I probably shouldn't be telling you that."

Wally grimaced but didn't say anything.

"I guess, really, I was curious about what went on in the class." She continued. "I wanted to see what ideas other people would have."

"So, something you wanted to know. Is there anything you could do with that?"

"Well, I wanted to know what other people want to know. I suppose. But it's just curiosity."

"That's what all of this is – curiosity. So how could you find out what you want to know?"

"I don't know. I guess I'm going to find out by going to class and listening to their presentations. But so is everybody else."

"How about..." Wally thought for a moment. He straightened up in his seat and leaned towards her. "How about if you were to keep a list of what everybody else is doing and categorize them?" Thinking about it, he wouldn't have been surprised if this was what he was supposed to do at the end of the term. "You know, like Personal, Science, History, Societal, stuff like that. Keep track of their original purpose and what they found out."

Cindy was quiet for a while, thinking it through.

"You know, that just might work. It could be interesting to determine what everybody else thinks is interesting. That's kind of cool." She smiled at Wally, which distracted him mightily. "You're actually pretty good at this." Then she frowned slightly, which now worried him. "But I'd have to wait till everybody else was done with theirs before I could even really do it."

"Okay, you might have to be last to present, I grant you that. But I think you could actually do the research before that. I can get you a list of who is in class and you could ask them what they are each studying. Of course, there will be a few who will wait to do anything till the last minute, but I don't think Dr. McElroy is going to mind if you miss a couple. After all, this is your interest, not his."

"This is great." She wrote some things in her file. "I think this can get me going. You have been a big help. I really appreciate it. But now ...," she closed her file and sat up, looking directly at him. "Now..."

He tensed. It had been a long time since he had heard a woman use that tone, and he knew he was feeling like a teenager again.

"Now I have to study for my Baltic Literature exam tomorrow. In that class I truly have no idea where the tests are going. But it is interesting reading. Again, thank you so much for everything."

She stood up, so he stood up. She came over and gave him a big hug and a kiss on the cheek, then gently pushed him toward the door.

"Uh, great. I was glad to help." The kiss had definitely been nice, as had been the hug come to think of it, but the end of the evening was kind of abrupt. "Uh, look, I was meaning to ask you. If you weren't doing anything Friday night ..." Back to being the bumbling teenager again. "Though I know Friday nights are usually busy. But there is a department get-together, a kind of party, at Dr. McElroy's house, and I was wondering if you might be interested in going. It's going to be the profs and the graduate students – I don't know how exciting it's going to be, but I thought you might be interested in it, just to see what these things are like ..." He realized he was rambling, but hoped he had gotten across that he would like her to go. With him.

She looked up at the far corner for a minute.

"Friday night. This Friday night?"

He nodded slowly. He thought it was this Friday night, but right now his thinking process was slogging through mud, not quite sure where it was going to step next.

"Yeah, I think that could work. There's an away game on Saturday, so Darryl will be gone. Yeah, that sounds like fun." She smiled at him, through the haze brought on by the mention of Darryl's name. "I'll make you proud of me."

The door shut. The exhilaration of having an actual date with Cindy was tempered with the realization that it was only because Darryl was going to be out of town. But ... Darryl was going to be out of town for the weekend.

CHAPTER 17

MyFate

You asked her to the Psych Department party, didn't you?
Well, if you didn't, you better go back there and ask her right now.
You only have so many opportunities to make that first impression.

CHAPTER 18

For some reason, Wally didn't get much sleep that night.

The next morning, as he went to go downstairs to pay his rent, he paused in front of Cindy's door, willing it to open up while he was there. It didn't, but he still smiled. After a moment, he continued down the steps, but barely felt them at all.

He rang the bell next to Mrs. Weidenbach's door. He had set up a bank account and was now able to pay with a check. It was check #003, but it was a check.

There was no answer. That was somewhat surprising as she always came to the door quickly. He figured she was usually right there because she wanted to keep an eye on the tenants' comings and goings.

He knocked this time, hard, and the door popped open. After a few seconds he realized it had opened on its own, not from being pulled.

"Hello? Mrs. Weidenbach? This is Drew Wright. I'm here with the rent check."

He took a step in and stopped.

"Hello. Anybody here? Mrs. Weidenbach?"

It occurred to him that Mrs. Weidenbach, though not considered extremely elderly, was of an older generation and possibly not always in the best of health. Maybe she had fallen or had an attack of … something. He took another couple of steps forward, hoping he wasn't going to be stepping on her.

The place was much larger than his. He had been in this apartment only once before, to the kitchen to move the refrigerator and had not looked around at all. His only memory was of Mrs. Weidenbach bending over with the top of her shirt unbuttoned and he had been anxious to get out as soon as possible. To the right was the open living room area, and three doors to the left along a short hall. The first was half open, and, as he came closer, he could see it led back to a bedroom, with another closed door at the far end and the sounds of a shower.

"Oh, oh!" He did not want to intrude on that. As he backed away, he noticed that the next door was also slightly ajar and, now that he was aware of the specific sounds, another shower was going.

Two showers. A one-woman apartment. More information than he wanted to deal with. Now or at any other time. He was not going to investigate that third door.

He held out the check as if he was going to set it down somewhere, but decided it was better that he wait until another time. No need for Mrs. Weidenbach to know anything about his having been in the apartment at all.

He glanced at the bookshelf on the opposite wall of the hallway, which he had been about to set the check on. A few titles caught his eye and he bent to look closer. There was an old copy of Huck Finn, Charles Dickens' *A Christmas Carol, We Cuss a Little,* and Ernest Hemingway's *For Whom the Bell Tolls,* as well as at least twenty other classic titles, many in editions he had never seen before. He pulled out the Hemingway and opened it, discovering a signed first edition. Now opening them more gently, he realized that most were signed first editions. *Huh,* he thought. *This is quite a nice collection. Who would have believed it?* He put two of the copies back, stood up, and recognized that one of the showers had stopped.

Replacing the last book, he quickly exited and shut the door firmly behind him. As he went to reclimb the stairs, he glanced out the front door. A figure was walking away on the far side of the street. From the back, if he hadn't just heard the showers, he would have sworn that it was Mrs. Weidenbach. But he shook his head. That could very well be anybody. Around here, from behind, one older woman could look just like any other older woman. He just knew it wasn't a pretty young female student. Those he could tell from their behinds.

CHAPTER 19

Another student, Mark Duckworth, was ready to present his Issue of Paramount Unimportance to the class. Well, sort of ready. He looked like he just wanted to get it done and over with before he could be compared with too many others.

He stood on the stage in front of the auditorium and shuffled his note cards for several minutes, cleared his throat, then cleared it again, looked out at the class, shuffled the cards again, then started to speak so softly that no one could hear him.

"Please use the microphone on the lectern, Mr. Duckworth." To his credit, Dr. McElroy did seem to know the names of all his students. "If you wish, we can go back in time for the past five minutes and pretend that class hasn't started yet."

"No, no! That's okay," Mark looked at the wall clock in horror. He didn't need to add another five minutes to his presentation. It wasn't going to be very long as it was. He stepped closer to the mike.

"I, I wanted to look at, if it mattered if you dressed when going to class, I mean, how you dressed. The types of clothes you put on, not whether you were naked or not." Students started paying attention once the word "naked" entered the discussion. Certain words will activate the hearing sonar and that is one of the words guaranteed to do that. Wally idly wondered if maybe more students should start their presentations with that word. "If a student would take the class more seriously if they dressed more, um, formally, not a coat or tie, I mean, or a formal dress, but more than say a dirty T-shirt and ragged blue jeans, or shorts. Not to say shorts can't be good-looking. But maybe a polo shirt and khakis on a male, or, uh, a nice blouse, or coordinated outfit for a female. You know what I mean?"

From the response of the class now that they realized nudity was not going to be the primary topic – yawning, more laptops being opened, more whispering or low talking, it was pretty clear that this issue was of paramount unimportance to them. His first objective had been met.

"I," he stuttered again. "I started by keeping track of how many notes I took in class based on whether I dressed very informally, just casually, or in some of my better clothes. However, it appeared that my amount of note-taking had more to do with the class subject or the speaker -- not you, Dr. McElroy, than with my attire, how I dressed.

"So, I, um, started paying attention to how the other students dressed, mostly in my smaller classes. There were too many in this class, though, I guess, I could have gone with only so many of them, maybe ten, or fifteen, I guess. But I didn't think of it. Till now. Anyway, I did other classes." He looked down at his notes, pulled out one from the bottom.

"I didn't do a power point. I didn't know we needed to ..." He looked at Dr. McElroy.

"That's alright, Mr. Duckworth. That was not a requirement. Though it might have been helpful."

"So anyway, I don't have pictures or charts."

A student raised his hand and, Mark, thankful for a distraction, nodded at him.

"How did you determine what was dressing well and what was not? Aren't you making a subjective judgment? Maybe some people couldn't afford better clothes or don't have many choices. I mean, I'd rather dress better for a date than for class."

"No, you don't," said a young woman next to the young man asking the question. "You always wear the same thing you've got on now." It was a 1985 Toledo Mud Hens t-shirt and a pair of jeans that might have been blue at one time, though it was hard to tell. "To tell the truth, you wear the same thing for everything. I've never seen you in anything else." She straightened up. "Unless you're also dating someone else, and dressing up for her."

The young man grinned but didn't look at her.

"To answer your question, I didn't, I wasn't looking at why someone was dressed that way," Mark responded. "Just what they did when they were dressed. The way they were." He looked around, but there were no other hands.

"I judged it on how I would have dressed for doing yard work, or getting together with friends, or, as he said, going on a date. So I had three columns. I asked the prof if I could have a couple of minutes at the end of class sometime, and then asked the students to just let me see the notes they took, if I could just glance at them, either in notebooks or on their laptops or tablets, whatever they had, you know. I told them it was research for a class. Most of them were okay with that. Then I just had columns for less than a page, one to two pages, or more than two pages. Sometimes columns for more than that, depending on the class."

He lifted his head, but there weren't too many actively listening by now. Maybe a few just to see where Mark was going with this.

"Your findings, Mr. Duckworth?" Dr. McElroy prompted.

"Uh, yeah. There were almost no students dressing what I would call formally."

"Almost none?" asked McElroy, stressing the almost.

"Well, there was one. And she told me she had to hurry because she had to get to work. So nobody dressed nicely for class. Of the ones dressing casually, I guess, versus dressing down ...." He was trying not to look at the student who had interrupted before. "The ones dressing casually did have roughly twice as many notes. So my conclusion is that how you dressed did make a difference in the amount of notes you take."

A hand shot up from the middle of the room. Wally craned his head and saw that it was Cindy.

"Mark, do you have any information on whether it made any difference in learning the material?"

"No, no, I don't. I would have to see the grades and I didn't think anyone was going to let me do that. Besides, this is too early in the term to tell how grades are going to be."

"For most of the students, Mr. Duckworth. But not all." McElroy stood up. "If there are no more questions?"

"Actually, I do." Cindy wasn't done. "I notice, Mark, that you are wearing a polo shirt and khakis now. As a matter of fact, you look good enough to go out on a date with, better than anyone else in here." There was some laughter, mostly from females. The males were rolling their eyes. "I am curious as to how you dress 'down' when you were trying to do it yourself."

"I, ah, borrowed some clothes from my roommate. Only he didn't know that, so don't tell him, okay?"

"I don't know your roommate, so I don't think that's going to happen." Cindy smiled and Wally had trouble breathing. "Mark, did you draw any conclusions about why the students that dressed better took more notes? Do you think they were just better students?" Wally thought that Cindy herself was dressed smartly enough to take anywhere. She was not in an outfit for doing yard work, though she probably would have looked good in that, too.

Mark held up a finger and pulled out another card.

"I was going to get to that. I think, and this is just a guess on my part, I think that the students who took the class seriously enough to dress differently for it than for, say, playing Frisbee football, also took the class seriously enough to want to make sure that they took enough notes to get the information they needed. That doesn't mean, I don't want to imply, that other students didn't get the needed information, they just didn't take as many notes. So that's what I think."

Dr. McElroy looked pointedly at Cindy. She shrugged and sat back down.

He turned to Mark. "Thank you, Mr. Duckworth. I look forward to getting your completed report. I know that I, personally could care less about your results, but there may be ..." He looked around the auditorium, "There may be some in here that could take your presentation to heart."

Once the students started exiting, Wally maneuvered himself over to Cindy before she could leave. "Those were good questions. That may have helped Mark to get across his point."

"Thank you, Drew. Well, if I am going to be a teacher, maybe I should be aware that how a child enters the class might be impacting how ready they are to learn. I'm not sure it's the same once you get to this level. I think most of these students already know what they want to get out of the class, but little kids may not have that sense yet. But, if they're dressed differently than when playing at home, they may treat class differently and figure they should pay more attention."

"That's a good observation. You look like you were dressed to learn today, if I may say so."

She put a finger to his chest. "You don't know where I am going the rest of the day. Maybe there's something I care about more than this class."

And she smiled and walked out.

CHAPTER 20

Wally took more time than he usually would have to get ready to go somewhere. Recalling Mark Duckworth's presentation, he had gone out shopping, and bought a new dress shirt, a sweater, and a nicer pair of pants than any that had been originally packed in his suitcase. He was surprised that his previous self hadn't considered this. Well, maybe he did, and decided that the present self should be responsible for some things.

And then there was the question of when to arrive at this sort of a party. His old younger persona would have been obsessive enough to get there right on time. His new older image was thinking that, it's a party, people come and go. Nobody gets there right exactly on time.

Unless Cindy was planning on being ready to go at that exact time. In the movies, when the main characters get to a party like this, it's always already in full swing. Always. But Wally realized that it also meant that most other people must have arrived earlier than those main characters, so somebody has to be getting there close to when the party is supposed to start. And he belatedly recognized that he was a main character only in his own mind.

While he was dithering, he heard a knock on his door, and his decision was made. I guess I'll go when she's ready to go. Which has been pretty true of men all over the world.

He opened the door and his heart stopped.

"You look … gorgeous. I mean beautiful. I mean really something."

She was wearing a slim blue dress that moved in and out in all the right places. "Thank you. I was planning on you saying something like that. That I looked nice anyway, but your words sound better."

"More than nice. I'm almost afraid to let anyone else see you like that." Wally grimaced. "I'm sorry. That's kind of ... possessive of me, considering we don't have that kind of relationship. Yet."

She smiled her world-class smile. "That's okay. That might be the nicest compliment anyone has ever said to me. Much more mature than the guys I'm used to seeing."

"Well they need to work on their lines then if they want to keep seeing you." Maybe he had learned something since high school -- maybe he was growing up.

Fortunately, it was a nice night for walking, and the McElroys didn't live too far away at the edge of campus. Wally had never bothered to get a car. All of the buildings on campus were easy to get to and the town had grown up surrounding the college. Derek had driven them the few times they had needed to go somewhere else, but Wally had never figured he'd be here long enough to justify buying or renting or stealing that car. His stay was already much longer than he would have originally thought. It was almost like he was actually going to school.

Cindy might have had a car. He didn't know, and he wasn't going to ask her to drive them the first time they go out. Maybe the second time. Keeping his fingers crossed for a second time.

"So, ... have you enjoyed Bradford State?" Wally wanted to start the conversation with something safe.

"Yeah, it's been all right. It was sort of what I expected. My high school had done a pretty good job of preparing me for college academics, and, though it isn't far, I was ready to get away from home. How about you?"

Wally shrugged. "I don't know what I expected. But I guess this is where I was supposed to be. After all, I met you, didn't I?"

Cindy gave him a sideways look before responding.

"A lot of people say, 'High school is the best time of your life. Enjoy it.' It wasn't, believe me." Wally was surprised. From his perspective, her high school life had appeared to be going as good as it can get -- very popular, doing well in class, top tennis player, homecoming and prom courts, plenty of other activities. "And then they say that college will be the best times of your life, so you better enjoy that. I don't know. I just think that life should keep getting better, so I should have more to look forward to. If this has been the best time of my life, then where do I go from here? I want to be happy with what I do with the rest of my life, not just look back at what was, or what could have been."

She stopped and looked at him. "I don't expect to find all my dreams in high school or in college. Does that make any sense?"

"Yeah. Yeah, I think it does."

"I want to take from this moment on and move forward. No regrets. No wishing I could change anything. No going back."

Wally wasn't sure what she was saying about having met him now under his current circumstances, but he was willing to certainly "move forward" in whatever direction she was going.

He replied, "That's very different from what Dr. McElroy wants to do, at least in his research."

"What do you mean?"

"He wants to stop time. Sort of stop it. Kind of pause it, maybe. Like a time-out. Or even go back and change what has happened. He has several watches set to different times so, if he doesn't like what he has just done, he can go back and use a different watch to repeat the last five minutes. Not really, but sort of, in his mind. He wants me to keep track of what happens when he does that – if events get better or not."

"That seems really strange." She laughed. "But I hope I never get to a point where I want to travel back in time. I think you've got what you've got, and you figure out how to work with it."

She took his arm. "But we've got right now. And I for one am going to appreciate the moment."

Wally couldn't argue with that. Even though the comment about traveling in time had hit home.

He was enjoying the walk and simply being with Cindy so much that he was actually disappointed when they arrived at the house. He recognized some faculty going slowly up the walk, almost as if they weren't sure if they were supposed to be here yet. He glanced at his watch and, realizing it was the exact time to the minute that the party was supposed to start, slowed down slightly.

"Are you okay?" Cindy asked. "Shouldn't we be going in now?"

"Ah, probably. It's just that Dr. McElroy has such a hard time with … time that you never know when is the … right time for him. Do you know what I mean?"

He looked around. A few cars were parked on the street, but certainly not enough to say a full-blown party was in progress.

"I do hear some talking from inside the door," Cindy tilted her head toward the house.

"How about if we walk around the block one more time? To be honest, I don't know a lot of staff or even the students to talk to and I'd rather have a few more people when we do go in. Okay?"

"Whatever you want, Drew. I'm here to follow you."

He smiled at that. "This is where many of the professors live and I've never been over here to just walk around. It might be interesting just to look at the homes anyway."

As they moved past a few homes, they almost literally ran into Dr. Askovarik hurrying around the corner. Wally and Cindy stepped out of his way.

"Sorry, excuse us."

Askovarik nodded at Wally. "Mr. Trueblood. I see you do not have that Mr. Smart-mouth Wright with you tonight. I must say your taste has improved." He turned his head to look back where he had come from. "But are you not going the wrong way? The department gathering is this direction."

"Dr. Askovarik, this is Cindy Connor. She is a senior in education." Wally wanted to maintain what he had been taught were appropriate manners, and to avoid getting into an unnecessarily long explanation about why he wanted to spend more time just walking with Cindy.

"I took your class in the Psychology of Daydreaming last year," she shared. "Fascinating. But right now, we're just enjoying the nice evening for a few more moments, then we will be in." Her explanation was better than his would have been anyway, and the "enjoying" touch brought another smile to Wally's face.

"Very well. Pleased to meet you, Miss Connor. I suspect you were very inspiring in class. I will see you shortly, then." He walked on, but kept walking past the McElroy house, in the direction where they had come from.

Cindy turned Wally to face her. "So, what was this 'Mr. Smart-mouth Wright' and this 'Mr.', what was it, 'Trueblood'? Do you have another name you're not telling me about?"

Well, yes, Wally thought to himself, but that's for another time. "He thinks I'm another student. I mean he has always had our names mixed up. Which is probably just as well. Otherwise he might be mad at me instead of the other guy. It's not a long story, but it's not worth the telling."

They watched Dr. Askovarik continue to walk up the street. "I wonder where he is going? Apparently, he lives this way and he obviously knows the house ..."

"Come on," Cindy pulled his arm. "I wonder which house is his. Let's see if we can find one that matches his personality."

They first picked a large two-story that was dark and foreboding, not welcoming at all, but then a much smaller ranch with everything neatly trimmed and just so. As far as Wally knew, the professor was not married and lived alone. Of course, he didn't really know anything about him. Askovarik could like the Gothic look or the Tudor style or a split-level, or anything else for that matter. But it was fun trying to figure it out, as long as Cindy was laughing and smiling next to him.

CHAPTER 21

There were several more cars parked along the street as they finished the walk around the block, and four or five people coming up the walk, and much more noise coming from inside. It did appear to be time to make an appearance.

Wally held the door open for Cindy and they entered into the front hallway. Most of the talking seemed to be coming from the right and they moved in that direction. He was looking for Dr. McElroy and for other students that he might know but was spotting neither. There were some professors that he knew by name, and they nodded to him but most of their attention appeared to be on who he was with. As his would have been in their shoes.

A woman, vaguely familiar to him, approached them. "Hello, I'm glad you could come tonight. I don't believe we've met before. I'm Heather McElroy, Sam's wife. And the so-called hostess for this affair."

She was primarily looking at Cindy as the right age for a student, but Wally first grabbed the offered hand.

"I have been looking forward to meeting you. I'm Drew Wright. Dr. McElroy's graduate assistant. That's where I know you from, your picture is on his desk. I mean, you looked familiar when we first came in, but I couldn't remember where. Now I do. I'm sorry, I'm rambling."

"He tends to do that," Cindy added.

"Oh, I am so happy to meet you," Mrs. McElroy smiled back at him. "Please call me Heather. I am so glad Sam was finally able to get his graduate ass, as they say, though, personally, I've never cared for the term. For some reason, the department has been reluctant to provide him with one." She lowered her voice. "I suspect it has something to do with his lack of, shall we say focus? Would you believe I had to remind him an hour ago of this party?" Wally grimaced, but nodded. "But he seems to be so pleased with your help. He has had to rely so much on the secretary for the department, Sandy Fochs."

He put his hand on Cindy's arm. "This is Cindy Connor, she's a senior in education."

"And I am in Dr. McElroy's Beginning Issues of Paramount Unimportance class," Cindy offered.

Heather rolled her eyes. "He has always called it 'Beginning Issues', but I have no idea what 'Later Issues' would be. Let's hope we never find out."

A sudden noise by the front door drew her attention. Wally and Cindy heard the sound of children's voices. "But what are we supposed to do? They never let us watch television."

The apparent mother responded. "You have some books and games with you. Find a corner and keep yourself occupied. Mommy and daddy will be busy."

The apparent father had already separated himself and was trying to find the drinks table.

"Oh my," Heather sighed. "They promised they would not bring the children this time."

The mother, who Wally now identified as Dr. Lucille McCulligan, Derek's supervising faculty member, called across the room, "Oh, Heather, dear, I hope you don't mind. We simply were unable to find an appropriate sitter for tonight."

"Which means either they didn't look till the last minute, or the sitters knew better than to be available. Probably both," Heather whispered to Cindy.

"Harrison and Belinda will be absolutely no trouble." Dr. McCulligan continued to yell, ensuring she was the center of everyone's attention. "They are such angels." Then she followed her husband, leaving her heavenly offspring by themselves.

The faces of the children, looking to be about four and six, did not present as angelic. They were already arguing over the backpack that must have held their activities and materials.

"You'll have to excuse me. I will need to see to this." Heather walked toward the battling youngsters, carefully arranging a smile.

"I feel so badly for those kids," Cindy sighed. Wally looked at her. He had been feeling sorry for the rest of the people at the party.

"It sounds as if this has happened before. I'm sure Mrs. McElroy, Heather, will have some place for them to go."

Cindy stared at him. "Some place for them to go. That sounds so cold. As if they were coats to throw on a bed somewhere."

Wally felt a hand slap on his shoulder and turned around, wincing, to find Derek standing there with Peggy Mishkavitz.

"Hey, Drew, glad to find you here. I'm trying to stay away from mingling with the profs, particularly McCulligan. She's likely to want me to do something with her kids."

"I think that situation may have been dealt with. Mrs. McElroy is taking them somewhere, I mean is making sure that they are enjoying themselves."

"Yeah, I heard them come in, but I kept myself scarce until she went into the other room." Derek put his hand on Peggy's elbow. "You remember Peggy, don't you? And ...?" He inclined his head toward Cindy.

"Oh, this is Cindy Connor. Derek Trueblood and Peggy ... Mishkavitz?" Peggy nodded at his question, but Drew was never sure if she was ever listening to him when Derek was there.

"The Derek Trueblood?" Cindy asked.

Derek raised his eyebrows at Wally. "You've been talking about me?"

"We ran into Dr. Askovarik earlier and that's what he called me. You know, he still doesn't know which one of us is which."

"And I intend to keep it that way."

"Yeah, you're not the one whose name is on his shit list." Wally sighed.

While Cindy and Peggy were asking each other general "getting to know you, sort of" questions about their class loads, Derek took Wally's arm to draw him a few steps away.

"Hey, I didn't know you were bringing a date. I do have to admit you have good taste. But I didn't just bring Peggy. I also asked Lori, because, not knowing about Cindy, I thought you might like some company too."

"What, Lori's here?" Wally looked around, then saw her across the room talking with Dr. McElroy, and, surprisingly, he appeared to be listening to her. Wally had never seen McElroy actually listen to anybody. He even wondered about the presentations in class. "Actually, Cindy is why I am here."

"You mean, here as in at this party?"

"No," Wally realized he had no way to explain that comment. "No, never mind. But you brought two dates?"

"No, one was for you. Well, I guess, now they're both for me. But I didn't know about Cindy. You've never mentioned her."

"She ..." Wally wasn't ready to tell Derek yet about how he really knew Cindy. "She lives across the hall from me. I just met her."

"And I have a class with Dr. McElroy, so that's why Drew, if he is really Drew and you are really Derek, invited me." Cindy rejoined the conversation. "Fortunately, I do not have a class with Dr. McCulligan." She turned to Wally, "Lori?"

"She's also in McElroy's class," Wally quickly responded. Derek and he must not have been standing as far away as he had hoped. "We, Derek and I, ran into her and Peggy at a football game. Peggy is her roommate. Right, Peggy?" He wanted the conversation to go in a different direction.

Peggy nodded at the sound of her name and grabbed Derek's hand. "Can we get something to drink now? And I'd like to try those deviled eggs. Derek, I think your prof has filled up her plate and wandered off."

"Sure, sure. I think we're safe. Check with you later, Drew." Derek was dragged by a hungry-looking Peggy in the direction of the appetizers.

"Would you like something?" Wally gestured toward the same table for Cindy.

"I'm willing to see what they have."

They filled their plates and found some punch to drink. Wally couldn't tell if it was alcoholic or not and he noticed that his plate appeared twice as full as Cindy's. He started looking for a place to set his cup so that he could actually take a bite from his plate instead of just hold it for the rest of the evening. He could never figure out how other people managed to eat with both hands occupied. The realization hit him that Cindy had already taken a few bites without spilling anything and without him being able to tell how she did it.

As they took a couple of steps away from the food table, Lori and Dr. McElroy approached, still in discussion.

"I think we can work something out with that, Miss Gibbons." McElroy was now doing the talking. "But you'll have to get with my assistant, Mr. Wright, to go over the details. Ah, there he is now. Mr. Wright, have you met Miss Gibbons? She is in the Beginning Issues class and will want to meet with you regarding her project. I know I could care less about it."

He noticed the table as if for the first time. "Oh, food!" then he looked around the room and seemed to also see all the people for the first time. "A party." Across the room, his wife was entering from a hallway, wiping her brow and sighing. "Our party! The faculty and graduate party!" A puzzled look came over him. "Am I supposed to be doing something?"

He looked at a wristwatch and shook his head. He pulled one out of a pocket and smiled. "That's better. Now, at just the right time, this party should be ready to start."

Noticing Cindy for the first time and turning back to Lori, "Miss Connor, Miss Gibbons, it is nice to see you both tonight, but how did you get into this affair? Undergraduate students were not invited. That one is later in the spring."

They responded simultaneously, "Drew invited me." Then looked at each other in surprise.

Lori recovered first, "Well, actually, Derek Trueblood asked me, but said, um, never mind."

"That's okay then, as long as you came as somebody's guest. I just wanted to make sure I was in the right place." McElroy stepped away from them and grabbed a plate, disappearing around the table.

"I am sorry," Lori apologized. "I shouldn't have said it that way. I must have misunderstood what Derek said. But," she cocked her head at Cindy, "I thought you were seeing, oh, you know." Cindy raised her eyebrows. "Forgive me, I'm speaking out of turn again."

Wally answered, "He has an away game this weekend. Cindy lives – in the same building as I do." To Cindy, "And Lori lives in the sorority next door."

"Oh."

And another "Oh."

Both young women were sort of still smiling, but Wally had no idea what that was supposed to mean, just that somehow he was in trouble and didn't really know how that had happened.

"Uh-oh." Cindy was now looking over his shoulder at the same hall doorway that Heather McElroy had entered. There were two small heads peering around the frame, staring at the food table. Their parents were nowhere in sight. "Excuse me for a minute, Drew."

She handed him her empty plate and cup (*how had she finished them? And how was he supposed to hold them and his still full plate?*) and made her way over to the door. "Hi, are you guys hungry? We can probably fix you something. Come on." She brought them back to the table and became busy finding finger food they would be willing to eat.

Lori took Cindy's plate and cup from Wally and she placed them on a small table next to the wall, which seemed intended to hold the used dishes. "She seems nice."

Wally took a sip from his glass and then set it down momentarily on the table. He still hadn't been able to take a bite yet, so quickly took one -- something on a cracker or maybe a dry piece of toast, not quite sure but at least it didn't seem to have Bradford seasoning -- before answering.

"Yes, she is. At least as far as I know. I don't really know her all that well. We just met. Kind of. I mean, I had seen her in class. With Darryl Thomas, I mean. But I just found out that she lives in my building. One time we entered the lobby at the same time. I'm babbling again, aren't I? I do that sometimes when um, I get, uh …"

"Yes, I've noticed." At least her smile seemed a little more real this time. And struck a distant chord in him. It was more familiar than just recognizing it on her.

"Look. I do apologize. I had no idea that Derek had invited you here for me. As a date for me, I mean. Or however he explained it."

Lori laughed this time. "Actually, I think he intended it to make Peggy more comfortable in coming here with him. Not to be the only undergraduate here. Though now it seems like there are several of us."

She took a deep breath, and then another. "Drew, there seems to be something different going on with you. I don't mean bad, but I think there's something odd. I don't think you are here as a graduate student just to get a degree. There's something more. Your laptop said you would tell me about it sometime. And that was really weird in itself, that your computer had a message for me." A third deep breath. "Maybe it's time?"

Wally watched Cindy take the children, both carrying full plates in one hand while holding on to one of her hands with the other, to the hallway.

"Alright, I probably do need to talk with someone." He spoke in a low voice and looked around. "But not here. And not tonight. How about Monday if you come in during my tutoring time? We're apparently supposed to be talking about your project anyway."

"That will work." She nodded and glanced toward the doorway. "Oh, look. Dr. Askovarik has brought a date too. At least I don't think it's his wife. I thought I heard that he wasn't married."

Wally followed her gaze and stood in shock for a moment.

"That's Mrs. Weidenbach! My landlady!"

"You know her?"

"She owns my building. At least that's who I pay my rent to – I assume she owns it. But ..." He was trying to determine which persona she was using tonight. She seemed to be dressed sedately enough, but there was still a little swing to her hips and a smile that seemed to promise something more. And, come to think of it, he had never seen Dr. Askovarik smile before either. "I had no idea they even knew each other. And dating?" He shook his head.

"Well, I think that's nice for them. They look good together. And he certainly seems happy. But you said 'Mrs.' Is she married?"

He shook his head. "No, at least I've never seen or heard of a husband. I think she's widowed."

Lori looked back to the hall entrance. "I do believe Cindy has gone somewhere with the McCulligan kids. And I am betting she could use some help. I'll talk to you in a little bit." And she was gone in the same direction.

Wally wasn't sure what to do now. Theoretically he had two dates for this evening, but, in a very practical sense, he was with neither one of them. Not the way this was supposed to go.

And now Professor Askovarik and Mrs. Weidenbach were heading in his direction. When they were still halfway across the room, Derek, oblivious to the approach of the others, appeared at his elbow.

"Hey, where are all your women?"

"At the moment, they seem to be taking care of your supervisor's children, since nobody else is. Well, Heather McElroy was, but she had to get back to hostessing. Speaking of females, where is yours? I thought she never left your hip."

"Peggy is back at the food and drink table," Derek pointed. "She can't get enough of those deviled eggs -- guess she never makes them."

"Have you ever made them?"

"What, deviled eggs? No, but then it's not one of my favorites. She's also mixing her drinks."

At Wally's raised eyebrows, Derek shrugged, "I think it's orange juice and ginger ale. That's her party drink. She doesn't drink alcohol."

By that time, Askovarik and Mrs. Weidenbach had reached them and it was too late for Derek to slide away.

"We should as well get this over with, gentlemen," Askovarik started. "Mr. Wright, Mr. Trueblood, may I present Eleanora Weidenbach. Eleanora, these are two of my so-called students, some may be less called students than others."

"Mrs. Weidenbach." Wally nodded to her while Derek simply stood with his mouth open. Fortunately, Askovarik hadn't indicated which student was which. As his landlady still didn't always call him by the right name, she didn't need a third choice thrown into the mix.

"Oh, I know Mr. Wright," she said, batting her eyes in the general direction of both of them. "We live together."

"In the same building." Wally was quick to point out. "She's ..." he suddenly remembered he wasn't supposed to be Mr. Wright to Askovarik, "a, uh, a landlady."

But Askovarik didn't seem to have noticed the eye-batting or the awkward response. He merely said, "I am sorry to hear that. Eleanora, would you care for some refreshments? Then we will find out what is left."

As they moved away, Wally heard her say, "Sorry? I could have sworn I had finally got it right." She giggled, "Wright. Did you hear what I said, 'right' for 'Wright'?"

Derek finally closed his mouth. "Somebody dates him? Willingly?"

"That's my landlady," Wally repeated. "I was afraid she was going to confuse the issue even further with our names and who is really who."

Peggy reappeared next to Derek with a plate full of her deviled eggs. "I got the last of them. I'm good for the night."

"Great," Derek smiled. "Let's enjoy them in another room."

But as they moved through the doorway, they literally ran into Lucille McCulligan and Peggy almost dropped her plate. Almost, but she managed to keep the eggs from sliding off.

"Derek! There you are! I've been looking all over for you!" He really hoped that wasn't true. "Have you seen Harrison and Belinda?" At his blank face, she added, "My children! You know, the little ones that came in with me."

"Oh, I think they are with …" He looked at Wally who inserted, "a Miss Connor and a Miss Gibbons. They are being well taken care of."

"So thash where Wori went." Peggy spoke around a mouth full of egg and mayo.

"Oh, good!" McCulligan beamed. "I knew they wouldn't be any trouble." She poked Derek in the chest. "But you just take care of it if they are." And off she went.

"But they are being trouble," Wally muttered, not caring if anybody really heard him or not. "I'm not spending any time with my date, or even my other could-be date."

The three of them wandered for a few minutes, trying not to spend any meaningful moments with any of the faculty. Some of the students had started a card game at an empty table but it was already in progress with no empty chairs to join.

Heather McElroy spotted them and came over.

"I hope you're enjoying yourselves. Drew, I so appreciate your Cindy. She is helping out so much with the McCulligan children. And her friend too. I'm afraid I don't know her name."

"Lori Gibbons, she's another student in Dr. McElroy's class," Wally told her.

"Well, she is being such a help too. I don't know what I would have done without them."

"I'm sure they're glad to do it. Cindy is in elementary education so she enjoys kids of that age."

"Thank them for me again. Oh, it looks like we're out of deviled eggs. I'll have to see if there is any more in the kitchen. Excuse me."

Derek and Peggy were looking at him, Peggy trying to hold the last egg out of sight of the departing hostess.

"That was Heather McElroy, Dr. McElroy's wife. She was not happy when she saw the McCulligan children come in. I suspect this is not the first time they have shown up unexpectedly."

Derek smiled. "I expect it's not unexpected from someone's point of view. If Dr. McCulligan believes that she got away with it once, she'll do it again, just assuming that other people will adjust to what she wants." He shrugged. "There are people like that. And then they will act offended when someone finally confronts them. The only way to deal with it is to not do what they want the first time."

"Has that been working for you?" Wally asked.

"No." Derek sighed. "Most people, like me, are too nice, thinking surely they can't be that presumptuous to ask me to do that again. And then they do."

"That's terrible," Peggy said. "I'd make them watch their own kids. I think I'm going to go find those kids right now and tell the girls that." She strode to a doorway, but Wally had no idea if she was heading in the right direction or not.

"I'm sorry, Derek, but it looks as if you may have lost your date for the night too."

"She'll be back. I think there's some bacon-wrapped shrimp left and she loves those too. I don't think she really eats much on her own because she doesn't like to cook, so she likes to take advantage of free food when she can get it." He looked around. "I think I'm going to go watch the card game. I have no idea what game they're playing, but it seems to involve a lot of drinking and throwing things at each other. Join me?"

"No thanks, I think I'm going to check with Dr. McElroy and make sure he still remembers this is his party."

McElroy may not have remembered that it was his party but he was enjoying himself. He was in a small group trying to tell some story about a guy lost in the woods, but kept messing up the punchline about meeting the mother bear – Goldilocks kept entering the story and somebody was nakedly bare – but it didn't matter since the rest of the group had already had too much to drink. The funniest thing was that it didn't appear as if McElroy had had anything to drink at all. It was just his usual confusion. Everybody else kept laughing, which messed up his sense of the story timeline. He nodded at Wally but didn't stop talking and Wally didn't want to interrupt him.

He felt a hand on his back and turned to find Cindy there.

"Oh, hi, you're back."

"Only for the moment, I'm afraid. I told the kids I'd get them each a cupcake. I hope there are some left."

"I think so. The faculty seem to be more interested in the drinks."

"Lori and …" She searched for the name. "Peggy are reading a story right now, taking turns with the voices. The kids are really good kids, just out of place at an adult party. I don't know what their parents were thinking."

"I think they were thinking they wouldn't have to pay for a babysitter. And they were right. You're doing it."

At that moment, Askovarik and Mrs. Weidenbach entered the room. Wally pointed them out.

"Did you know Mrs. Weidenbach is here?"

"No, I didn't. But which one is it?"

Wally looked at her in surprise. "Which one? You mean, which personality? I think it's the fun-loving one, the one who likes to flirt."

"I meant which sister. Eleanora is the more playful one. Surely you knew which was which."

He almost spilled his drink, tried to catch it with both hands, and ended up finally spilling only a little on his shirt. "There are sisters? I thought there was only -- there's more than one? They're both a Mrs. Weidenbach? Wait a minute. I've only seen one at a time. Are you sure?"

Cindy lowered her voice. "They are twins. Not every one is supposed to know that -- that's why they dress alike, but I thought you would know it by now. You're supposed to be a psychologist, can't you tell the difference?"

"Well, about that ..." he started. "I could tell there was a difference, yes, of course, but I just thought she was weird."

"Like a split personality?"

"No, just ... weird. I've never seen them together." He was having trouble getting his head around the concept. "They're two different people, but they have the same name?"

Cindy looked around and spotted two empty chairs in a corner. "Let's go over there." Once they were seated, she continued, speaking quietly, "They married brothers. The brothers were not twins, but they were brothers. Both died a short while ago, in a paint store fire, where Isadora's husband worked. Isadora is the more sedate one, the one who dresses and acts more conservatively, I guess you could say. But it may not have been an accidental fire. Apparently, Eleanora's husband was there to talk to his brother about something that he was involved in that he wasn't supposed to be. I'm not exactly sure of all the details, but I'll tell you what I do know."

Her eyes circled the room again, this time to make sure no one else was listening.

"Isadora's husband was legit, but Eleanora's apparently got into trouble gambling and owed a lot of money. He robbed a couple of bars late at night to get the money, and the story is that one of the bars was a front for the gamblers themselves, and that they kept all their money there. Which he took. He didn't know it was theirs and he didn't know at first that it was so much. He used some of it to pay them back for his debts and then somehow, they figured out it was their own money. It's complicated but they apparently killed the brothers trying to get the rest of it back and now are after Eleanora, figuring she may have it. Now she is living with her sister and they are pretending to be one person, Isadora."

"I don't believe this, there are two of them." Wally shook his head, not yet ready to process the rest of the story. "But Askovarik called her 'Eleanora'."

"Oh, that could be a problem. He's not supposed to know that name." She put her hand on his arm. "Look, we'll talk more later. I did promise those kids their cupcakes before they're gone." She stood up and hurried to the table.

"But, but ..." Wally couldn't get any words out fast enough.

He sat for a while and watched the professor and his landlady, or rather one of his landladies, wander. Askovarik was carefully avoiding coming to Wally's side of the room. Eleanora was being consistent with the flirtatious side that he had come to fear. Now that he was paying attention, Wally didn't see any of the more straight-laced, sedate personality coming out. Maybe there really were two of them. That would explain a lot, but, as far as he was concerned, it didn't explain nearly enough.

CHAPTER 22

As the party went on, the crowd began thinning out. Apparently, Dr. McElroy's stories could only hold attention for so long, and, once the deviled eggs were truly gone, and the alcohol choices were becoming limited, people were saying their goodbyes and looking for their special treats elsewhere.

Derek sat down next to Wally and informed him that the other graduate students had taken their card game to someone's apartment, where they could become louder and more inappropriate with their actions than they could among professors determining their futures. Wally was still so stunned by the double Weidenbachs that he had trouble engaging in much meaningless small talk, and they just sat for awhile and watched the outrageous behavior that the remaining faculty thought they could get away with. Dr. Miriam Bluebaugh hit on just about every male present, available or unavailable, subtly or not so subtly, and eventually walked out with a first-year associate professor. Derek commented that he didn't think it was soon going to matter much if she was wearing underwear or not, but Wally was barely listening. Though Derek had long ago decided that she wasn't wearing any. Doctors Avery and Mendelschmidt insulted each other's research, but were too intoxicated to remember why, just kept calling it "shit", sometimes "immature shit", or "uneducated shit", or "shitty shit", when they couldn't recall what they had already said. This was apparently a common enough exchange that everybody else totally ignored it. Their spouses eventually took them off home.

Peggy showed up, licking her fingers from the last of the bacon-wrapped shrimp.

"The kids are finally asleep. You'd think the parents would realize this needs to be an early evening, but no, they're still going strong."

Lori came up behind her. "I think they are going to take advantage of not having to be with them for as long as possible. Cindy is still there watching after them. Drew, she is a very nice person. I really like her."

Wally just nodded, "Yeah." Lori had spent much more time with his date than he had, and probably now knew her much better.

Peggy took Derek's hand and pulled him out of his seat. "I think it's time we were leaving. While I'm still awake, if you know what I mean."

Derek's eyes widened.

"And I guess you're still my ride home," Lori added.

His eyes widened even more.

"Okay, then, we are off. Take care, Drew." He put out both arms for the ladies to take and escorted them to the front door without a single look back.

Most of the guests had departed when Cindy finally reappeared.

"I kept waiting for the McCulligans to come claim their children, but I finally gave up and just told Heather where they were sleeping. She said she'd take care of it, but that I should have come back to the party sooner."

Wally sighed, but tried not to make it too audible. He then attempted to make up for it with a supportive comment.

"Well, no one else was going to take responsibility for those kids, especially not their parents. That was extremely nice of you to do that. You're a very caring person."

She shrugged. "I think the small talk among the PhDs would have gotten pretty strained. There's only so much psychological analysis that I can take. After a while I think some, not all, but some of the academicians can get caught up in research findings and not in how it makes sense in people's lives. No offense."

"None taken. Most research applies to groups and the likelihood of a certain response rather than any individual case. None of it means that this particular person will act this particular way in this particular situation, only that there is a ninety per cent chance, or an eighty per cent chance, or a fifty per cent chance that he or she will. Or he or she won't. There's a purpose to it, but sometimes it's hard to get too high and mighty about it."

He stood up. "Are you ready to go? Before the kids wake up and the McCulligans decide they want just one last drink?"

"Yeah," she joined him. "It's past my bedtime too. And soon I turn back into a pumpkin."

"I don't think you ever could become less beautiful than you are. But I don't think that's how the story really goes. She just loses her glass slippers and her fancy gown." He paused. "Maybe that's not such a bad idea."

She didn't respond. They waved goodbye to the McElroys from across the room and slid out the front door before anyone else, particularly the McCulligans, could catch them.

Wally's hopes were not quite as high on the way back to their apartment as they had been on the way to the party. He hadn't had as much of an opportunity to charm Cindy and to impress her with his wit and maturity as was his original intention when he arrived in this time period, and it was way too late for any of it to work tonight. As a matter of greater priority, the concept of the two Weidenbachs was still at the forefront of his brain, emphatically blocking his libido.

"You said you would tell me more about Mrs. Weidenbach and ... Mrs. Weidenbach. How did you find out all this?"

Cindy glanced behind to make sure there wasn't anybody walking within hearing distance.

"One day I was walking back from the laundry with one of them and we came upon the other checking the mail. They both looked distressed and asked me to come into their apartment. They swore me to secrecy, 'except of course for that nice Mr. Wright' for some reason. That was a big reason I assumed you knew. Anyway, they told me all about having to pretend to be the same person. The gamblers had apparently threatened Eleanora after her husband's death. That was the first she claimed to have heard about all this. They didn't seem to really believe that she didn't know anything about their money and said they would be back. She didn't want to call the police because, well, her husband, Gus, did like to gamble and it was all too possible that he had done what they said he did. So she packed up some clothes and left her home in Oldstown to come here. She and Isadora came up with pretending to be the same person, and then there wouldn't be an extra somebody to have to explain. If the gamblers thought it was only Isadora here, they would look elsewhere. Eleanora could sort of hide in plain sight."

"And this works?"

"You didn't know there were two." She stopped walking. "Oh, you're not one of the ones looking for them, are you? And I've given it away?" But before he could answer, she shook her head. "No, no, they said to keep it a secret from everyone but you. So you can't be one of the bad people."

"Well, I didn't know anything about it. But I also don't know why I'm supposed to be an exception to their secret."

Cindy shrugged. "That's all they said. Unless you're not the 'nice Mr. Wright' they were talking about. After all, you told me they keep messing up your name."

She stopped and looked behind them again.

"But I am worried. Dr. Askovarik was not supposed to know Eleanora by her real name."

"Maybe that means he knows there are two of them. Maybe, if he is dating, I almost hate to use that word with him, but if he is dating Eleanora, maybe they thought he needed to know. Then he wouldn't accidentally, oh Jesus, kiss the wrong one." Wally shuddered at the thought, but realized it was not as revolting a thought as it would have been a few hours earlier.

"That could be. But he introduced her that way."

"That didn't mean anything to me. I didn't know her first name, or either of their first names anyway. I didn't catch anything."

"But the gamblers would have."

"If they would just happen to be at a faculty party at Bradford State University. Not one of the things you go to unless you have to." Cindy shot him a glare. "Or are invited to go. By someone that has to be there.

"I didn't see anyone strange," he added. "Or, let's put it this way, I didn't see someone who was out of place, wasn't supposed to be there."

Cindy nodded, "You're right, there wasn't any catering or wait staff. And, I assume, anybody not actually a known faculty or a known graduate student, would have been a spouse or a date. But it still bothers me that, if he used her real name there, he's likely to use it other places – somewhere where he can be overheard. By the wrong people."

By this time, they had arrived back home. Wally was surprised he found himself thinking of it as home. It wasn't what he would call homey, but it was where he was living. At least in this time out of time.

They trudged slowly up the steps and stopped outside Cindy's door. She turned to him and showed off her megawatt smile.

"This has been fun." End of date words if he had ever heard any. "I have enjoyed this, even if much of it was spent watching somebody else's kids. And not getting paid. And I liked meeting your friends. Lori is very nice." She sighed. "I have to get up early. On Saturday mornings, I help cook a breakfast for a food pantry. Maybe you could help sometime. It's kind of late to set up for tomorrow, but how about next Saturday?"

Wally's brain was not ready to process the next morning, but "Sure" for the next week worked.

"Anyway, we'll do this again. Or maybe not this but something. Really I want to do that." She leaned forward and kissed him on the lips. He held her arms as he wasn't going to be the one to first break the kiss. It seemed to him that, though it wasn't a full-bodied passionate embrace, she did hold it longer than a simple peck would have been. To him it was forever, yet not nearly long enough. She smiled again and disappeared behind her door.

CHAPTER 23

MyFate

I hope you enjoyed the party.
*Well, as much as you could while she was babysitting, so to speak.
I know I enjoyed whatever time I did spend with Cindy.*
But ...
And it's a big but.
*But maybe, just maybe, Cindy isn't the only reason you're back here.
Maybe, just maybe, the two Mrs. Weidenbachs may have something to
do with it.*
Think about it.

CHAPTER 24

Wally didn't happen to run into either of the Mrs. Weidenbachs over the weekend and he couldn't think of a legitimate excuse to deliberately knock on their door. But he also couldn't get them out of his mind. Even though they weren't the females he wanted to be thinking about. Not at all.

When he went to the grocery store he found himself looking at everybody with suspicion – the guy stocking the fruits (*was he here last week, and, even if he was, just when was he hired?*), the woman gazing at him from behind the fresh bagels, the man with the hiking boots striding quickly away, the young lady with a cart full of breakfast cereals and two little kids. Was someone not who they were pretending to be – someone sort of staking out the Weidenbachs? Okay, probably not the one with the little kids, but the hiking boots reminded him of something. Possibly, but not for sure.

He did knock on Cindy's door both Saturday and Sunday, but didn't get an answer. However, he already knew that she was both busy and popular, words that didn't typically fit himself. He told himself that he wasn't familiar with when she might not be busy, and he knew she was always going to be popular.

Monday morning was his open office time to help the undergrads. He had promised Lori some time to talk about … time. He had been avoiding thinking about this conversation, so he opened The Laptop as he sat down at his table.

MyFate

You've been avoiding thinking about this conversation, haven't you?

I don't blame you, but it's going to happen anyway. Lori is going to be here any minute and she is the one you tell about being from the future. Yeah, she'll think you're nuts at first, but what else is new?

In order to prove that you are telling her the truth, you could tell her that the Cleveland Browns win the Super Bowl, but that's too far off in the future (still far off in the future) to mean anything to her now. And frankly, that would be too unbelievable anyway. I know, tell her that the star running back for the Bradford State Bees, Marshall Jefferson, breaks his ankle in practice today, which actually enhances Darryl Thomas' draft status, as he now becomes the focal point of the team's offense. She may not really care about "draft status", but she will find out about the broken ankle.

Actually, she's not going to be that hard to convince, as she already knows that something about you is different. Significantly different.

You'll figure it out.

Just as he finished reading the entry, he looked up and saw Lori waiting in the doorway.

"How long have you been standing there?" he asked.

"Long enough to see that puzzled look on your face. Is that concern about talking to me, or is there something else that's bothering you?" She sat opposite him, not waiting for an invitation that didn't appear to be coming.

He looked off to the left for a second, not changing his puzzled look, but then spun The Laptop around. "You better take a seat."

"I am sitting."

"Oh, yeah, well, take hold of your seat then. And read this."

She read silently for a minute, then sat silently for two more minutes, looking back at the screen a couple of times as if to confirm for herself that the message was really there.

"You're nuts."

He sighed, "I thought you'd say that."

She pointed at the screen. "Well, it said I would say that, so I thought I would get it out of the way. This is nuts anyway. Wait a minute," she paused. "Something else is appearing." She glanced up at Wally, "And, unless, you are really good at time-delay writing, you're not writing this." Her eyes went back down, and then she pulled her own laptop out of its case next to her.

"What are you doing?"

"Hold on, it says to open my computer." She opened it and turned it on. Her eyes opened wider. "My screen says, I can't believe this, it says, well, just look …" It was her turn to show the screen to him.

Good morning, Lori …
I know you are surprised. I was surprised too.
Believe Drew (by the way, that's not his real name, but he will tell you about that in a minute). There's no way to really explain it in a way that makes sense, but he is from the future. Really. Truly. In fact.
Listen to Drew. He needs you to believe him, because it will matter, believe me.
From Lori. (Yes, I am you from the future, or some other time anyway. It is a lot to hold onto, but trust me).

Lori sat back and took a deep breath. She stared at Drew for at least a moment. During that time, another man, a little bit older than a typical student, appeared at the door.

"Excuse me, but could I see you about my project?"

Wally stood up and went to the door. "I'm with someone right now. Could you take a seat, or better yet, could you come back in about half an hour. This is going to take a while."

The shorter man took a look at his watch. "How about an hour and a half? I'm on my way to a class right now."

"Yeah, yeah, that will be fine." As the student started to leave, Wally called after him, "Oh, and bring something to eat. I'll be hungry then." He shut the door, which probably should have happened earlier.

Wally sat back down and shuffled some papers just for something to do while not looking back at Lori. Without looking up, he said, "Marshall Jefferson will break his ankle today."

"Who?"

"Marshall Jefferson. The running back for the football team. He will break his ankle in practice today and Darryl Thomas will become a bigger star and go high in the NFL draft."

"Okay. I know the program said to say that, but why tell me that particular information? I don't really know the players on the team. I think I told you that Peggy and I go to the games to look at their butts."

He pointed at The Laptop. "As you said, my program said to tell you that so that you would believe I'm from the future."

"Oh, I wasn't really questioning you being from someplace else. Yet." She tilted her head. "So what is your real name?"

"That's the question you start with? Not how did this happen or what are you doing here? Or where is security when you need them?"

"I need something to grab on to. Something that makes sense. Sort of, I guess."

Wally shifted in his seat. "My real name is Wally Stephens. Wally."

"Wally. You're a Wally. Huh. So how did you get the name, 'Drew'?"

"That's the name on the ID they gave me before I came back here. Drew Wright. Well, Andrew Wright. Drew was just what I pulled out when somebody asked me what I was called. The last name, 'Wright', has led to some problems, but that's another story. I have no idea where the name came from in the first place. If there's any significance to it or if it was just random."

"Okay, ... Wally, how far ahead in time are you from?"

"Call me Drew. That's my name here and I'm not ready for someone else from this time to become confused with my name. That's already a problem for my landladies -- landlady, and Askovarik."

"Drew." This time she rolled her eyes.

"From six years ahead. I'm actually 27, the same age I look."

"I'd have said you look 30, but, okay."

"Really, I always thought I looked young for my age, but maybe because you're younger, I look comparatively older. I think that sometimes ..."

"Drew. I was kidding and you're rambling."

"Yeah, I do that."

"I know." She put her hands to her cheeks and lightly rubbed them. "So you're from six years into the future. Hardly worth coming back. Not much difference here."

"Some technology. This Laptop is way out of date. In my time, I have a watch that I use to talk with other people. And we also have flying cars, that sort of thing."

"Flying cars? Really?"

"No, it was my turn to be kidding about that. Technology will just keep getting smaller and focusing on communication, without really improving how people do communicate with each other. It just makes it easier to say things of less importance. More apps on cell phones … and the watches. It seems as if the best minds just continue making more apps, rather than going in an original direction."

"So you have a job and a separate life. You're already out in the world. Are you married? Do you have a family? Or do you still live with your mother?"

"I'm the manager of a small used bookstore." He shrugged. "I like it, but it doesn't take a Master's degree. I'm not married, but I don't still live at home, though my mom does still do my laundry sometimes. She insists on it, or so she says. As if she doesn't trust me to wear clean clothes. I don't have a serious relationship with anyone. That's probably why I was willing to do this."

"To do what, exactly?"

He drummed his fingers on the table.

"Well-l-l …"

"Well, what? Your … computer program or whatever said you're supposed to tell me. So tell me."

"Keep in mind, this isn't what I picked first. I wanted to go back to something important, something significant. You know, a famous date or time?"

"You're rambling again."

He looked down at the table, not wanting to meet her eye.

"I used to know Cindy Connor in high school …"

"Yes?"

"They told me …"

"They?"

"Dr. Vernon Sheffield." Lori pursed her lips and she raised her eyebrows. "The guy in charge of this time travel organization." Wally shifted uncomfortably in his seat. "He told me I'm supposed to come back and ... get to know Cindy better. That was my motivation for wanting to go back in time. Sort of an 'if I knew then what I know now' sort of thing. I was pretty shy in high school and never asked her out."

"Really? To get to know Cindy 'better', did you say? And has that happened? Did you get to know her 'better' the other night?"

"Well, kind of, but, no, not what you mean. Or what you thought I meant, anyway." He pulled his Laptop back to his side of the table in a desire to move the subject somewhere else. Anywhere else. "Anyway, my program, which I guess is me, is now saying I may be back here for something different."

Lori crossed her arms. "Why are you telling me all this stuff? What am I supposed to do about it?"

"I don't know. Seriously. I guess you're the one that's been asking the questions about what I'm really doing here. Maybe you're supposed to help me with something or solve some problem I don't know about yet."

"So I'm supposed to help you get to know Cindy 'better'? You seem to be doing pretty well with that already."

"If you have any ideas in that direction, I wouldn't say no." He saw the look in her eyes and straightened up. "But maybe it has to do with this other thing my computer brought up."

Lori brought up her hand. "Wait a minute. Before we get into that, you mentioned a Vernon Sheffield? You do know that was who came to the door when we first sat down."

It took a moment to bring it back. "No, I didn't. I didn't recognize him." Wally paused. "He looked much older when I first met, first meet him, six years from now."

"Well, that will be six years from now."

"No, even older than that. Like close to forty, not roughly my age."

"Now who's bad at estimating ages." Lori smiled. "Actually, he is older. He's, oh, about thirty, I guess. He's one of those perpetual students – keeps getting degrees so he doesn't have to go out and face the real world. Still searching for himself, as they like to say." She shrugged. "Personally, for me, school is just something I have to get through to go out and really do something. For me, it's a stepping stone -- for Vern Sheffield, it's a slow drive down a long, long road with no apparent exits. Or a need for any."

"So how do you know him?"

"He's in an apartment on the other side of the sorority. Has been there ever since I've known him. He used to date a senior that was in the house when I was a freshman, but she graduated two years ago. He still comes over and is sort of like our big, well older, brother. I don't think that's what he always wants to be, but that's how we think of him."

"At some point, he's going to have to be involved in this. Because he's the one that gets me here."

"And just how did he get you here?"

"Well, there's this chair..."

"Yes?"

"And I sat on it ...!"

"That's usually what chairs are for."

"And Sheffield pushed a button on the chair ..."

"And?"

"And I was here."

"And you were here."

"And I was here."

"Just like that?"

"Just like that. No noise, no fading in and out, no traveling down a time tunnel. Just here."

Lori turned The Laptop around to face her again and studied it for a minute. Then she shook her head and sat back. "Where is this ... chair?"

"In my room at my apartment."

"Can I see it?"

"I suppose. Sometime. My program didn't say anything about it, so it didn't say you couldn't. See it. No touching though."

"Vern must have touched it."

"He will. In the future. I guess he touches it at some time, but probably not the button. You know, THE Button."

"So he didn't use it himself to go through time?"

Wally paused to consider that point. "I don't know. I don't think so, but it never came up. He just said 'You're going, so sit down'. He put The Laptop on my lap, and a suitcase in my arms, and pushed the button. And off I went."

"But he did tell you that you were supposed to get to know Cindy Connor 'better'. Somewhere in the middle of that business of getting you into that chair and then pushing that button.

"So." She pointed a finger at him. "Now what? What are you supposed to do now? And why am I involved in this?"

"This…" He tapped The Laptop. "This now says that I may be here for a different reason altogether. Something to do with my landlady, who, as it turns out, is actually two landladies – twin sisters."

"Yeah, I knew that. So what's their problem?"

"You knew that they were twins?"

"Yeah, once you pointed out she was your landlady, I realized I had seen them before as neighbors and it was obvious. Are you saying you didn't know?

"Not till Saturday night. How did you know? No one is supposed to. It's supposed to be a secret."

"Afraid it's not a secret. Once you meet each of them, you realize they are two separate women. Couldn't you tell?"

Wally avoided answering the question directly. "Apparently, there are bad guys – organized crime, after one of them, for something her dead husband did. Both of them are widows and they are trying to pretend to be the same person so the bad guys don't know that the one they are after is there."

Wally expected Lori to need more explanation, or at least to look puzzled. But she just nodded as if it made perfect sense.

"Okay. I can see that."

"So that makes sense to you?"

"Enough. Let's just say it makes more sense than you being from another time. What are you supposed to do about it?"

"I don't know." He put up a hand. "And don't say that I say 'I don't know' a lot. I know I do. And that's because I don't know. I got sent here with no real explanation of what I'm to do. And this thing," he gestured at The Laptop, "only tells me something when it wants to. And then it can be pretty vague."

He ran his fingers through his hair. "I guess they haven't found her yet – Eleanora, I mean. The one who's hiding. And I am probably supposed to help keep her from being found, or to help keep her from being hurt if she is found."

"And you have done this sort of thing before? Save people from 'bad guys', as you call them?"

"No, not really."

"Not really?"

"Well, no. Just no, I haven't done anything like that."

"And I'm surprised that she hasn't been found out yet. Maybe they just sent males and it's a 'man' thing not to recognize the difference between them. I mean, you couldn't tell."

Wally looked at her as if he wanted to argue, but ended up conceding she probably had a point. "Okay, maybe."

Lori looked at her watch, the non-communicating kind.

"Look, you just laid a bunch of stuff on me, but I do have a class I have to get to – and you have to meet Vern Sheffield yet, right? We do have to get together again to figure this out. You're supposed to be here to do something, or at least do something else, but you don't know what yet, and I'm supposed to help you with whatever, but I don't know how yet. Something like that?"

Wally sort of bobbed his head as if he wasn't sure whether to nod in agreement or not.

"Here's my cell phone number." She read him a string of digits and he picked up his phone and entered them. "Call me sometime, soon, I mean it." She leaned over and took his hand. "We'll work it out."

She let his hand go, grabbed her bag, and left.

CHAPTER 25

There was a knock at the door and Wally looked up. There was no one in sight. He had left the door open on purpose for Vern Sheffield, but, Vern, after noisily interrupting earlier, and not knowing just what he had really interrupted but that it looked intense, knocked on the far side of the door without looking in. Not getting an immediate answer, he knocked again.

Wally still didn't see anything but a hand, so he said, "Yes? Is someone there?"

This time, Vern stuck his head around.

"Is it okay, now? Are you alone?"

Wally looked around and said, "Yeah, I think so."

Vern stepped into the room and Wally added, "But apparently not any more."

Vern blinked at that comment. "Oh, uh. I can come back."

"I meant you. You're here now, so I'm not alone. Come in and sit down." Wally waved to the seat. "You wanted to meet with me?"

"Uh, yes. Here's your lunch." Vern held out a grease-stained bag. Wally took it and opened it to discover it full of Bradford French Fries. He could tell because they appeared to be covered in Bradford grease, and, from experience, he knew they tasted just like the Bradford Onion Rings and Bradford Mushroom Balls.

"Thank you, but I didn't really mean for you to bring me a lunch. I was just kidding."

"Oh. I'm not very good with kidding, ... but I'm working on it. My name is Vern Sheffield. I'm in Dr. McElroy's class." He held out a grease-stained hand that had held the grease-stained bag that had held the grease-stained fries.

Wally pulled out the cleanest napkin that he could find from the bag before shaking the proffered hand, then wiping his own hand. He started to say, "I know who you are," but realized, just in time, that he wasn't supposed to know Vern yet.

"I appreciate the -- I think they're fries, but what can I do for you, Vern?" He pushed the bag to the end of the desk, near the wastebasket, to make it easier for just shoving in later. "Maybe something to do with time travel? That seems to be popular at the moment."

Vern looked startled. "No, that wasn't what I had in mind at all. What makes you say that?" He paused for a second. "But ..., now that you mention it ..."

He started thinking about it. For one minute, then two. At three, Wally finally broke the silence.

"Was there something you wanted to talk with me about?"

Vern looked up, as if surprised there was someone else in the room.

"Oh, uh ... yeah, I think there was ..." He shifted in his seat. "I'm interested in doing something for my project regarding 'echoing'."

"Echoing?"

"Yeah, just like that."

"Well, I don't know anything about the science of echoes. You probably have to talk to someone in physics, working with sound waves. But I don't know what you'd research about it for Professor McElroy's class."

"Oh, not that. I've already done the science of echoes. Physics, with an emphasis on auditory reception, was one of my earlier majors. You know, I have developed a sort of crude resonating machine. That produces its own echoes. Maybe you'd like to see it? I can show you how it works."

Wally was already familiar with the working model and wasn't anxious to repeat the experience.

"Maybe ... maybe some time in the future." That was accurate enough. "Tell me what do you want to do with 'echoing'?"

Sheffield sat forward, his face showing an eagerness that had been absent from most of the other students coming in to see Wally.

"Just what you did a minute ago. I said something and you repeated it, as if you hadn't heard it right."

"As if I hadn't heard it right."

"Yes, just like that. As if you hadn't … wait a minute, did you just do that on purpose?"

"Do what on purpose?"

"Repeat what I just said. Are you playing a game with me? Like little kids do – constantly repeat another just to bug the hell out of them?"

"Okay Vern, I'm not trying to bug the hell out of you. Maybe the heck out of you, but not the hell." Wally decided he'd had enough of trying to get back at Sheffield for something he wouldn't do for another six years. "I understand what you're talking about, but what do you want to know about people repeating what someone has just said? We all do it. Just like going to the bathroom." He was thinking back to Emily Pressman's presentation.

"Yeah, we do all do it. Some of us more than others." That hit home to Wally, as he was too aware of how often he repeated previous statements. "But we all do it." Vern tapped the table in emphasis and continued.

"But what do we expect the original speaker to do in response to it? My theory is that there are three possible reasons why we repeat something we have just heard." Wally thought there were too many "th" words too close together in the previous sentence (theory, that, there, three), but didn't want to go into it, because "thinking" also started with "th". "First is because we really didn't think we heard it right. Second, because we thought we heard it, but want to confirm it. And third, and quite possibly the most common reason, is because the original comment was so unexpected, that we can't believe it, and want time to process it. By repeating it, we are giving ourselves some extra seconds to think through how we really want to respond."

Wally shrugged. "A fourth reason could be that we want the first speaker to hear what he or maybe she just said and give them a chance to rethink it."

Vern sat back as if a light had just gone on, somewhere in the deep dark recesses of his brain.

"Wait a minute, wait a minute …"

Wally didn't point out that repeating oneself might also be meaningful. Or not.

Vern waved his fingers as if going through some computations in his head. "I think you've got something there."

"You mean about giving the speaker time to rethink what they said?"

"No, no, I don't care about that. They should have thought about it before they said it in the first place. I mean that 'he or she' comment you made. It hadn't occurred to me before, but I'm not sure that females do it as often as males. Maybe it's more of a male thing. Maybe that's what I could do as my project, compare how often men and women do it – repeat what they just heard. Is there a gender difference? That could be something worth checking into."

Vern stood suddenly and reached over to shake Wally's hand.

"Thank you. Thank you so much. I think we may be seeing each other more often in the future."

"I don't know about more often, but I can definitely say we will be seeing each other in the future."

"Oh, oh yes, in class. I meant I'm going to be checking in here to get more of your feedback."

And he was out the door and gone. Wally sighed and looked for another napkin to wipe his hand again, then pushed the bag further in the direction of the wastebasket. He couldn't wait to see Vern Sheffield later. Well, maybe he could, like about six years, give or take.

CHAPTER 26

MyFate

You are about to have another visitor. You're probably thinking, wait a minute, you didn't warn me about the last two; what's so special about this one?

You're right. This one you need to prepare for. This is a crucial day. Hopefully you have shared why you are here with Lori, and you have met Vern and implanted the concept of time travel in his mind. You did, didn't you?

Wally didn't know whether the thought had really been implanted, but he remembered that he had mentioned it.

Yeah, you may want to repeat it. It's hard to know what he's going to do next.

But this next one is different. This is someone who is looking for Eleanora Weidenbach. And now you know who I'm talking about.

CHAPTER 27

Wally looked at the screen for a few seconds, then slammed the top down. Maybe he could get out of the office before this "next visitor". He didn't feel ready to face somebody who was looking for Eleanora Weidenbach. Not yet. Probably not ever, but definitely not yet.

But before he could even rise from his seat, a shadow fell over the desk. He looked up and found a figure blocking the doorway. Maybe not actually blocking it, but certainly filling it up. The moment he had spent processing the computer passage had cost him his escape time. *I have got to start reacting faster,* he thought.

"Mr. Wright?"

"Yes ...?" He really had wanted to say no, but that moment was gone.

"Or is it Dr. Wright? I'm sorry, I really don't know the appropriate protocol."

"It's not doctor. At least not yet," he added to give the impression that he expected to get there sometime. "How...." He cleared his throat as it sounded too squeaky to him. He deepened it in overcompensation. "How can I help you?"

The man took a step into the room. As he did so, Wally noticed his hiking boots, boots that somehow seemed familiar, boots that struck a chord in his memory.

"I am Officer Terry Miller." He pulled a wallet out of his back pocket, and flashed it open and closed so quickly that Wally could barely register what appeared to be a badge, before returning it to his pocket. "From the Oldstown Police Department. I was wondering if I could ask you a few questions. It would just take a minute."

Wally had always held the belief that, if the police wanted to talk to you, you were better off giving them as long as they wanted. However, the police were not who he had been expecting. There had been no mention of police. And those boots were bothering him. But maybe this was about something else entirely.

"Okay." Wally rose and slowly shook the extended hand. "Have a seat." Almost too late as Officer Miller was already settling into the chair.

"I understand you have just recently moved in to town. At the beginning of the term, is that right?" Miller began.

"Yes. I just started in the graduate program." Wally did not want to ask how Officer Miller knew he had just recently come to be here.

"Oh, really? Are you enjoying it?"

"I don't think you are supposed to enjoy graduate classes. Just sort of survive them."

Miller laughed. "I suppose not. I wouldn't know. It's not been one of my experiences." He sat forward. "But that's not why I am here. Are you familiar with an Eleanora Weisenbach?"

Wally tried to take a deep breath without appearing to. This was not about something else. "No."

Miller frowned. "Isn't she one of your landladies?"

"One of my ...? There is a Mrs. Weidenbach who is my landlady, the only one that I know of, but I have no idea what her first name is. If it's Eleanora, then I do know her. Well, not really know her, just to see her in the hall. Give her the rent money, that sort of thing. No, I don't know her. I mean, I do know her, but I don't know anything about her, if that's what you want to know." His voice trailed off. "They tell me I tend to ramble on at times."

"Yeah, I can tell." Miller coughed. "We, the police, are looking for a Mrs. Eleanora Weidenbach, as you said. Sorry for the mispronunciation. Her husband, a Mr. Gus Weidenbach died about a year ago in a suspicious fire. As well as his older brother, Dieter. His widow is your landlady, Isadora. That's probably the one you say you know. She has been the landlady there for some time, I understand."

He paused and made direct eye contact with Wally.

Wally didn't know how his face was supposed to look – surprise, shock, dismay, guilt. He was working too hard on it not showing anything.

"I'm sorry. I didn't know any of that. I knew that she was a widow, well, I assumed she was a widow, because I never saw any Mr. Weidenbach around, but I didn't know about the fire. As I said, I didn't even know her first name. Our relationship is not on that kind of a basis. She's just always been Mrs. Weidenbach to me." Wally stopped, thinking he had said enough for the moment.

"Eleanora is her twin sister." Wally attempted to raise his eyebrows, as if in surprise. "I know, it was twin sisters marrying two brothers. Probably a good thing they didn't both have kids, huh? Could have been confusing as hell. Maybe even have gotten up to triplets, who knows."

Miller leaned on the desk and spoke in a lower voice, implying that what he was going to say was confidential – not for anybody else's ears.

"Between you and me, kid, Eleanora has disappeared, and her disappearing right after the suspicious fire really looks even more suspicious, if you know what I mean. It could be arson. Maybe arson that went wrong, or maybe even arson that went right. We'd really like to talk to her. Straighten it out if she had nothing to do with it. Could be she's okay, but it would be good for her if we could get her story." He sat back. "There have also been stories that there are really two women living in your landlady's apartment."

"Stories?"

"Well, talk. From neighbors. That sort of thing."

"I have only met Mrs. Weidenbach. I haven't seen any sign that she might be living with someone else. Oh, you mean that there might be two Mrs. Weidenbachs." Wally thought back to the sound of two showers and the sight of a Mrs. Weidenbach on the front walk at the same time. Could there be more than two? No, Cindy had talked about only two. Maybe Askovarik ... Wally stopped imagining right there. "No, only the one."

"Only one? You sure?" When Wally didn't respond with a nod or a shake, he went on. "No harm in me asking, huh?" Miller took the top note from a pad on the desk and wrote something on it. "You know, it's in her best interest to come talk with us. Maybe her story clears her of any involvement in this fire. Maybe she's got a good reason for disappearing. Who knows, if she's gone?" He handed the paper to Wally. "If you see or hear anything, this is a number where you can reach me." He stood. "Hope to hear from you soon. It would be real helpful."

Wally stood too and shook the proffered hand again. He'd been doing a lot of hand-shaking this morning, but this one was a bit firmer – too firm really as if Officer Miller was making a point. He tried to disengage but the officer apparently wanted to ensure that the point had been made before he let go.

After Miller left the office, Wally took some time to look at the note on his desk. Not an official card. And not apparently the number of the police station. A personal number. On a post-it note. He quickly gathered all his things and left the room. He didn't care if he had any office time remaining, this had been enough for one day.

As he came out of the office area, he dumped the bag of too-greasy and too-cold-to-eat French fries in the nearest trash can and looked around. No sign of the hiking boots or the man who wore them.

CHAPTER 28

Dr. McElroy gave Wally a piece of paper with the name of the next presenter on it and took his normal seat in the front row.

Wally stepped to just in front of the stage holding his microphone and read from the paper. "Delique." He glanced back at the speaker to ensure that the two-syllable pronunciation was the correct one. She smiled and nodded. "Delique Holmes will today be talking to us about her research into Inter-Religion and Inter-Denominational Dating Practices." He frowned for a moment. "Okay, dating outside your own religion or your own denomination, I guess. Unless she's talking about determining how old religions and denominations are, but probably not." He raised his eyebrows. "Sounds like she's been busy. Take it away, Delique." He pointed up at the pretty dark-haired young woman at the lectern, then walked up the aisle to the back of the auditorium to his usual spot.

Delique gave a tentative smile and a tentative wave to a few students she knew, but her smile became much bigger when they waved back.

"I am not talking about my own dating history." There were a few more waves and smiles out in the audience. "Well, not for the most part."

She took a deep breath.

"My interest in this subject started because I am a Catholic and I met this cute Presbyterian boy. At a party. We just started talking and I realized I wanted to see more of him. To see him more, I mean. More often. But my parents have always wanted me to settle down with a nice

Catholic, so that I would stay in the church. The Church, both words capitalized, to them. Even though they're both Christian. Protestant and Catholic, they actually have the same beliefs.

"And I started thinking, its just college right now. I mean I'm not ready to settle down yet, for heaven's sake." There were a few chuckles at the "heaven" reference. "So to speak. It got me thinking, maybe there are others with the same issues out there, wanting to date someone outside their own denomination, even their own religion. That doesn't mean they're going to marry them, does it, but is it still an issue even to date?

"As I said, we're in college and we meet a lot of different people from different backgrounds. We don't hang out usually only with others based on religion, or even race or ethnicity or sex. I mean gender. Yes, I know there are some that hang out together based on sex, but that's not what I mean." Now more people were paying attention, once the word "sex" had been brought into the conversation.

"We get together based on who we have class with, or who is in our dorm, or who we meet as friends with someone else. This is our chance to get to know other students who are different, who may have different religious backgrounds. Are we willing to date them, not just have them as friends? I've always thought that the best couples started as friends, so why should religion interfere with that?"

Dr. McElroy interrupted, "Miss Holmes, are you going to start singing 'Kumbaya'? Is this a 'change-the-world' moment?"

"Oh, no, no. I just wanted to date this cute guy, and I thought it might be an interesting idea to do my research for this class on it. I was just curious." She cocked her head at the professor. "And isn't that what you first said, that this was to satisfy our personal curiosity? I don't care who you date, Professor McElroy, or get married to, I guess, as you're already married. So you shouldn't be dating, I wouldn't think."

He nodded and waved a hand. "Continue, Miss Holmes. To satisfy your own curiosity."

She smiled again. "Well, that's what I did. I wanted to know. So I did a survey." On the screen behind her flashed a questionnaire. The printing was too small to read at first, but she pushed a clicker a few times and the print became larger, but now only showed the middle of a question – "...one who attends a ..." She clicked again and now the whole line appeared but probably still too small for the back row.

"OK, I think this is as good as it's going to get. Sorry about that, but, if you want a copy of the survey, you can let me know after class."

"How about if we want a date?" A voice came from the middle of the room.

"Um, well, maybe that too. But remember, I am a good Catholic girl."

"Well, darn. I would have said 'damn', but you're a good Catholic girl." She still couldn't tell where the voice came from, but Wally was now pretty sure it had been Darryl Thomas, sitting next to Cindy. Wally had already been looking in that direction. Others nearby were laughing, but Cindy was frowning. That seemed to be a good sign.

Dr. McElroy had turned around as if he had wanted to admonish somebody, but couldn't figure out exactly who. "Alright, people. Remember, each one of you will have your turn up here. Respect the speaker as you would want others to respect you when you are speaking." He tried to give his "I am serious" look, but he wasn't very good at it and there were still smiles throughout the class.

Delique pulled out a card and held it in front of her.

"Since the screen is still hard to see, I'm going to just summarize. The survey questions were along the lines of what religion do you observe, if any, what denomination or sect do you consider yourself a member of, how long have you been in that religion or denomination, how often do you attend services, have you ever dated outside of that religion or denomination, how many different people have you dated in those circumstances, how many dates for each, how intimate did you become." She stopped for a moment and looked out at the class. "This was anonymous, but I did get some interesting answers on that last question. But you will have to imagine them as I am not going to include them in my report." She looked back down at her index cards. "How serious did you, or do you believe that relationship to be, are you still in that relationship, and do you expect or hope this relationship to become permanent?" She put the card down and looked around the auditorium. "I handed this survey out to fifty guys and to fifty girls at the student union, mostly people I didn't know. Forty-two guys and thirty-one girls gave them back to me. I'm not sure what that means, but maybe guys are more willing to talk about their dating practices with strangers than girls are. I did receive two marriage proposals – one was Catholic and one was Jewish. I did not give one to that cute Presbyterian, so the seriousness of that relationship is still pending.

"Fifty percent of the males and thirty-two percent of the females have dated outside their denomination, but only ten percent male and three percent female have knowingly dated outside their religion. I say knowingly, because there were many responses that did not know the religion or denomination of some of the people they had dated. The question apparently never came up for one reason or another. One from each sex was engaged outside their religion – Jewish and Methodist, probably to each other, as I am guessing they were together when I handed the surveys out. Half the girls thought their current relationship was going to be permanent, but only ten percent of the guys. I hope those weren't from couples. But only the one engagement was reported."

A young woman in the front row called out, "Have you shared the results with your parents?"

"Not yet." Delique shrugged. "First I want to figure out if I want my parents and the guy to meet. It could happen – I'd like to think that the relationship might get there, but, if it doesn't, then they will never need to know. When I was a sophomore in high school, I met this guy who had just graduated. It was in a group at a friend's home. I really liked him and he must have liked me because he asked me out a couple of times, but I wasn't allowed to date someone who was out of high school at that time. My parents didn't think I was old enough, or mature enough, or something." She sighed. "You know how parents can be. The next year, when I was allowed to, I called him but he was already seriously involved with somebody else by then. So I wasn't going to let this chance slip by. I'm going to see how this relationship works out, then tell them. Maybe."

"Your conclusions, Miss Holmes?" Dr. McElroy asked.

"Well, nothing really conclusive. But, in college, I don't think most people care about the religion or denomination of others. When dating anyway. Maybe more in serious relationships, but not just going out together. So, I'm not going to worry about it. If something happens, it happens."

Wally saw Darryl turn his head towards Cindy and wink at her, but she was pointedly ignoring him and had turned to talk with the person on the other side away from him. Darryl shrugged and got up to move down the row. Wally smiled. Maybe there were clouds in paradise.

CHAPTER 29

At lunch, as Wally was unwrapping his Bradford BLT, which seemed to be bacon, lettuce, and tuna, with a secret sauce, he saw Derek coming to the table with another man about his age. He looked somewhat familiar, but Wally couldn't immediately think of his name. They sat next to him and started opening their identical unrecognizable meals.

"Hey, Drew. How's your day going? Anything unusual anywhere?" Derek took a bite of something crunchy.

"No, just the same old morning. Another student presenter down. Only too many more to go."

"Drew, you remember Steve Getty, from our department?" He indicated the young man next to him, who was also trying to not look at what was in his lunch. "He didn't get to the party. Had something more important to do. Which could have been practically anything else."

"Oh, yeah. I don't think we've ever talked, but I've seen you in class."

Getty nodded, his mouth full and stuck out a hand to shake. He swallowed. "I was there when Askovarik mixed you two up in his room. I learned to keep my mouth shut in that class, I can tell you." He took another bite and swallowed again, seemingly without chewing or tasting, which may have made sense with a Bradford Special. "Drew tells me you're the grad ass for McElroy. Well, somebody had to be, I suppose. Me, I'm with Dr. Howard, RJ Howard, though I have no idea what the R and J stand for. He teaches only graduate-level classes and doesn't want me to mess up whatever they're doing, so I end up not doing much of anything." He shrugged. "That's okay with me. They tell me I'm kind of lazy anyway, so that works." He laughed good-naturedly, which probably meant that he was really the opposite, but didn't want anyone to know.

"What's your background, Steve? Did you work for awhile before coming back?"

"I majored in psych, here at good old BSU. But what are you going to do with a psych major, right? I was an assistant activity therapist at the Goodfellow Mental Health Center here in town for a few years, but decided I should probably be doing something more, so here I am. What about you? You look a little older than a straight to grad school student, sort of like me."

Derek laughed. "Drew here ran a bookstore. I keep trying to tell him to use that for something with his thesis. It's easier if it's something you already know. Any luck with that, Drew?"

Wally shrugged. "I'm working on it. My assistantship seems to be keeping me busy right now."

"Oh?" Derek raised his eyebrows.

Wally shook his head. He had probably already said too much. "Just a lot of undergrads needing help with their projects. McElroy's directions haven't been too clear and most of them don't have any idea what they should be doing. And the ones that have been presenting have just been muddling through. My advising hours have been pretty full."

Steve finished his sandwich and wiped his mouth with a napkin. "Anybody unusual showing up during your advising time? Somebody that you didn't expect, maybe not a student?"

"What do you mean?" Wally was a little surprised at the question. "It's been mostly just the students."

"Mostly?" It was Derek that asked the question, but both he and Steve had cocked their heads at the comment.

"Yeah, I mean, just the students." Wally put down his half-eaten bag of Bradford Chips, which gave no indication of taste, either written on the bag or in the chip itself. "Only students from the class. Nobody else." From his tone, he probably wouldn't have believed himself either.

Steve shrugged. "Okay. I have advising hours myself, but no one ever comes. Except for this one guy, said he was a cop, looking for somebody that I never heard of. A Mrs. Weisenbach?"

"Weidenbach." Wally said it before he was aware he had opened his mouth.

"Oh, you know her? I could have sworn he said 'Weisenbach'."

"Well, a Mrs. Weidenbach is my landlady. If that's who he meant." Wally looked at Derek, but he was pulling what appeared to be a pickle out of what was left of his sandwich. "Well, that's who I know with that name anyway. Weidenbach, with a 'd'."

"This cop said she disappeared after her husband died in a fire."

"Whoa, really?" Now Derek looked up in interest. "Does he think she did it? Drew's landlady? She was at the party with Askovarik."

"Oh, that's who he was with. I heard he had a date, which seemed to be worthy of people talking about." Steve shook his head. "But nah, that's not the impression the cop gave, just that it was kind of curious. I really don't know. Maybe he was just trying to downplay it, but it sounded more like he just wanted to find her. Did he come see you about her, Drew?"

Drew paused then slowly shook his head. "No, I haven't seen any cop. And I don't think it could be my Mrs. Weidenbach that he's looking for. I mean she's not being secretive. She's right there. If he was looking for her, he would have found her."

"Unless there's another Mrs. Weisenbach, or Weidenbach." Derek laughed. "That would be something, wouldn't it? Two Mrs. Weidenbachs. Hah!"

Wally felt that the conversation was steaming at full speed into areas he wasn't prepared to discuss yet. He stood up, packed up the remains of his lunch and looked at Steve Getty. "Well, I only know one Mrs. Weidenbach. And I don't think that's who this cop guy, or whoever he is, is looking for."

Derek cocked his head to follow Wally leaving the dining area, then looked back to meet Steve's eye. Steve winked back at him.

CHAPTER 30

MyFate

I think it's time to meet with the Weidenbachs, don't you? They should be aware that you know. And you should learn whatever you can -- whatever they want you to know.

Oh, and take Cindy with you. They know her, she knows the story, it just may make it easier. Actually, she's available right now in fact. In case you wanted to do this ... right now. As in, get up and go do it.

CHAPTER 31

Wally closed the door to his apartment and strode without hesitation across the hall. He was about to knock when the door suddenly opened and Cindy looked into his startled face.

"Uh, I was just about to, you know, …"

She interrupted. "I heard your door close and I wanted to catch you before you went somewhere else. I think it's time we talked with the sisters Weidenbach."

Wally just gaped at her. "That's, uh, what I was, uh, just going to suggest, that, we, um, go meet with them to, yes, talk about … things."

"Good." She stepped into the hall and closed the door behind her. "Then you're ready to go." It was not a question.

Cindy went ahead of him and rang the doorbell for the Weidenbach apartment on the first floor. Wally slightly rocked on his feet and wondered which sister was going to answer.

It was apparently Isadora, the sweet one. "Oh, hello you two. It's so nice for you to stop by. And it isn't even rent day. Is there something I can do for you?"

Cindy straightened her shoulders while Wally kept rocking. "We'd like to talk with you and your sister."

"My what, dear?" Mrs. Weidenbach looked pointedly at Wally and slightly inclined her head, as if trying to silently say, "with him here?"

"Your sister. Eleanora. We'd like to talk with both of you. Drew knows – I told him. I thought he needed to know."

"Oh." Isabella frowned slightly. "Well, in that case, I guess you better come in." She opened the door wider. "Excuse the mess, I've been so busy this morning."

There was no mess. But apparently this is what women say whenever they invite someone in, just in case they might have missed something somewhere. They walked near the bookcase. This time, Wally tried not to make it obvious, but he noticed some L. Frank Baums and a mint Doctor Zhivago.

"Just take a seat on the couch. I'll be right back." She disappeared down the hallway, calling back behind her, "Don't go anywhere."

Wally whispered to Cindy, "Now what?"

She looked back at him. "You wanted to come talk to them."

"So did you," he whispered back. "But what do we say? I hadn't thought that far ahead."

Mrs. Weidenbach returned to the room. Smoking a cigarette and with the top two buttons of her blouse unbuttoned. "Hey, how are you doing?" Apparently, the other sister.

"Good afternoon, Eleanora." Cindy smiled back. "We're doing fine, thank you." Wally couldn't help smiling. She had said "we", which implied a certain togetherness, which warmed his insides. "We" could do anything.

Eleanora pulled a cushioned chair with ease up closer to them. "You wanted to talk with me? Well. I'm here."

"We wanted to talk with both of you. Together. It's important." All Wally heard was the "we' again. He had better start paying attention.

Isadora slowly poked her head around the corner. "Are you sure, dear?" The rest of her also slowly came into view and she moved into the room, sitting stiffly in a wooden chair, a little further away.

Cindy looked at Wally, who shrugged and held his hands up, pretty much saying, "Go for it, I don't know where to start." She turned back to the sisters.

"I told Drew everything that you had shared with me. We saw Eleanora," she tilted her head in that direction, "at the psychology department party and I said something about which sister you were. I'm sorry, but I thought he already knew. I thought he could certainly have been able to tell. And you said, 'Don't tell anyone except Mr. Wright,' so I assumed you had let him know too. So anyway, now he knows."

Eleanora stubbed out her cigarette in an ashtray, then leaned back and pulled out a pack of cigarettes and a lighter from inside her blouse. Everybody watched her take another one out, light it, and stick in her mouth. "I believe we said to only tell the 'right' person." She offered the pack, but no one took her up on it. "So he knows. Now we're going to have to kill him."

Cindy said, "No! What?" and Wally said, "What? No!" at the same time.

Eleanora laughed and Isadora rolled her eyes. "I'm just kidding. We don't do that. That's what the people after me are trying to do."

Isadora leaned forward. "Mr. Wright, you're not going to tell anyone, are you?"

"What? No!" He was still trying to transition from single-word knee-jerk responses. "No, I'm, I'm not going to tell anyone. I haven't so far."

Cindy turned to look at him and raised her eyebrows. "So far?"

He grimaced and said, "There was someone in my office yesterday."

He paused. Eleanora held a hand out and Cindy prompted, "Yeah?"

"He said he was a cop." He paused again, but continued before Cindy could hit him. "And he asked if I knew an Eleanora Weisenbach." To their puzzled faces, he added, "I told him 'no'. That I only knew a Mrs. Weidenbach."

"Did he show you any identification?" asked Cindy.

"Well, he flashed a badge, but I didn't get a good look at it."

"Did he have a gun?' Eleanora wanted to know.

They all looked at her. Wally said, "Not that I know of. I never saw one, but then I wasn't really looking for one."

"Dear," Isadora asked sweetly. "Did he give you a name?"

Wally reached into a pocket and pulled out the post-it note. "Yeah. He wrote it down along with a phone number. It's Officer Terry Miller, from Oldstown Police."

"A post-it? He wrote it on a post-it? He didn't have a card?" Cindy looked disturbed.

Wally pointed at her. "I know! I thought the same thing. I really wonder if he's with the police at all."

Eleanora reached for the phone on the end table next to her and picked it up, starting to dial.

Dialing? Wally thought to himself. *A, what do they call it, a rotary dial? On a landline? It's on a cord. I didn't think anybody had one of those anymore. But maybe, six years ago, they were still around. Though I don't remember anybody I knew that had one. I wonder if it's considered an antique.*

"I make it a point to know police department numbers by heart. Not the one on the post-it," Eleanora said. "You just never know." Someone must have answered at the other end. "Yeah, hello, I was trying to get hold of Officer Terry Miller. Do you know if he's available?" The others could hear squawking from the other end, but nothing understandable. "Oh, really? I guess I haven't seen him in awhile. I didn't know that." More squawking. "Nope, that's okay. There's no problem, I just wanted to ask him something. No big deal. Thanks." She hung up. She did not push a button ending the call, she just put the phone back in its cradle. On its base or whatever it was called. Wally was surprised that he was so surprised by the procedure. Sort of like having to get up to change the channel on the television. Historically educational, in a way.

Eleanora turned back to the others. "Well, there used to be an Officer Terry Miller. Not any more. It's just Terry Miller. He resigned from the department about a year and a half ago, about the same time that Gus and Dieter died, maybe soon after that."

"Oh my." Isadora put her hand to her mouth.

"So," Cindy hesitated. "So, he's not with the police now?"

Eleanora shook her head. "Nope."

Cindy turned to Wally, who didn't know what to say, and was desperately searching his memory to make sure he hadn't said anything to "Officer" Miller that he shouldn't have. And hadn't done anything that might have made him look nervous. Ah hell, he had been nervous, but would it have been interpreted as a suspicious nervous, or just a the-police-are-questioning-me nervous?

"Wally, are you sure you didn't say anything?"

No, he wasn't. "Well, I said things. Of course, I said things. But I didn't say anything about there being two of them. No. I'm pretty sure of that."

"Pretty sure?"

"No, no, I'm sure. I didn't say anything about that."

All three of them looked at him as if they weren't nearly as certain, but eventually they looked away.

"Well, now what?" Eleanora asked.

Cindy shrugged. "I guess we keep an eye out for him. And for anybody else asking questions. There may be more than one of them. But now we know who he is, anyway. Anything else, Drew?"

"He was wearing hiking boots and a sports coat. I know that that is not that uncommon on a college campus, but I have a vague memory of having seen those boots before. They came up higher than most do and he had his pants legs tucked into them."

Isadora nodded. "I do recall a young gentleman dressed like that, inquiring about a room, shortly after you came here, Mr. Wright. But then we didn't have any rooms left. Of course, we wouldn't have rented him your room. That one was saved for you."

Wally sat up. "What do you mean, saved for me? Cindy also mentioned before that you were saving that room. Did you know I was coming? I didn't know I was coming."

"We just knew that we wanted the right person for that room, dear." Isadora smiled. "We can't have just anybody staying here."

"Well, he had to be cute, too," Eleanora added. "Easy on the eyes."

"Anyway," Isadora continued. "You seemed to be the right kind of person. Shy, well-intentioned, a little bit desperate."

"Oh." Wally wasn't sure how to take that last remark, but, figured that, sometimes, it was better not to pursue it.

Cindy spoke up again. "We just wanted to let the two of you know that Drew did know about you now. We thought you should be aware. I didn't know that this Officer Miller, I guess he's not really an officer, this Mr. Miller had been around, but now we do know that too. Drew," she turned to Wally. "I think we should go now, unless there is still something else for you to add?"

"No, no, I think that's it. I don't have any other," he was about to say "secrets", but thought better of it, "anything else."

"Are you sure you need to go?" Isadora asked. "We did just bake some lemon bars."

Wally hesitated, but Cindy stood up. "Thank you, but no, we'll be going." She took Wally's hand and pulled him up. He was going to follow that hand-pulling anywhere.

After they had pulled the door closed behind them, Cindy started toward the front door rather than upstairs. "I have a class now, and I'm sure you have to go to classes sometimes too. We'll talk again later."

And she was gone, leaving Wally to look at his watch and realize that he needed to get to an appointment with Dr. McElroy.

CHAPTER 32

Wally found himself in the outer office, waiting for Dr. McElroy, again. Mrs. Fochs was ignoring him, again. It wasn't that she disliked Wally, but that both of them knew they couldn't help each other with Dr. McElroy's schedule. He kept his own time. Well, Wally knew he kept his own times, several sets of them.

Dr. McElroy's office door opened and the professor poked his head out. Wally had already knocked twice before with no answer. "Mrs. Fochs, is there anything that I should know?"

She lifted her eyebrows at finding him already in his room. "Oh, there are several things that you should know, I am sure. But as of immediate relevance, just to remind you that there is a staff meeting this afternoon at four. But I suspect they wouldn't miss you."

He looked at the watches on both wrists. "But which four o'clock is it?"

Wally spoke up. "I would go with the earliest one. Just in case. Then you know you won't be late. Probably."

"And Mr. Wright has been waiting for your appointment." Mrs. Fochs inclined her head toward Wally.

McElroy looked at Wally for the first time. "We had an appointment?"

"Twenty minutes ago."

McElroy pulled out his pocket watch from his vest, then one from his shirt pocket. "Oh, here we go. This one says we're right on time. Come on in."

Wally followed him into the office and, as usual, moved a pile of folders from the chair to the floor before sitting down. He briefly wondered about the content of the folders, because he had never seen McElroy actually look at any of them. And he could have sworn they were the same folders every time. The top one had TOP SECRET stamped all over it.

McElroy sat down across from him and asked, "Was there something you wanted to talk with me about?"

"Um, this was our weekly meeting just to touch base?"

McElroy sat for a moment. "Yes, I knew that. I'm just starting with finding out if there's anything you wanted to talk with me about. Well?"

"No, no, I don't have anything in particular." Wally wanted to stay off the topic of his thesis.

"So how is your dissertation coming?"

"Um, fine. Just fine. No problems." Wally was thinking furiously, trying to come up with a possible topic.

"And what did you decide to do? Anything I can help with?"

"It's about … the …" Wally saw the watches sticking out from under McElroy's sleeves. "The efficient use of time."

"There is no efficient use of time. Time uses you. You either flow with it, or you fight it, and, believe me, fighting it takes up all your time. What are you going to do with it? Stick to one time, whether it makes sense or not?"

"No, I'm going to use it in bookstores, in selling books. In how bookstores arrange their books so that buyers can use their time more efficiently."

"Do book buyers want to use their time efficiently? Personally, I find that bookstores are one place where you can get away with not paying attention to time."

Wally sat forward a little. "Actually, that's exactly what someone else said. So, do bookstores arrange their stock so that browsers can enjoy spending more time, but people who want something specific can find that and get out? Are the more popular books easier to find, and does the genre browser get to be in a more comfortable, more relaxed setting? That sort of thing."

McElroy shrugged. He was going to do what he wanted to in a bookstore, no matter how they set their stuff up. "So where are you going to do your studies? I wouldn't think university bookstores would be the type you're talking about."

"Uh, I was thinking of ...." Wally was desperately trying to come up with bookstores from the area. "Thalman's and, ... Ye Olde Bookshelf." Ye Olde Bookshelf was where he worked. Or had worked. Maybe still worked.

"Oh, I know Sid Thalman. I'm surprised he's going to let you mess with how he has things arranged. They've been that way for years. He does not like change. I'll make sure to stop in and see how things are going. But I don't know, what did you call it, The Old Bookshelf?"

Damn. He hadn't thought about the fact that Ye Olde Bookshelf was actually pretty new and may not have opened yet. And, yeah, come to think of it, Sidney Thalman had always been an obstinate old cuss, stuck in his ways. And now, if McElroy knew him, he was going to have to go talk to the guy. Really. Double damn.

"Well, I may use Thalman's as the comparative, as the one that doesn't change compared to the one that does do things differently."

McElroy chuckled. "Hah, that I can see." He stood up. "Well, if there's nothing more?" He looked at both watches. "I'm sure I've got somewhere I'm supposed to be. I think I remember having an appointment this morning. At least I thought it was this morning. Is today Tuesday by any chance?"

Wally didn't want to remind him that this was the appointment, because McElroy may just want to do it all again, just to make sure. He probably had a timepiece somewhere that would have told him that now was the right time for their meeting to start.

CHAPTER 33

Wally wrote a note reminding himself that, as soon as this student office time was over, he needed to get over to Thalman's bookstore to discuss the possibility of a research study, even though Wally had absolutely no intention of ever doing it. Dr. McElroy needed to believe that something was going to be done. And he supposed he'd better come up with a name of a real bookstore in close proximity where he could also fake the rest of his study.

There was a knock on his door and he jumped. Normally the door would have been wide open, but, after recent events, Wally had decided to leave it closed in case he needed to pretend that he wasn't here or even give himself time to duck down behind his desk. He didn't respond to the first knock, but it came again.

"Drew, are you in there?" The voice came through the door. "This is me, Lori. I know this is supposed to be your office time. Look, I'll wait if you're with someone, and I apologize for interrupting."

He hurried over to the door and cracked it open. "Are you alone?"

She looked both left and right. "There are people going in and out of other offices, but there's no one with me."

He pulled her arm leading her into the room, shutting the door again behind her.

Lori looked around. "Are you okay?" she asked. "Why do you have your door closed if you're not with someone?"

"I had a surprise visitor last time, after you and Vern Sheffield. A police officer and it shook me."

"The policeman was after you? About traveling in time?"

"No, no. It was about someone else. It just made me nervous. I, I wasn't expecting him. But no, I'm not in trouble or anything like that. He just wanted to see if I had seen somebody. Somebody in particular. Somebody that you don't know. And I don't know. That nobody knows. As far as I know. At least not me."

"You're rambling again." Lori pointed out.

"Yeah, probably." Wally took his seat on the other side of the table.

Lori sat down opposite him. "Anyway. I heard that Marshall Jefferson broke his ankle and will be out for the season."

It took Wally a moment to appreciate what she had said. "Oh, the running back for the Bees. What I told you was going to happen. Or what the program told you. Which was really me, I guess."

"What you told me was going to happen. So, you really are from the future. Like you said."

Wally shrugged and put his hands out. "Yep." And added, "I knew you were going to say that."

"Really?"

"No, I just made that part up."

Lori rolled her eyes. "So now what? What am I supposed to do to help you? That Cindy can't?"

"Well ..." Wally ran his fingers through his hair. "That guy that I told you came in and surprised me, that police officer? And I just told you that I didn't know who he was looking for? Well, I lied. He was looking for my landlady's twin sister, the one that I said 'bad guys' were after? Only he's not really a police officer, not any more anyway. Though he told me he was. And you already told me that you knew about the Mrs. Weidenbachs, so I don't know why I said it was about somebody you didn't know."

"Drew ..."

"What? Oh, yeah, stay on topic. Do you understand what I'm talking about?"

She nodded. "It's like learning a new language, but, yes, I'm getting the gist of it. He wanted to know if you had seen the second Mrs. Weidenbach."

"I told him 'no'. At least I think I did. I'm pretty sure I did."

"What does he look like? So I'd know him if I see him."

"Probably about my height, a little bit, I was going to say skinnier, but I think slimmer is a better word. Overall, not as wide, but more likely more of it is muscle. Blonde hair, parted on ..." Wally waved his finger from left to right to left again in front of him. "His right. Slightly longer than mine. No glasses. Wears a tan sports coat and hiking boots. Wait a minute." He sat up straight and looked straight at Lori. "I've seen him before. I knew he looked familiar. I've seen him at different times around campus. When I was following Cindy."

"So he was stalking – either you or Cindy, while you were stalking Cindy?"

"Yes. No, I wasn't stalking Cindy. I was just following her, to see where she was going."

"You were following her. Without her knowing it?"

"It sounds bad when you put it like that."

Lori tilted her head and looked at him. "So do you think he was ... following one of you?"

"I don't know. Maybe he was just keeping an eye on the house. To see who was coming and going. To find out who might be there. That could be how he knew I lived there." Wally suddenly sat back. "I think he tried to get a room in that house, right after I arrived. Mrs. Weidenbach said so, but I remember those boots, too."

Lori raised her eyebrows.

"I was at the top of the stairs when Mrs. Weidenbach, the first one, I think, answered the door and all I could see were these boots outside the door asking about a room. She told him there weren't any and he left. But I think it was him."

"Did he give you a name?"

"Yeah. Terry Miller. And I think that's his real name. The second Mrs. Weidenbach, Eleanora, actually called the police department to ask about him and they said he was no longer with them."

"Alright. So I should just sort of watch out for somebody that looks like this guy to see if he's around asking questions, or seeming to watch your building, or showing up somewhere else?"

Wally nodded. "I don't know what else to do. And I don't know what to do about it if we do see him again. This isn't exactly what I am experienced with."

Lori stood up. "Okay. You're from the future, and your computer program says we're supposed to be protecting the sisters Weidenbach. Somehow. Okay. Seems like a cinch."

Wally walked her to the door, opened it a crack, and peered out. "It looks okay out there."

He opened the door wider. She took a step outside, then suddenly turned back and kissed him. She whispered into his shocked face. "I'm sorry, but I think I see him at the corner to your right. Don't look. I needed an excuse to turn back to tell you." She hurried off in the other direction.

Wally was still reacting to the kiss and not the words, so it took a second before he risked a glance down the hall as he closed the door, just in time to glimpse a tan sports coat and the heel of a last hiking boot turn the corner.

CHAPTER 34

Thalman's Bookstore looked crowded. Not with people, there were only one or two of those, but with books. Actually, not just crowded, but overwhelmed. Just like Wally thought a good used, rare, antiquated bookstore should look.

He wandered a bit, to get the sense of organization and to compare it with Ye Olde Bookshelf, his own shop. Okay, not actually his shop but the one he managed. The owner, Kevin Creager, liked the idea of owning a bookstore, but not the reality of running a business. So Creager had named it and hung around frequently, checking on new books and chatting with customers, but let Wally do pretty much what he wanted to with it.

Both shops had a counter near the entrance for checking out and a workspace behind it. Thalman kept his rare books up front in locked cabinets so he could control access to them. Wally kept a few of the rarer tomes in display beneath the counter, but most of them further back in the shop. Wally actually kept his desk back closer to that area and one of the other employees stayed up front to handle most of the selling, calling Wally up when there was a specific question, or someone was trying to sell interesting volumes that might have some value.

Sidney Thalman always sat at the front counter and watched the customers closely. If you wanted something in particular, you had to come to him. Wally liked to wander and help out in the stacks -- among the physical contents of the shop, talking to the potential buyers, discovering their likes and dislikes. Occasionally finding couples doing things they weren't supposed to be doing. Particularly back in the little-used travel section, but also sometimes in the erotica aisle, having apparently been inspired.

There were a few benches here in Thalman's, more for perusing than for reading, and definitely not for long-term comfort. Ye Olde Bookshelf had two open areas with easy chairs intended for people to spend some time. Wally had discovered that the readers didn't always purchase what they were reading, but they usually left with something, and, if not, they came back often enough to finish what they had been reading and to frequently buy something else. They were regulars and, more importantly, they became friends. Creager encouraged that relationship and worried less about making money and more about having people enjoying books. Wally worried a little more about the making money – that was his part of the business.

He approached Sidney Thalman, after determining that nobody appeared likely to be making a purchase within at least the next fifteen minutes, if not for another hour.

"Mr. Thalman?" In another six years, he would call him "Sidney" though the older man always cringed at it.

"Yes? Do you wish to know where something is?" Thalman had noticed that Wally was empty-handed.

"No." Wally realized he was now probably going to have to buy something before he left. "Actually, I wanted your help with something else. To ask for your help, I mean. My name is Drew Wright and I'm a graduate student at Bradford State."

"Drew?" Thalman interrupted. "Is that short for Andrew?" Wally now remembered that the older man always called him "Wallace" and, come to think of it, he had never heard anybody ever refer to Thalman as "Sid". Except for Dr. McElroy.

"Yes, sir, it is."

"Alright, Andrew. What is it you wanted to ask me?"

"Well, sir." Wally took a deep breath. "As I said, I'm a graduate student in psychology, and I'm doing a research study on how bookstores display their products in order to increase sales or customer comfort or foot traffic."

"I am not changing anything. I have the customers I want and the books that I want."

"Oh no, sir. I am not suggesting any changes or for you to do anything at all, really. I used to work in a bookstore in ... Liggetsville. And ..."

"What bookstore?"

"I'm sorry?"

"What bookstore did you work for in Liggetsville? There haven't been very many."

"Um." Wally searched his memory for a store that would have been there long enough to be in this time period. "Readmore. For Mr. Watkins."

Thalman nodded. "Yes, James Watkins. Very commercial establishment. A lot of nudist magazines, if I recall. Not my cup of tea. Unless they're vintage. There are collectors for that."

"Well, I wasn't there very long. And he probably won't even remember me. I was just part-time."

"So, Andrew, you want me to do something for you. But something that doesn't involve my actually doing anything. Is that correct?"

"Yes, sir. I am the graduate assistant for Dr. Sam, Samuel, McElroy. He said that you might be willing to let me just come in and observe a few times. For my thesis." Wally was aware he was stretching the truth beyond any reasonable expectations, but what the heck. "I'm also going to observe in The Book Look. Hopefully -- I haven't actually asked them yet. I thought I would give you the respect of asking you first."

Thalman looked around, but saw that no one else was yet approaching him to give him an excuse to end the conversation. "Do you have an outline of your study yet? To say what you would be observing?"

"No, not yet."

"I would want a copy of that first." Damn. "In order to ascertain that it would be appropriate and not disruptive. Let me see that and I will consider it. This is a reputable establishment and I will not have it used for anything flippant. Do you understand?"

"Yes, sir, I mean, no, sir. I wouldn't do anything like that."

"Do you wish to buy anything?" Thalman was returning to the business of what, after all, was his business.

"Uh." Wally looked around. He spotted a copy of *The Body on the Roof*, a signed first edition that was much cheaper than in his own time. He could fit that into his luggage to take back. "I'll take that book there. I'm a fan of his."

***

The Book Look was easier. Matt Dubois, the owner, was much younger, much more laid back, much more willing to entertain the thought of some changes.

"Hey, man, that's cool." Dubois winked at a seventy-five-year-old woman passing by as he conversed with Wally. He believed in multi-tasking. The woman giggled, which made his day. "I'm up for anything that could make this place more the flavor of the month, you know what I mean?"

Wally knew what he meant. The problem was that he also knew that, no matter what changes would be made, this place would not still exist in six years. Dubois' skills at multi-tasking led to his not being able to fully commit to any one thing at a time. He was always half thinking of something else and that's a skill that only really works when you're already wealthy enough to hire somebody else to follow through on each separate task. "Flavor of the month" was a good way to put it because Dubois would be sampling a different flavor next month.

Wally focused on what he needed today. "That's great. I'm going to want to move just a few things, not much, maybe rearrange the reading areas a little for more light. I don't want to do too much because you've got a good … vibe here and I don't want to mess that up."

"Whatever, dude. You know I'm here for you." Dubois clapped his hands and pointed a finger at him. He raised his voice and called out to the older woman. "Hey, Judy, I see you fondling that copy of the Kama Sutra. Any more of that and I think you have yourself a relationship." She giggled again and raised her hand as if pushing him away, but she didn't put the book back.

He turned back to Wally. "Feel free to come in here anytime you want. Go get a doughnut from the table in back." He raised his voice once more. "Unless Fred there has eaten them all." An older man across the room guiltily switched his half-eaten bagel from one hand to the other, apparently trying to hide it.

Wally smiled and walked away. This was definitely not the quiet reading room of the library. But this was more the relationship he always enjoyed with his customers. And, he realized, the changes he was suggesting would make it more like Ye Olde Bookshelf, his own place back in his time. Ahead in his time, he mentally corrected, and hoped he hadn't said that out loud.

CHAPTER 35

As Wally headed back to his apartment, he passed the convenience store where he sometimes bought a few things, and realized he didn't have anything for dinner that night. Or, come to think of it, the next night or the night after that, but he only wanted to deal with one meal crisis at a time.

The shop had limited options. After all, it was for convenience, not variety. In the frozen meal section, there were only three choices – a vegetarian, good-for-you-but-absolutely-tasteless something with unfamiliar Peruvian beans and unidentifiable Ecuadorian root vegetables, a lasagna with something that resembled meat and something that resembled bread, and a Salisbury steak with mushrooms, mashed potato paste, and cheese-covered brussels sprouts. He was glad he wasn't having to choose more than one and he didn't dare look at the "Best By" dates. He pulled out the lasagna and grabbed two packages of peanut butter crackers (just in case). He had survived on those crackers in his undergraduate days.

As he was checking out, he heard a voice behind him.

"Dr. Wright! Fancy meeting you here."

He knew the voice and the "Dr." reference could only come from one person. Turning around and dropping his change of forty-seven cents on the floor, he saw former officer Terry Miller. As he bent down to pick up the coins that had rolled near the now-familiar hiking boots, he reminded himself, *don't think former, I'm not supposed to know that, just think officer.*

"Hello, Officer ... Miller, is it?"

Miller smiled broadly, as if they were supposed to be happy to see each other, and pointed to Wally's package. "That any good? I try to eat a little healthier myself. Keep myself in shape." And he patted his non-existent stomach to emphasize the "in-shape" comment. To Wally's ears it sounded like a drum.

"I honestly have no idea." He was suddenly acutely aware of his own lack of fitness. He tried to run every once in a while, but it had been awhile since he had once run. "I just needed something quick for supper and there weren't many choices."

"I thought the South American Vegetable Medley looked good."

You would, Wally thought. "I'll take your word for it." He stepped away from the counter and realized Miller didn't have anything in his hands to buy, not even that South American whatever. Miller moved with him.

"So, you thought anymore about what we talked about the other day?"

"About what we talked about?" Too many "abouts", but he was just repeating what Miller had said, to give himself time to think of something else to say. And tried to remember if that was one of Vern Sheffield's choices.

"About your landlady. You know, anything out of the ordinary."

Wally took another step and shifted the bag from one hand to the other as if to open the door, but Miller stepped to the side to let others out and Wally was forced to slide in that direction.

"Well? Anything new?"

"I don't know her enough to know what 'out of the ordinary' would be. But there's nothing new. I still don't know anything about, I think you said it was her sister?"

"Yep, her sister, Eleanora. Nothing, huh? Hey, okay." Miller clapped his hand on Wally's shoulder, hard enough to let him know who was in control here, and almost caused Wally to drop the grocery bag. "Just saw you and wanted to check. You know, let you know I hadn't forgotten you."

"And I haven't forgotten you either, Officer. I hope you enjoy your vegetable meal from, somewhere else, and I'll enjoy my lasagna from ... Italy, I guess."

Miller glanced down at the package. "I think they made it in West Virginia."

Wally made another attempt at the door. "You're probably right. Maybe Little Italy, West Virginia. I guess there's a little Italian in all of us." He pushed through the door, glad it opened in that direction and walked away, thinking that was a pretty inane comment. After about twenty feet, he risked a glance back and saw Miller standing outside the door, watching him. Just watching him.

CHAPTER 36

MyFate

Now, where are we supposed to be?

Lori knows about your time traveling, but Cindy doesn't. The landlady sisters know that you know about them. "Officer" Miller has talked with you, and, hopefully, I'm metaphorically keeping my fingers crossed here, you haven't told him about the sisters. In case you don't already know, he's not really a police officer anymore — take my word for it. Try to avoid him at all costs.

And both Cindy and Lori should have kissed you by now.

I'll let that simmer for a moment.

Now, where are we supposed to be going?

The sisters Weidenbach will not be safe until one of two things happens:

The bad guys get their money and give up on trying to find Eleanora, or

The bad guys get caught and get sent away where they can't bother anyone anymore.

Make sense? I suppose we could add that the bad guys could get killed, but that's a little morbid and I can't see you (me) doing anything like that or, for that matter, anybody else involved.

Eleanora, whether she knows it or not, is still the most likely one to know where the money is. Which is sort of the bad guys' point. That is why they are after her. You will need to talk with her some more, find out what she knows that she doesn't know she knows. (Oh, I'm as bad as you, which, yes, I know, makes sense)

Catching the bad guys is a good idea whether they have the money or not. But that's going to involve somebody from law enforcement. There just may be somebody you can trust, but that's all I can say right now...

CHAPTER 37

Wally rolled over in bed and slightly opened one eye. Only slightly because it was Saturday morning – he paused for a few seconds, but, yes, he was pretty sure it was Saturday – and he didn't have any classes or help-with-projects time scheduled. But something was nagging at the back of his head. Something that he was going to do today.

His cell phone beeped and there was a knock at the door at the same time. At the very same time. Instantaneous. He groped for the phone by the bed and croaked out an "Hello?".

"Drew? This is Cindy. I am standing right outside your door. You promised to help me with breakfast at the food pantry this morning. Remember?"

"Wait, wait a minute. There's somebody knocking on my door." He pushed back his blanket and pulled on the jeans from the previous night. Still holding the phone, he yelled at the door, "I'll be right there."

"I can hear you from both ways, the phone and your yelling. Open the door."

He opened the door and said "Morning" into the phone.

"Drew, put down the phone. You can just talk with me. Ooh, that tee shirt looks like you slept in it."

He looked down at his shirt, which said *Wake Me Up When It's Over,* and picked at it. "I, I did. It's what I sleep in." He yawned and stretched before he became aware enough to realize that Cindy was not seeing him at his best. "I'm sorry, I'm just not awake enough yet. The food pantry, right. Are we supposed to be there now?"

"No, we have an hour before we have to be there, but I thought I had better make sure you were up and had enough time to get ready. You can get a shower, and get … better dressed. Knock on my door in half an hour and we'll walk over." She walked back to her apartment and Wally slowly closed the door. He looked at the phone in his hand and hit the end call button.

Twenty-eight minutes later, looking more presentable considering it was still a Saturday morning, Wally was standing in front of Cindy's door. He raised his hand to knock, but before he could connect, the door opened.

"Okay, let's go." She did look much better in the morning than he could ever hope to.

As they walked, Wally asked, "So, tell me a little more about this food pantry. What is it we're going to do?"

"It's in a local church. People who are in need can come there on Saturday mornings, and pick up groceries for the week for their family. Members of the church also provide a hot breakfast for everyone that shows up."

"How did you get involved? Do you go to that church?"

"No." She shook her head. "I just volunteer to help out with the breakfast. It was one of the things that was posted on the volunteer board at the union."

"There's a volunteer board?"

She stopped and looked at him. "A big board. Just inside the front door of the student union. I can't believe you haven't seen it. The one with 'Student Volunteer Opportunities' written across it in bright blue and red letters."

"Oh, yeah." Wally had walked past it many times, rarely paying any attention to it. One of those student life activities that he had never expected to be here long enough to become involved in. "That board."

They went around to the parking lot at the back of the church. About twenty people were already in line waiting to go in. Cindy opened the door and Wally followed her in and up some steps to what seemed to be the fellowship hall with many tables set up for eating a meal. They went through to the kitchen.

Two people were already there, setting out the materials for the breakfast.

"Good morning, Tameka." Cindy grabbed two aprons off a hook and handed one to Wally. "Hi, Emmett. This is Drew. He's going to be helping out this morning."

Tameka smiled and said, "Hey, Cindy, Drew." Emmitt grunted. "Yup. Hope he's good with eggs."

Wally looked at Cindy. "Eggs?"

She smiled back. "I usually help with the serving as they go through the line. It looks like you'll be scrambling the eggs. Put your apron on. You will probably be needing one more than me."

Emmitt waved him over. He lit one of the stovetop burners and set the biggest skillet Wally had ever seen on top. He poured cooking oil from the biggest oil can Wally had ever seen into the skillet, and then poured pre-scrambled eggs from a bag in on top of the oil. He handed Wally a spatula. "Keep stirring it so it doesn't burn on the bottom. When it's firm enough to eat, scrape it into the serving tray on the back burners. Do it all over again."

"So I make sure it doesn't burn."

"Yup, just like I said."

"And if it does burn?"

Emmitt looked at the others to make sure they weren't listening. "Just don't tell me." He opened the stove below Wally and pulled out a tray of biscuits. Wally saw there were also trays of roasted potatoes. It was a better breakfast than he was used to.

"How long do I do this?" Wally asked.

"Until I tell you not to."

A few more students came wandering in to work, and one of them, introduced as Joey, came over to do his own pan of eggs. Joey seemed less awake than Wally felt, and kept sipping from a thermos full of what Wally hoped was coffee, or at least caffeine based.

Once the customers started coming in, Wally did not have free time to talk with Cindy, but enjoyed watching her interacting with the other people. She appeared to be very comfortable, and many were familiar with her. He realized it was a good thing that she was out front and that he was not.

At one point, Emmitt told him to get his own plate to eat and he went up to the servers to get it filled. Cindy asked him, as she put extra potatoes on his plate, "Having fun, yet?"

"Yeah, sort of. It gets kind of hot back at the stove, but this isn't bad. Makes me glad I don't do this for a living, but I do respect the people that do. What about you?"

She threw her hair back. "I enjoy this. Makes me think I'm actually doing something that people appreciate, you know what I mean?"

Wally paused and nodded, "Yeah, I do."

He moved on to the eggs and took two ladles full from Tameka. "Whoa, enough."

She put a little more on. "You're kind of cute, but you're too skinny. You need some more weight on your bones."

"Hey," Cindy broke in. "You're already married. You stay away from Drew."

Tameka laughed and winked at Drew. "You never know. I can still look, can't I? No law against that."

Wally looked out at the still long line and stiffened when he recognized someone. He backed behind Tameka. She said, "Well, alright, Drew, but not now".

He whispered to Cindy, "About eight people back, the guy looking around the room. That's 'Officer' Miller."

She looked out. "Oh, I see him. The guy with the muscles and the sports jacket."

"Yeah. What's he doing here?" Wally retreated back to the stove area with his plate and crouched down behind the preparation island.

Joey stared at him. "What are you doing, bro? I wouldn't get down there. That floor's kinda dirty."

Wally sat down with his back against the island. "I, uh, I prefer to sit when I eat. And there aren't any chairs back here."

Joey shrugged. "To each his own, I guess."

Emmitt came around the corner from delivering more biscuits and saw Wally on the floor. He looked at Joey who shrugged again. "Don't ask me. I just work here."

Wally was trying to guess when Miller had gone by, when he heard Cindy raise her voice.

"And what can I get for you, sir?"

The familiar deep voice of Miller's came back. "Oh, just a little bit of the eggs and one biscuit. No potatoes, thanks. Too much starch, I'm afraid. They don't have any tomato juice, do they?'

Tameka answered, "Nope, just orange juice and milk. And coffee."

"That's okay. Thanks." He started away then turned back. "And, if you happen to see Dr. Wright, tell him I said to have a particularly nice day."

After he left, Tameka asked Cindy. "Who's Dr. Wright? I thought you came with Drew."

Cindy shook her head. "That is Drew. Well, he's not a doctor, yet. He's working on it."

"A doctor? Well, tell him I got this pain in my hip. Here, I can show him...."

"Not that kind of doctor. He's working on his PhD." She nodded toward the retreating Miller. "This is one person I happen to know he's trying to avoid." She turned around and called softly. "Drew. Drew? Where are you? He's gone."

Wally slowly raised his head up, then his whole body. Joey and Emmitt looked at each other and they both shrugged. He placed his plate on the table and finished his breakfast, still checking the customers outside, just in case Miller wanted seconds, or even thirds.

When Wally was told to stop cooking eggs, he moved to the sink and started washing some of the pans and trays. Joey stayed at the stove, scrubbing away the eggs that they had both accidentally spilled, a little more on Wally's side than Joey's.

After everything was cleaned and put away, they said goodbye. Tameka gave him a hug, and Emmitt grunted, "Yup, okay. You'll do."

As they walked back to the apartment building, Wally kept looking around and peering behind every bush. "He must have followed us there."

"He could have just spotted you when he got in line, before you ducked down." Cindy was trying to be positive, but gave up. "You're probably right. That's not the sort of place he would just have wandered into, hoping for a free breakfast. Maybe he thinks you're going to lead him to Eleanora."

"Who?"

"You know, Elea...."

Wally lowered his voice. "Shh, maybe he's listening. Remember, we're not supposed to know whoever he's looking for."

Cindy brought her voice down to match his. "Oh, you're right. We have to be paranoid all the time." She giggled.

Wally sternly turned his face towards her. "He was at the breakfast, wasn't he?"

The rest of the way back, they stayed silent, which Wally considered a waste of the rare time he could spend with her. As they neared the front door, he spoke up. "What are you doing the rest of the day? We could go do something else and take Miller on another wild goose chase."

"I'm sorry, I'm going to the game with some friends to watch Darryl. I'd invite you, but it's just females talking about female stuff instead of football. I just promised Darryl I'd be there."

Wally's "Oh" had a depressed tone to it. A mostly, with the exception of Miller's appearance, enjoyable morning had been spoiled by the mention of Darryl Thomas. He knew from Darryl's reputation in the future that it was not a permanent relationship, but it sure messed up the current moment.

CHAPTER 38

Tim Gravesend was the next speaker in class. He stood next to Wally waiting to be introduced. Wally himself was waiting for the class to quiet down, but soon realized that probably wasn't going to happen on its own. He waved his hand, but nothing changed. He clapped his hands above his head, but, again, the noise remained the same.

"Hey!"

That worked somewhat, but now any conversation was along the lines of "What did he say?"

"We have another speaker. Mr. Tim Gravesend is going to talk to us about ...?"

Wally turned toward him and raised his eyebrows.

"Yep. I'm going to talk to the class."

Wally looked back at the class, now quieting enough. "Okay, I guess we'll all be surprised. Tim, take it away."

"Good morning, Bradford!" Gravesend's voice boomed, shutting down any stray conversations. He pointed to a young man in the front row. "You, sir, do you have any idea what I'm going to talk about today?"

The man shrugged his shoulders. "Not a clue. And I don't really care." Which drew a chuckle from the audience.

"You, ma'am?" pointing to the young lady sitting next to the clueless man. "What do you think?"

She giggled. "I have no idea." And giggled again. "But I hope it gives me an idea for when it's my turn to talk. And I've never been called 'ma'am' before."

"Anybody have any idea what my subject is today?" He raised his arms to the rest of the class.

A hand popped up about midway back, but Gravesend ignored it. The hand started waving back and forth, but Gravesend tried hard to look anywhere else.

"I do! I do!" the hand called out. People were turning to look. "I do!" By this time, there was practically only one person, well, actually three, in the auditorium not watching the waving hand. The other two – Wally and Dr. McElroy – kept their eyes on Gravesend.

The hand went higher, bringing the rest of its body to its feet, exposing a short bespectacled young man. "You told me you were going to talk about secrets."

Gravesend finally brought his gaze to the young man. "And what did I tell you to do?"

"To … not … talk about it."

"And what did you just do?"

"I told you what you were going to talk about."

"As well as telling who else?" Gravesend gestured to the rest of the room.

The young man wisely did not answer the question and resumed his seat. The audience turned back to Gravesend.

"Secrets. Exactly." Gravesend paused for effect. Wally figured his major was probably in the drama department. "Everybody has them." Some squirming and grimacing occurred. "And most of us probably know somebody else's." Now students were glancing at their neighbors, who were glaring back, as if daring them to say something.

Wally was trying to catch Cindy's eye, but she was maintaining her vision toward the stage. He was now always aware of where she was sitting, and she was helping out by pretty much sitting in the same place every class. Darryl was next to her but she wasn't looking at him either. She appeared unfazed, as if she had never kept any secrets in her life.

He then looked in Lori's direction, who was staring intently at him. Uh-oh, too many secrets. Well, two big ones anyway. He didn't respond to her stare and quickly turned his head, hoping Gravesend would go somewhere with this lecture.

Gravesend spread his arms as if engulfing the room. "They are everywhere." He grabbed the microphone and took a step to his left. "Too many secrets. Too many to keep." He took a few more steps in that direction. "So what do we do with them?"

Wally wanted that answer.

"I don't know." Gravesend walked back to the right. He was keeping everyone's attention now, though McElroy rolled his eyes at the last remark. "Really, I don't know. As you can already see, I told one other person what this talk was about, and he blabbed right away. So much for that secret.

"So, I did a questionnaire about how other people handle secrets." He pointed a finger out at the audience. "I deliberately did not choose anyone from here. And I told those who responded that I would not share their names, that I would keep them confidential. And I will, unless somebody tries to seduce me, in which case . . ." He shrugged. "I may spill the beans. I do have my price and I know what it is." There was some tentative laughter. Gravesend resumed his pacing.

"Anyway, back to secrets. What I found intriguing, but probably not unexpected, was that few people would admit that they had their own secret, but they always knew somebody else who had one, or two, or more. And I noticed that they usually looked at the person next to them when they gave that answer. A person who had just said that they also had no secrets. As I said, a result to be anticipated."

He stopped walking and brought his focus slowly from left to right, covering everyone in the auditorium.

"The interesting part." He brought his mic down briefly, then lifted it back up. "The most interesting part is when I asked how they kept secrets, the secrets of others, they all said they simply didn't talk about them or share them with anyone else. However, it didn't occur to any of them, that by initially admitting that there was a secret to keep, they had already given away part of it."

Here he brought the microphone right up to his mouth, so that it sounded like he was in a cave when he talked, or like he was pretending to be God. "If you already know a secret exists, you can begin making assumptions about what it may be, and, that can lead to actually discovering the secret. It makes it much easier to figure out."

A hand was raised several rows back to the right. Gravesend pointed to her. "Yes?"

"Do you have any secrets? Besides the one that was shared at the beginning of your talk?"

Gravesend stared at her for a full ten seconds, then smiled.

"No."

He waited another ten seconds. "But then, the best way to keep it hidden is to tell you I don't have one." Gravesend then walked off the stage. There was silence for a few moments until everybody realized he was done, then conversations started again. They started to pack up their bags and leave.

Wally didn't believe that any new territory had been covered with this presentation. His problem was that he had already shared some of his secrets, because he had been told to (by himself, he had to admit). The biggest issue was that Officer Miller kept asking him about the landladies, which meant that he probably already knew Wally had a secret, which also meant he had a good chance of figuring it out. Wally shook his head. He didn't dare look at Cindy or Lori.

CHAPTER 39

Wally knocked on Cindy's door, but got no answer. He had tried her cell phone earlier, but also no response. The thought that maybe she was in the shower had prompted him to pause, then hurry out his door, then pause again in front of her door before knocking. The mixed internal messages were still confusing him, just as they had done in high school. He was supposed to be past that, but ten years of supposedly added maturity hadn't cured his indecisiveness. His initial rap was tentative at first, but got louder the second and third times.

He fidgeted for a moment. He wanted to talk with the Weidenbach sisters and thought that Cindy would want to be with him, but, apparently, she was not at home. He would have to brace them by himself.

Walking down to the first floor, he took a deep breath and knocked on their door with what he hoped would have been perceived as confidence.

The sister who opened the door, smiled and said, "Oh, hello, dear. We were just talking about you."

Noting that her top button was undone, Wally made an assumption and began, "Eleanora, I was wondering if we could have a little talk ourselves. With both you and your sister, I mean."

The sister blushed slightly and reached up a hand to fix the button on her blouse. "Oh, I'm Isadora. But, certainly, come in, come in. We were just having some tea. Would you care for some?" Without waiting for an answer, or even expecting one, she led him in to their living room.

Already seated was Eleanora with her cup. Now that he saw her, he did recognize that he had certainly been mistaken at the door. Both her top two buttons were undone.

As he turned toward the couch to sit, he discovered Cindy was also already there. Her buttons were where they were supposed to be.

"Hi, Drew. I thought you might be coming down here. We were just discussing that possibility." She slid over slightly, to let him know he was supposed to sit next to her, on her left. As if he would have sat anywhere else.

"Yeah." Eleanora took a sip as Isadora entered the room and handed Wally his cup. "You probably want to ask us some more questions, and to make sure that you know everything that you need, before the next time you have to talk with that Officer Miller."

"Uh, yeah, that's exactly what I came down here for, you're right." Wally took the cup, which didn't have a saucer and realized it was hot. Really hot. Too hot to just hold. The side table was on the other side of Cindy, and he had to reach across her to set his cup down, but couldn't find something to set it on except the bare wood, so he wavered with it in the air.

"Here." Cindy's voice breathed into his ear from that distance. "Let me take it and you can hold mine."

"But it's hot. I mean, hot."

She switched the cups and held the hotter one comfortably in her lap. "That's okay. I'm a woman. I can handle it."

Her cup was also still hot, but much more livable and he decided he'd better not complain. His eyes drifted in the direction of the bookcase with the collection of first editions that he had noticed before, but he couldn't make out any more titles from where he sat. The sisters both took sips from their steaming mugs and smiled at him.

"Uh, you're right." He started again. "I've seen Officer Miller a couple of times since we last talked, and he seems to really believe that I know something. I think he's following me to see if I go somewhere or do something."

Isadora spoke. "But you're not going somewhere or doing something, are you, dear?"

"No, but he doesn't know that! I'm afraid I'm going to give something away. About the two of you." He took a sip before he remembered it was Cindy's tea, then sucked in a deep breath as hers was still really hot.

"Look," he continued once he could again speak. "Last time we talked, it was more in general terms. Just that there were two of you and an ex-cop was looking for Eleanora. But we didn't talk about why you are in hiding. Maybe we need to know a little more about that so we know just what we are protecting. Right now, I don't really know what I'm not supposed to say. Do you understand what I'm saying?"

The sisters glanced at each other. Isadora spoke first. "It's your story, Eleanora. You had better tell him what you do know."

"Yeah, I suppose." Eleanora sighed. "You know that we married brothers, that Isadora here got the quiet, practical, hard-working one, and I got the fun one – the one that took chances and didn't mind a little trouble. For the most part, considering our own different personalities, it worked out for both of us.

"But then Gus got in a little more trouble than he could handle. He liked to gamble – cards, the horses, football, whatever he could lay a bet on. When he won, it was exciting and we partied and went on trips. The problem was he always spent it all, never put any aside for the times when he wasn't winning, which was more often than not. I admit I enjoyed the fun times and there were enough of them that I didn't complain. Too much. I also enjoyed my roulette, at times. But when I got ahead, I was smart enough to keep it for a rainy day.

"Well, Gus got on a losing streak. Longer than any he'd had before, and he couldn't pull out of it. I think he was taking bigger risks trying to get a big win from longer odds, but it wasn't working. His bookies wanted their money, and they weren't too particular about where it came from. I think you can guess what I mean. At first he asked Dieter to loan him some money." She looked at Isadora and slightly raised her shoulders. "I could say I didn't know, but I suspected. But then it became too much for that and he wasn't able to pay anything back to Dieter."

Isadora patted her on the knee. "You know I would have done whatever I could to help."

Eleanora patted her back on her knee. "I know, dear, but we were already owing Dieter so much, and I didn't want to bother you any more with my problems. You had already been so helpful."

Isadora returned the pat, just a little bit harder. "That's what sisters are for."

Eleanora set her teacup on the table next to her and used both hands to pat Isadora's knee even more forcefully. "I couldn't let you do that. It was our problem. Not yours."

Isadora now set her cup down and her patting became a drumming. "That would have been my decision to make."

Wally was fascinated and wanted to see how far this no-longer-hidden tension would go, but Cindy broke in. "Ladies, please, can we get back to what happened next? Please?"

Isadora raised her chin and gently brushed a hair back into place. Eleanora smiled as if she had somehow won something and picked her cup back up to take a gulp. Then she turned to Cindy and Wally.

"As I was saying, Gus owed the bad guys a lot of money. How much, I don't really know, just that it was a lot. He didn't tell me, but, by now, I could recognize when there were money problems. He'd get moody and short-tempered, and wouldn't want to eat. Not even schnitzel, and he loved schnitzel. And he would drink more beer, much more beer. This time, it was worse. He would barely talk to me or even spend time in the house. He was constantly gone."

She took another gulp of tea and was silent for a moment. "I'm sorry. This ain't easy to talk about."

Isadora reached out a hand again, but Eleanora quickly moved her knee out of the way. "I think this is when he started picking up … additional money, I mean robbing places. Mostly the bars where he was drinking the beer. He later told me he just started by picking up the tips left on tables or money left on the bar for the bartender. There were four or five places he frequented so it wasn't just one place he could be tied to. A couple of times he'd take cash from a till that had been briefly left open. There were also some guys who'd leave their wallets on the bar next to them while they drank and then they'd turn to talk to somebody on the other side of them, you know how that is. According to Gus, it was only when the opportunity was there.

"But then he started going to new places, places where they didn't know him, and getting a little more bold about taking wallets out of jackets draped over seats or handbags left on an open barstool next to a drinker. Just taking a few twenties at a time, counting on them not knowing just how much money they'd started the evening with. And it usually worked. If somebody caught him with their wallet, he'd say he just found it on the floor, give it back to them, then leave immediately."

Wally was so engrossed in the narrative that it wasn't until he looked down that he realized that Cindy had taken his right hand in her left. He smiled but then also noticed that she had shifted her purse to the other side of her body, away from where he could reach it. So was she holding his hand out of affection or protection?

"But it wasn't nearly enough." Eleanora was gripping her cup with both hands. "He worked at an auto parts store, but he was still smart enough to not touch any money there. Almost all his paycheck was going to keeping the bookies at bay as well as the little he was stealing.

"Then one night he was at a place called Mattie D's, somewhere he'd never been before. A man came in, sat down a few stools away, and placed an expensive-looking briefcase up on the bar. He opened it, took what looked like a hundred dollar bill out of it and gave it to the bartender. The bartender gave him a beer, but no change. Gus' first thought was to wonder what beer cost a hundred dollars and could he get some of that, maybe just a sip anyway. Then he noticed that the guy never touched it, and just walked away and out the door, leaving both the beer and the briefcase. Gus looked around, saw nobody watching him, and reached over to pull that beer next to him. He took a sip, was surprised to realize that it tasted just the same as the one he was already drinking, thought "well, that ain't worth it", and pushed it back to where it had been, his hand brushing up against the case. The next thing he knew he was walking out the door with the briefcase. Didn't even consciously think about it, just took it and left."

Eleanora and Isadora now just sat and looked at Wally and Cindy. Cindy took her hand out of Wally's and lifted what had been his cup for a sip of tea. Wally swiveled his head from Eleanor to Isadora, then from Isadora to Eleanora, then repeated it.

"And?"

"And there was a lot of money in it. I mean, a lot. A lot of a lot. More than enough to pay off what he owed. Nothing in it but money. Two hundred and twelve thousand, to be exact."

"Wow." Wally leaned back. He hadn't realized that he had been on the edge of his seat till then. "So that's the money they're looking for."

"That's the money they're looking for," Eleanora agreed. "Gus paid off his bookies the next day. At first they were happy. Surprised but happy. Then they must have started wondering about the size of the bills. To make a long story short, well, actually, it probably isn't that long. The owner of that bar was the one who ran the bookies. Gus had paid them back with their own money that he had stolen from them. So they put one and one and one together." She held up a hand and counted off on her fingers. "A large amount of money was stolen from them, Gus pays them back the next day, the bartender apparently identifies him from a picture as having been in the bar that night."

Now it was Cindy's turn to say, "Wow." Only she leaned forward instead of back. "So they came after him?"

Eleanora inclined her head. "Not immediately. I mean, not that day, anyway. I think they must have decided to follow him for a few days. To see where he had the money and what he was doing with it. He didn't know it was theirs at first. He was expecting the police checking on somebody that had a briefcase stolen. He told me that a man did come to see him, flashing a badge, but the questions were just general about whether he had seen anything at that bar. Probably that Officer Miller of yours. After about a week, his bookie, Sammy Jessup, came up to him in the street with a couple of bigger men. Muscle, Gus called them, though Sammy referred to them as 'associates'. That's ..." Eleanora wiped a tear from each eye. "That's when they said they knew about the theft and they first threatened him. Return all the money plus twice what he first owed them. Within two days. Or he would be a lesson.

"Not that he would learn a lesson, but that he would be a lesson. That's when he told me everything and to get out and hide. I came here. Two days later, he and Dieter were killed in the fire at Dieter's paint company."

Wally stirred. "You said he told you everything. Did that include where the money is?"

"No." She shook her head. "He said it was in a safe place, that no one would think to look for it there, but he wouldn't tell me. He was trying to figure out how to get the rest of the cash they now wanted and he was going to give it back all at once. He thought if he gave them their money back, they might just cut their losses and him at the same time. As long as they still had hope of getting the rest back, he figured he was still alive." She shrugged. "I guess they ran out of patience and probably didn't think the money would be as hard to find as it is."

"And you still have no idea where he could have hidden it?" Cindy asked.

Eleanora looked at Isadora, but they both shook their heads. "No. I know they went through everything at our apartment – tore it apart. Isadora went to check there shortly after the brothers died. Everything was ripped apart, nothing worth keeping. I don't know of any secret bank account or safety deposit box. If he physically hid it, I have no idea where."

Isadora nodded her head in agreement. "If he buried it somewhere, we would not know where to start."

Wally was silent for a minute. "You also said they followed him soon after the robbery, so they would have known if he had gone somewhere different to hide it. It must be somewhere he would normally have gone that didn't seem suspicious." Now he shook his head. "Have you told the police?"

Isadora answered, "They came to me after Dieter and Gus had died, of course. But Eleanora was already hiding here and we couldn't tell the police about the bookie's threats and his gambling debts without them discovering where she was."

Wally and Cindy looked at each other, not knowing what to say.

CHAPTER 40

Wally was eating lunch in the Bradford Union. Something called Bradford Stew, which wasn't bad as far as stews go. And you didn't get too curious about the ingredients.

Derek Trueblood slid into the seat across from him, holding a bag from a fast-food place down the block. He held it up briefly. "My stomach felt a little queasy after Askovarik's class, so I didn't want to chance anything with Bradford seasoning or sauce today. Just good old familiar grease."

Steve Getty sat down next to Derek, carrying the same type of bag, and shrugged. "We were walking together."

"So, anything new going on?" Derek pulled out his sandwich.

"No." Wally set his spoon down and shook his head. "Nothing new. The same-old, same-old. Everything's old. At least six years old." He sipped from his cup of Bradford Lemonade.

"That's very time specific, but okay. Just haven't talked to you much in class lately."

"Well, you know, trying to keep up with my notes." He stared hungrily at Derek's very recognizable hamburger. There was nothing in the Bradford Food Court that resembled it.

"Huh, I didn't think you took any notes, particularly in Askovarik's class."

Wally shrugged. "Maybe it's getting harder."

"Maybe?" Now Steve was curious, enough to set his hamburger down after only two bites.

"Yeah, okay, I hate to admit it, but I'm understanding less as the class goes on. Maybe it's his accent." Wally also didn't want to admit to himself that he was going to be here longer than he had expected to be, that maybe he might have to pass a few tests, might actually have to demonstrate a little learning. And he had started with less knowledge than anybody else in the program.

Derek leaned in. "That's okay, we can get together to go over some of this stuff."

"As well as some other things." Steve added, looking at Derek as he spoke. Derek grimaced and spread his hands, scattering a little bit of what was recognizably catsup, and, just as recognizably, not Bradford sauce.

Wally had had enough of the Bradford Stew with the Bradford Seasoning. "Other things? What do you mean, other things?"

Steve took another bite before answering. "Do you remember that guy I asked you about before – that cop named Miller? The one asking about your landlady, Weidenbach? Has he been around to see you yet?"

Wally noticed that he had said the name correctly this time, with a "d", not an "s". He hesitated long enough for Steve to continue.

"Yeah, I thought so. He came back to see me, to ask if you had talked to me about any of this." Steve held a real french fry in front of him for a second before popping it in his mouth. Wally licked his lips. "I told him 'no', that you and I weren't real close, but he strongly implied that he had had a conversation with you and that he was very interested in your relationship with 'a Mrs. Weidenbach', not 'the Mrs. Weidenbach'. As if there were more than one."

He looked again to Derek, who was wrapping up the trash from his lunch. Derek paused, then nodded, and said, "Let me do it. Wally, it's time we were square with you about a few things."

Steve gathered up the trash from all three lunches and went to throw it away, leaving Wally and Derek alone for a moment.

"Steve and I are not just graduate students." *Well, neither am I,* Wally thought, and then briefly wondered if Derek was going in the same time-travel direction.

"We're actually undercover police officers from the Oldstown Police Department." Wally sat back. Okay, that was a completely different direction. "Investigating a gambling syndicate and the deaths of the Weidenbach brothers." He paused and stared straight into Wally's eyes. "You know about the murder of the Weidenbach brothers, don't you? You showed surprise about us being police officers, but not about the brothers being killed, or even about a gambling syndicate."

Wally just sat there, trying, apparently too late, not to show anything on his face. He didn't know what to say, or ask, or deny first, so he just sat there.

Derek continued. "We joined the force about the time this Officer Terry Miller left. He was in a different division and never met us. There were suspicions that he was somehow involved with the gamblers, but he resigned before any official investigation was begun. The department thinks he is still involved, and there were rumors he was hanging around the campus." He shrugged. "The higher-ups thought we could pass as college students and got us in place to see if we could get an idea about what he's doing here. Steve's dad has been on the Summerfield police force for quite a few years, so he's been around this law enforcement stuff all his life. I just sort of follow his lead."

Wally's mind got stuck on one thought. *This is why Derek never questioned my lack of knowledge in psychology. He doesn't know any more than I do. Is anybody in our class really here to study psychology?*

Derek was still talking, so Wally shook his head and decided he better get back to listening. "Now former officer Terry Miller seems to have focused on you and your landlady. Yes, her husband and brother-in-law were killed, and her twin sister has disappeared, but why does he want to know about you? It makes sense for him to stick around her, hoping her sister shows up, but what do you have to do with it?"

A chair was pulled back as Steve returned to the table and sat down. Wally turned to the noise, more as a way to give his thought processes time to start working again, before he faced Derek again.

"I ... don't know." His thinking apparently still needed more time.

They obviously didn't believe him and waited for him to add something. They were better at waiting than he was, and Wally spoke first.

"Look, do you have any ID? You still look like grad students to me – as much as I do anyway."

Each of them pulled out a badge and laid it on the table. Now that Wally had time to examine them, it was clear that these looked official and Miller's had not.

Derek put his back away. "Nothing personal, but you have never really looked like a grad student, like you belong here. There's been a deer-caught–in-the-headlights look about you, as if you didn't know what you were here for, or that someone else was going to figure out that you were a fake. For example, you rarely took any notes at first and you had no idea what you wanted to do for your doctoral thesis. I've never known of anybody that came back after several years that didn't have a better idea of why they were here. Maybe somebody straight out of undergrad, but not somebody giving up a real job and money to come back to being poor again."

Wally took a deep breath. "I have met Terry Miller. A couple of times. Once in my office, and once in a convenience store. I think he was following me. He asked me if I knew a Mrs. 'Weisenbach', like you did at first." He nodded to Steve. "I told him just my landlady, Mrs. Weidenbach. He didn't seem to believe me. But that's the one I know."

Derek leaned back and stretched his fingers, releasing a hidden tension. "When we ran into Professor Askovarik at the department party, he introduced us to his companion, Mrs. Weidenbach. Mrs. Eleanora Weidenbach. The sister that everyone is looking for. Not the sister that is your landlady."

"I didn't know that." Wally's voice rose slightly. "I didn't know her first name."

"But she knew you. She said 'We live together.'"

"I thought she was my landlady, just acting different." He wished he had something still on the table to take a bite out of, just something to give him time to consider what he could or should say. "She seemed to have some … personality changes, and I never knew what personality I was going to run into."

"But now you know that there are two of them."

Wally paused again and crumpled the one napkin that had been left. "Ye-yeah. Cindy told me. You met her at the department party. She just knew, told me it was a female thing to recognize they were different people. I swear I didn't know till then." But now he had spilled the beans, or the cat was out of the bag, or the milk was spoilt. No matter what metaphor was used, he had given away one of his secrets.

Steve leaned in as if he wanted to say, "Aha!", but he didn't. "You haven't told that to Terry Miller?"

"No! I'd rather tell him I came from the future. I mean, tell him anything else, make something up, rather than tell him about the sisters."

Derek looked at him and blinked rapidly after the "future" comment, but he didn't pursue what he was obviously wondering. "The sisters. Have you talked with them? Do you know anything about the gambling syndicate, or the murder of the brothers?"

"Look." By now the napkin had been shredded into tiny pieces and Wally was trying to put it all back together. "I've been told, well, I've been informed that I could trust somebody from law enforcement. I'm going to have to take the chance that it's you two."

Neither Derek nor Steve nodded, but Steve did shrug and say, "Well, you know you can't trust Miller. We're all you have left."

"I'm going to have to tell you some things. I have talked with the sisters." He didn't want to mention yet that Cindy had also been there. "Eleanora has been hiding out here, but she doesn't know anything about where the money is, or who it is that is after them, except that it's the group in charge of the gambling. She was threatened before she hid. The only name she mentioned was a bookie named Sammy Jessup, but I had the sense he was not the one making any decisions."

Derek nodded. "We know about Jessup. He's a little fish. He may make some threats, but he's not going to be the one that carries them out. It's who he reports to that we're trying to find. But what about this money? Is this why Augustus was killed? We knew he owed big money, but not that he had any."

"Uh." Wally gulped and looked over at the dessert counter without seeing it. "Apparently Gus stole some money to pay his debts, and it turned out that he stole it from the same gang he was paying it back to. So not only did he owe them money, he also stole from them. Double jeopardy, so to speak. And he still had some of it. Most of it. A couple hundred thousand, according to Eleanora." He brought his eyes back to the table. "But she has no idea where any of it is. So she can't give it back to them."

Derek drummed his fingers on the table as if he were listening to a tune that no one else could hear. "That's why Miller is here. He's looking for the money and thinks the sisters can lead him to it." He brought his hands to a crescendo bang on the table. "And apparently he thinks there's a reason you're in that apartment building. That you know something that nobody else knows. Well?"

Wally jumped back in his seat. "Derek, I don't know anything, honest. It was … recommended to me that I get an apartment there, and I think I got the only one left." An image of hiking boots suddenly came to him. "I think Miller tried to get an apartment right after me, but was told I had just taken the last one."

"But why are you here?" Steve asked. "We've established that you don't seem to be here as a student. So what are you here for?"

Wally couldn't say he was here to reestablish a relationship with Cindy, and it wouldn't sound any better to say he was here to meet girls in general. "I needed a change. And graduate school seemed like a good idea at the time?" He realized that comment had come out like a question and changed his tone. "I thought a graduate degree would give me more career options."

Derek tilted his head, not accepting that obviously ridiculous concept. "Okay, Drew, if that is your real name. It sounds like you've got a secret that you're not quite ready to share with us yet. I think we're going to have to live with that for now." He tilted his head the other way as if to get a different perspective of Wally. "I still think you're one of the good guys in this. Don't make me regret this."

He turned to Steve, nodded, and they both got up and left. Wally spent another couple of minutes trying to repiece the napkin before it occurred to him that he could leave the lunchroom too.

CHAPTER 41

Wally was not looking forward to his grad ass hours, the time he was being paid to be available for simply anyone to wander in, and either confront him or ask him unanswerable questions. His first visitor, however, was about the last one he would have expected.

Darryl Thomas' voice carried through to him from the open door, obviously talking to someone else. "Hey, buddy, you mind if I catch Drew for a couple of minutes first? Great, I appreciate it, man. Got some places I need to be, you know?"

He came into the room without knocking, checking off a column in his notebook. "Whoop, there's another one." Glancing up at Wally, he smiled his big I-know-you-like-me smile and closed the book. "That was a great idea for my study, Drew. I'm getting a lot of positive checks here. It pays to be me, know what I mean?"

Wally nodded in silent jealous agreement, but asked, "Who were you talking to out there?"

"I don't know, man. Just some dweeb in glasses from the class. Whoops, I should have shut the door first." He turned and slammed it behind him.

Relieved at first that it was only another student waiting for him, Wally now became concerned about being alone in the office with Darryl. They hadn't spoken since that time when he helped set up Darryl's ego-tracking system, but he didn't know what the football star knew about the time he spent with Cindy, and what he cared about that relationship. He didn't remember Darryl Thomas being in trouble for beating up someone in college, but, then, that might not have been considered newsworthy at that time.

"How, how can I help you, Darryl?"

"Oh, I just wanted to set up a time for me to do my presentation. I think I got enough stuff here for me to go ahead and get it done."

"Data."

"What?"

"Data. You said 'stuff'. You should probably call it data when you give your talk. That you have data regarding your interactions with others."

"Yeah, man. Good idea." He opened the notebook and wrote at the top of a page, hopefully the word "data". "Makes me sound like I know what I'm talking about. Though that hasn't bothered anybody so far." He laughed at his own joke.

Wally pulled up a calendar on his laptop. "How about next Thursday? I've only got one scheduled for that date so far and I think we can fit in another one."

"Great. Can I go first? Then I can leave and won't have to listen to someone else yak about their boring stuff, I mean data." He laughed at his own correction.

Wally shrugged, recognizing that any discussion about supporting the other students would not find a listening ear. "Sure, why not?"

Darryl made another checkmark in his notebook. "There you go. More data, huh? Thanks a lot." He turned and opened the door, calling outside. "Okay, buddy, your turn. Told you it was going to be quick."

Wally started to blow out a long breath of relief when Darryl poked his head back around the doorframe.

"Oh, hey. Cindy told me she talked to you about what she was going to do, and that she thought you were cool." He paused. "Glad you were able to help her out too." He gave the thumbs-up signal, then left.

Wally didn't complete his breath until Vern Sheffield walked in and closed the door behind him.

"Did he leave?"

"Who?" Vern asked.

"Darryl Thomas, the football quarterback."

"Oh, is that who that was? I don't follow sports, so I don't know him. Is he famous or something?"

"He will be."

Vern raised his eyebrows at that remark, but came all the way in and sat down.

"Okay, Vern, what can I do to help you?" He suddenly held up a finger. "But give me a minute. I hate to do this to you, but I need to check something first. I know you had to wait for Darryl, but I do really need to do this."

He hit the link for MyFate on his Laptop and it came up immediately.

So what are you waiting for? You have to tell him at some point or you never get back here. It might as well be now. Go for it.

It took him a few seconds to realize that Vern was asking him a question. "Wha-what did you say?"

"I said, are you all right? You seem distracted. Did that football guy say something to upset you?"

"No, no." Wally shut The Laptop. "I'm sorry. I had something else on my mind. But it didn't have to do with Darryl. That actually went better than I expected." He shook his head. "Thank you for waiting." He folded his hands on the desk in front of him. "So, you came to see me."

"Yeah." Vern leaned forward. "You know, last time you were talking about time travel?"

Wally slowly said, "I remember."

"And I was talking about echoing another's statements?"

"And you were talking about echoing another's statements."

Vern pointed a finger at Wally. "Are you doing it again? Repeating what I say just to annoy me?"

Wally tried not to smile. "Where are you with this study, Vern?"

Vern moved even more forward on the edge of his seat. Wally was glad there was a desk between to protect his personal space.

"I decided to look at gender differences. Between male and female in needing to repeat what someone has just said. And you were right, there is a difference." Wally didn't recall having said that, but he was willing to take credit for it. "Males said it about three times as often as females. Females are more likely to just say, 'what are you talking about?' I find that fascinating."

"Was this always in response to something that you personally said?" Wally considered that Vern Sheffield may get more people not following what he was saying than most other speakers. And his listeners may need to check for understanding more often.

"Well, for the most part. I found that when I tried to overhear other conversations and take notes, they became offended for some reason. I don't know why. I didn't tell them that what they said was stupid or anything. But I did get a couple times when they didn't know I was listening."

Wally picked up a spare paper clip to twirl in his fingers. "I think they probably felt you were violating a private conversation."

"I was just listening."

"Do you remember Tim Gravesend's study on secrets? That everybody probably has something they don't want other people to know?"

Vern shook his head. "I remember him talking, but since it wasn't supposed to be of any importance to me, I wasn't listening. I'm not going to be tested on any of these presentations, am I?"

Maybe you should be, Wally thought to himself. Then realized thinking to himself was just thinking, so he could drop the "to himself" when he was thinking, to himself. "So, are you ready to present?"

"Yeah, I suppose so. I could keep doing this, getting more data, but I might as well go ahead. I think everyone else will find it riveting."

Or something. Instead Wally said, "I've got a couple presentations scheduled for next Thursday, but it's an hour class and no one has gone over fifteen minutes yet. I would be surprised if there are going to be a lot of question-and-answers for any of these."

Vern nodded. "Okay, I think that will work."

"You think that will work?'

Vern looked at him, then smiled. "You're doing it again."

Wally nodded. "Yeah, I'm doing it again." Vern didn't seem to notice that one. "Before you go, Vern, you mentioned something about time travel when you first came in. Was there something you wanted to bring up about that?"

Vern shook his head. "No, I just remembered that you had asked me about it. I have no interest in that kind of thing. It's impossible."

"That's what I would have said. Six years from now."

"You mean six years ago?" When Wally shook his head, "Six years in the future?" Wally nodded. "That's crazy."

Wally nodded again. "But it's true."

"Then you're crazy."

"Probably, but that doesn't make it any less true. I'm from six years in the future." Wally realized he needed to be pretty direct in stating anything to Vern Sheffield. "And you're the one that sent me here."

"Then I'm crazy."

Wally laughed. "I'm not going to dispute that either. But I think I have to tell you now so that you can send me here from six years away."

"I invent a time machine, in the next six years?"

"You know, I don't know that you invent it. I think you just sort of have it. And it's not a big machine. It's just a chair. With a button."

"I will have a time chair. With a button."

"Yep. Now you're repeating what I say. It must be contagious. You don't seem to know how it works, but you push the button and I'm back here at Bradford State."

"You're crazy. But … it does sound sort of cool." Vern sat back, seeming to all of a sudden matter-of-factly accept the concept. "But why you? Why not send myself back?"

"That's a good question. My best guess is that I am already here. As this person from the future, so I can't change anything. But you are here only as you are now. At least that is sort of how you explain it to me. It is just that I am the one that did go back, nobody else, so I am the one that will have to go back. Why it was significant for me to be the one, I don't know."

Surprisingly, Vern seemed to accept this. "Yeah, that sort of makes sense." Wally was glad it made sense to somebody, but he wasn't going to debate it.

"Do you believe that I am from the future?"

"Sure, why not? You seem like an honest guy, Drew."

Wally scratched his nose. "Well, first of all, my real name is not 'Drew Wright". It's Wally Stephens."

"I can see why you changed it."

Wally wasn't sure how insulted he was supposed to be about that, but recognized that wasn't the point at the moment. He opened The Laptop and turned it around to face Vern.

"I have a program on here that tells me, in general, what I may need to be doing when, but gives me very little specifics. I have to figure out a lot on my own. But it did tell me that I have to tell you about being from the future. Because you're the one that has to arrange it, in six years."

Vern adjusted his glasses and leaned in to see what the program said.

Hi.

He sat back again. "Okay. Should I say 'hi' back?"

Wally shook his head. "It doesn't work that way. At least I don't think so. It's just sort of there when it thinks I need it. Most of the time. Sometimes. It told me to get a certain apartment and to register as a graduate student and to get this assistant job through Dr. McElroy. And, just now, to tell you what is really going on."

"So what do I need to do?"

Wally tore a piece of paper out of his notebook and started writing on it. "Right now, I think you just need to know. I'm hoping the program will give me more specifics on what you need to do later on. The only thing I do know is that you will have to send me a letter to arrive by this date." He paused for a minute and tapped the pen on the desk, then continued writing. "This is my name, address, and the date. And I think this is the gist of the letter you send me. I can probably get you the original because I think I still have it in my suitcase." He handed the paper to Vern.

"What would happen if you meet yourself? Your younger self, I mean."

"Thanks, I didn't worry about that before." Wally shook his head. "But it's not going to happen. I didn't go here for college. I went to

Western Oshawa, and I don't remember coming over to Bradford State for anything at that time. And I know I'm not leaving here to go there."

Vern shrugged. "Just wondered if you'd explode or something." He put the paper in his pocket and got up to go. "I guess I will be seeing you again. I mean, besides class." He sighed. "And I guess this also means that at some point I've got to quit going to college and go have a career." Vern shook his head. "In time travel. Who would have thought?"

After he left, Wally sat for a few minutes, waiting to see if Lori or Officer Miller or anybody else stopped by. Nothing else showed up on his MyFate page, no matter how much he willed it to. He looked at his watch and realized it was time for him to get to his bookstores. He had some observations to do, and, for the moment, he better keep up with his expected routine.

CHAPTER 42

Thalman's Bookstore looked as busy as ever. Which meant Sidney Thalman, sitting behind the counter, and about three other customers, perusing quietly and independently. Mr. Thalman looked up, saw that it was Wally who had just entered, and went back to whatever he had been doing, which was infinitely more interesting than Wally.

Wally nodded in the direction of the now downturned head, and moved back to halfway through the shop, where he had established a spot for him to sit. However, an older woman was now in his chair reading. Or at least starting to read. Her left thumb seemed to be holding down only about three pages. She lifted her head, fixed him with a "don't bother me" glare, and shifted her rear, getting more comfortable. She was planning on being there for a while.

From his previous trips, Wally was aware that there was only one other seat in the shop, back in an isolated corner where other customers couldn't see you, and, more relevant to Wally, that you couldn't see anyone else from. Good for private reading, but not for observing.

He picked an open area and leaned against the wall facing the International Bio section (he assumed it was Biography and not Biology), and between the Sexual Health and Paranormal shelves. Perhaps it was Biology across from him.

Opening his Laptop, he found it awkward to hold and keyboard. Looking to the front of the store to make sure Thalman didn't see him, he pushed a copy of Grey's Metaphysical Anatomy from it's display on top of a bookshelf down two feet next to Diary of a Frustrated

Housewife. He still wasn't sure what section those were supposed to be in, but it gave him room to set his computer on top of that bookcase.

He brought up his notes from his last visit. Not much there. He only kept track of number of customers over a certain time period and which areas were used more frequently. It was only going to be for comparison purposes to The Book Look. He was never going to be making any suggestions to Sidney Thalman for any changes. Six years from now, he knew nothing was going to be different.

Wally stopped. "He was never going to…" He was never going to do any of this. He was never going to finish this study and never going to write it up and never going to make any recommendations. What the heck was he doing? He had started out just going through the motions, but had found himself actually taking what he was doing seriously. As if he really had to do it.

A sudden blip on his screen drew his attention.

MyFate

You may possibly, barely, negligibly use this information in your own job when you go back to your own time. Maybe. It is still good practice for you to be noticing what is going on in the store.

However, you don't need to be doing much more in this bookshop. You could probably spend more time in The Book Look. There's more to watch there.

Wally was about to shut the lid when he noticed a middle-aged man approaching the Paranormal section. When he saw Wally standing there, he stopped suddenly and pulled a book from the shelf next to him without looking at it, then turned and walked quickly back the other way. At least Wally assumed he had been coming to the Paranormal books. Maybe it was one of the other genres nearby.

CHAPTER 43

After just sort of hanging around for another half hour and observing two other people avoid what he now figured was the Sexual Health area, Wally left Thalman's Bookshop and headed over to The Book Look. Even if he wasn't going to ever use his notes, it was more fun to wander there and think about what worked, and what didn't work, and what changes might work. The seats were more comfortable and he could ask questions of the customers.

One observation from his previous visits had stood out to Wally. Matt Dubois stocked much more contemporary books and he wasn't very discriminating, as if he had told the company that provided the books, "Just send me about six copies of your top one thousand sellers." Any rare or used books seemed to just be ones that were brought in for trade or resale. And Dubois didn't seem to care about the values of those books. He was probably making money on the new books, but not on the rare ones. Wally had earlier seen a signed first edition of Stephen King's *Carrie* for only two dollars and had snapped it up quickly. He knew that copy was valuable in his time and had probably been worth a lot for years. Dubois rang it up and never blinked, just told him he hoped he enjoyed that kind of stuff, it wasn't his own cup of java. Apparently, the bookseller wasn't in the business through a love of fine literature, but to simply make a profit. Nothing wrong with that, but it made Wally realize that he himself actually loved the books, that maybe he was in it for more than just something to do.

His chosen seat here was more comfortable than at Thalman's, probably too comfortable. Last time he had dozed off briefly and woke only when someone had dropped a large volume trying to reach across him. He hoped the dozing was short and that it hadn't been too obvious with any snoring. It was an unobtrusive spot, but had a good view of the front check-out area, as well as the comings and goings through the most popular sections. And he could slide down deep enough in the chair so that other customers couldn't see that he was watching them. The only problem was that it was in front of the historical romances, which drew many of the middle-aged women readers. And they liked to spend their time here, leafing through the pages to the already well-thumbed good places.

Today, the owner was wandering through the shop, making small talk with several people. He waved to Wally and came over. "Hey, kiddo. How's it going today? See you're still at it. Any suggestions yet on how I can make a quick fortune here?" He laughed at his own joke. "You know, some day, you're going to have to get out into the real world and make a living yourself. I'd hire you on here, but, with your degree, you're going to be too damn smart, and too damn expensive, for this kind of work."

Wally didn't feel too smart for working with books, even though he had almost convinced himself that he should be looking for some more meaningful career. But he felt comfortable back in the book community. That surprised him. He actually understood this world and enjoyed it.

"I don't know, Matt." Calling the owner by his first name was also cool. He couldn't do that at Thalman's. "Doing this study has been one of the best parts of graduate school. Makes me think working with books isn't a bad job."

Dubois grunted and shook his head, wandering over to get one of his own doughnuts. He kidded another customer, "Hey, Fred, there's never any sprinkles left after you've been here. Why is that, do you think, huh?" This was more the relationship Wally wanted with the people that came to Ye Olde Bookshelf.

The front door opened, ringing the little bells that hung over it. That type of signal at the door was a necessity in these small businesses, so that the employee at the front counter would have to at least look up from his phone or video game to check out the comings and goings. That was the idea behind it, but it probably took much more disruption than that to get part-time student workers to look up from their electronics. Maybe that was the reason for four bells instead of just one.

A man wearing a checked sports coat over an open-collared striped dress shirt, and carrying a briefcase walked to the front counter. "Mr. Dubois in?" A little dressier than the usual midday customer.

The young man currently filling the seat at the counter used a Harry Potter bookmark to keep his place in his copy of *War and Peace,* and looked around the shop. He spotted Dubois behind the last week's bestsellers, flirting with an older woman while winking at a younger one standing nearby. "Hey, Matt, you got a second? Someone here to see you."

"Sure." Dubois started walking back to the front, but his eyes narrowed when he saw who it was. He quickly resumed his usual jovial smile as he got closer.

"Thanks, Tommy, I got it. You can get back to the joys of your ancient literature." He took the new customer's arm and pulled him over to the side of the shop, but still within hearing distance of somewhat-hidden Wally. "What are you doing here? I told you never to come to this shop."

"I'm sorry, Mr. Dubois, but I just got this." He hefted the briefcase. "And your other place ain't open yet. I didn't want to carry it around all day, if you know what I'm talking about?"

Dubois glanced at the case. "Yeah, it looks so heavy. You could hurt yourself." He sighed and took out his cell phone. "Okay, Sammy, I'll call Tony and tell him to meet you there. He'll take it off your hands." He clapped Sammy on the back. "Just don't do it again, you got it?"

The man nodded and left, ringing all the bells again, and causing Tommy to look up once more. Dubois walked back to his small office in the rear of the shop, punching some numbers into his cell as he went. Wally could no longer hear any further conversation, no matter how hard he strained his ears.

Wally shrugged. He wondered if Matt Dubois' "other place" was another bookshop that he wasn't aware of. He guessed not. Matt wasn't into books enough and he certainly wasn't making enough money here to open another similar business. However, Wally knew him well enough to know that Matt enjoyed making money, so it wasn't surprising that there was another Dubois enterprise somewhere, probably a bigger moneymaker.

For the next twenty minutes, Wally continued making notes on how customers roamed the shop, where they stopped, what they came back to. Even though there was a more comfortable feel to The Book Look and more open, well-lit spaces, he realized that Thalman's had a more natural flow to it. The organization and order of the shelves made more sense and the customers seemed to find it easier to locate what they were looking for, but also to do more browsing along the way. A combination of the two styles may actually work the best.

The bells above the front door tinkled for the third time since the man with the briefcase, but this time Wally recognized the visitor. Someone who strode in the now-familiar hiking boots right past the front counter and toward the office in back. Wally slithered down further in his chair. He couldn't see the office, but he heard Dubois' voice raised in surprise. "You? ... You better get in here and shut the door."

As soon as he heard the door close, Wally decided enough observation was enough for one day, gathered his materials and headed to the front door, nodding at the top of Tommy's head as he went. He had no desire to have Terry Miller find him today.

CHAPTER 44

Wally wanted to talk with Lori. It struck him that was kind of weird, because he should want to talk to Cindy. But Lori was the one who knew he had traveled through time, not Cindy. One of the major points of this whole experience was that Cindy not know who he really was, and where he had come from. Not until the reunion anyway. And he needed to talk to someone about his conversations with Derrick and Steve and Vern. He did need to talk to Cindy about who Derrick and Steve really were and what they were doing, but he desperately needed to sort out which part she should know and which she shouldn't.

He called Lori's cell phone, but was only able to leave a message asking her to meet with him when she could. He looked at his watch. She was probably in class at this time and, come to think of it, he was supposed to be somewhere too. His weekly meeting with Dr. McElroy was supposed to have started ... right now.

Only three minutes behind schedule, but breathing heavily from the run across campus, he entered the department and asked Mrs. Fochs, "Is he in?"

She shrugged. "Probably. He's supposed to be, but being where he's supposed to be, when he's supposed to be, is not his idea of a schedule."

Wally knocked on the office door, heard, "Entre vous," and walked in.

McElroy looked up and seemed disappointed. "Oh, I thought it might be the French instructor, Professor Gabreau."

Wally was startled. "Oh, were you expecting him, or her?" He had never met him, or her. "I thought it was time for our weekly meeting."

McElroy shook his head. "No, I wasn't expecting her. At least I think it's a her. The first name is Rene, so that doesn't really help. But she's never been here, so I thought she might be paying a surprise visit." He glanced at the watch on his left wrist. "Aren't you late for our meeting?"

Wally took a chance. "Why don't you look at your right wrist?"

McElroy did. "Ulp, you're right. You're right on time. So, what do you want to talk about?"

"Um, this is our regularly scheduled meeting." As he said it, Wally recognized that "regularly scheduled" had no meaning for the professor. "Our meeting when we're supposed to discuss how things are going." He moved some books from the only chair to take a seat. As he set them on the edge of a table next to him, he realized they were the same books from the last time he had been in the office and had to move them. He wondered, for the umpteenth time, if they had been opened since then or just simply moved back to the chair because that's where McElroy liked to keep them.

He decided to start with the hard part of the meeting, his thesis. "I've been making regular observations at the bookstores for my project, and I think I have some insights into optimal arrangements, but I don't yet know how that impacts sales and profits. It's hard to tell how Sidney Thalman makes money, because he has much fewer customers."

"Great, great, great. Tell me about it when you write it up. I trust you know what you're doing. After all, you wouldn't be working for me if you didn't." McElroy swiveled his chair back and forth. "Have you thought any more about time?"

Wally gulped. "You mean the keeping track of time, by all the various timepieces you have?"

"I mean the flexibility of time." McElroy stopped swiveling. "There is no fixed moment of time, whether it's measured by this watch," he held out his left wrist, "or this one," pulling one out of his pocket. He glanced at it, then stared at Wally. "Are you sure you're not late? Never mind." He put the watch back. "Think of all the different time zones there are in the world. It's three hours behind in California, six hours ahead in Germany. In Germany, I'd already be eating bratwurst and spaetzle for dinner, instead of poached fish and boiled asparagus to still have to look forward to." He sighed. "There is nothing in nature that worries about what exact moment this is. There is no natural way to keep track of time."

"Except, maybe, by the passing of the sun?" Wally suggested. "You know, from east to west." He stopped for a second. "Yeah, from east to west."

"Aha!" McElroy slapped his hand down on his desk. "The sun has no concept of time. Have you forgotten that the sun does not move?" He shook his head. "Does not pass from east to west? The earth moves around the sun. The sun does not care about time. It just is. So earth is the object obsessed with time. And that brings it back to us, sitting here, getting caught up in knowing just what the exact minute is. And we can't make up our minds."

He stood up and pulled out all the different timepieces he carried from his wrists and his pockets, until there were seven laid out on the desk. "Look at that. None of them agree."

"But you're the one ..." Wally started, but quickly stopped when McElroy glared at him. The professor's mind was clearly going where no mind had gone before, and real life had no place there. Sort of like time travel. It didn't make sense, but here he was.

McElroy sat back down and shook his head. "Where was I going with this?"

Wally shifted in his seat, not really wanting to start the discussion again. "You were, um, talking about the, uh, flexibility of time."

"Oh." McElroy gathered up all his personal methods of keeping track of time. "You just keep thinking about all this. After all, you have all the time in the world. Time, and you, aren't going anywhere."

CHAPTER 45

As Wally was walking back to his apartment after leaving Professor McElroy's office, his cell phone whistled the old TV theme song, *The Fishing Hole*. For some reason, he always wanted to say, "Hey," when he answered.

It was Lori. "Hey, back. You wanted to talk with me?"

"Yeah, can we meet somewhere? It has to do with, you know, what my computer told you. There are some things I need to talk out with you."

"Okay. I have an evening class, a small group discussion about the psychology of small group discussions, so the only open time I have is for supper before that."

"Alright, how about I take you to eat somewhere and we can talk."

"A date? I thought you were supposed to be seeing someone by the name of Cindy."

"I mean, I can buy you dinner for helping me. You know what I mean."

"I know what you mean." Wally thought he might have heard a sigh at the other end of the line. "That's fine. I can work with that."

They settled into a booth at Barney's Burgers, Burritos, and Beans, and looked at the menu. Surprisingly the featured beans were lima beans. Lori ordered the lima bean fruit salad and Wally ordered the cheeseburger burrito, with black beans instead of lima. At least it wasn't a Bradford Special.

As they waited the two minutes to get served, Wally told her about his lunch with Derrick Trueblood and Steve Getty. What he now knew about them and what they now knew about him.

Lori waited until her salad was set before her and she took a bite. "Then they are actually undercover cops investigating the killings of the husbands of your landladies?" She chewed slowly. "Is anybody in the psychology department actually a student?"

Wally threw up his hands. "Probably not. And who knows what Askovarik really is. But they also suspect that I'm not really a student, that there's some other reason I'm here. That's why I needed to talk with you. You're the only other one who knows these things. And the only one I trust."

"So, what do you want me to do? I don't know your landladies."

"Actually, it's not just them. Vern Sheffield also now knows that I'm from the future."

"Vern? You told Vern?"

"I had to. I told you that he's the one who gets me back here, so now he's got six years to figure out how to do it. Besides, my Laptop told me to let him know."

Lori shook her head. "How did he take it? I expect Derrick and this Steve also had trouble believing that you don't know more about the Weidenbachs and the gamblers than you do."

"I don't know if the student-cops -- that sounds funny but cop-students doesn't sound any better -- if they believe me, but Vern had no trouble accepting my time-traveling. He said that I didn't really seem to fit this time period anyway. That I always acted as if I was just here waiting for something to happen." Wally shrugged. "He was right about that."

Lori put down her fork and looked at him for a moment. "Yeah, he's got a point. Most of us are trying to figure out what we're doing next, where we're going. You just sort of meander from one day to the next."

Wally sat back. "I don't know about that. I've been working hard at my assistantship. Much harder than I expected to."

"It's not that. But, outside of wanting to date Cindy, there hasn't been any real purpose to what you're doing. You're just ... doing."

"Well, now I'm supposed to be solving the problems of the Weidenbach sisters. Is that enough purpose?"

Lori finished her fruit and pushed the lima beans aside. "Maybe it is. Maybe that is your purpose for being here, not for finding the love of your life. Maybe you're here to make somebody else's life better. Did you ever think of that?"

Wally looked down at his plate and absentmindedly mixed the black beans with the rice. "Yeah, The Laptop said something about that, too."

"Oh. So, maybe that's what you're destined to do before you can go back to your own time."

"Before I go back." Wally sighed and took a sip of what seemed to be real lemonade. "I didn't think I was going to be here this long. I've been messing around with my classes, and with these stupid bookshops for my stupid dissertation." He paused, slowly set his cup down, and looked Lori full in the eyes.

"Wait a minute." He licked his lips. "The bookshops. Books. Making money from books. I managed a bookshop in my time. There has to be a reason why I am the one that is here. And all I know are books."

"Okay." Lori looked doubtful.

"Books! Don't you see, books! It has to be something to do with books." Wally stood up. "I have to go. Thanks for meeting me." He started to move to the door, but stopped and looked back at her. "You have really been a big help. Not just a help, that isn't what I'm trying to say, but …." He wiggled a hand in exasperation in trying to find the right word. "You have been maybe the most positive … aspect of this whole experience. More than that. Oh, you know I have trouble finding the right thing to say. One thing I know about coming back is that I was meant to meet you. Enjoy your class discussion about class discussions." He hurried out.

Lori called after him. "It's a small group discussion about small group discussions." But he was gone by then. She looked down at the table, at the mostly uneaten meals, and realized she was going to have to pay for this not-a-date.

CHAPTER 46

Wally pushed open the door to Thalman's Used and Rare Books, ringing the sole bell above it. Sidney Thalman was just putting on his sports coat, getting ready to leave.

"Mr. Wright, I am surprised to see you here at this time. I was just about to close up, so I'm afraid there is nothing for you to observe. It is time for me to go get my dinner."

"I know, Mr. Thalman, and I am really very sorry to disturb you. But I really need to ask you just a couple of questions. It's really important and I don't know how much time I have." He saw that Thalman was holding his CLOSED sign. "Here, let me put that in the window for you."

"There is a hook just to the left of the door. Bring the OPEN sign back to me. Keeping them separate reminds me if I have already changed them, or if I still need to do that. Years ago, one of my assistants forgot to flip over the CLOSED sign to OPEN on the other side and you can imagine the lack of business for that day." He shuddered in memory, took the sign from Wally and set it up prominently in front of the cash register. "You put so many 'reallys' in your last statement that I assume that asking me these questions is 'really' vital. Come around the counter and take a seat back here."

Wally sat in the chair that he hadn't even been aware was there. He felt honored, but wasn't sure where to start. Now that he was here, he had to make what he asked sound important enough to Sidney Thalman.

Thalman prompted him. "You also mentioned a lack of time. May I suggest you ask me what you need to ask. You have not abused the privilege of observing in my store and I appreciate that. My dinner can briefly wait. What do you want to know?"

"Mr. Thalman." Wally licked his lips. "Mr. Thalman, you have been running this shop for a number of years …"

"Thirty-eight. I am aware of that."

"Thirty-eight years. So you must have been making a living from it." Thalman nodded. "Forgive me, but I guess I need to ask you how. And the answer is really, I mean, very, important. How do you make enough to make a living? I have never seen more than a few customers here at a time. I also go to The Book Look and they always have many more customers. And I know Matt Dubois still has another business to keep him going. I recognize that it's a different clientele and his inventory is mostly contemporary works. But he still has to be selling more books per day than you can."

Thalman snorted, which was a surprising sound coming from him. "Mr. Dubois can keep selling those new so-called works of literature. Most of them are flash in the pans. A few may still be worthwhile in a couple of years." He pointed to his front window. "You might not have noticed, or maybe you did, you do seem to have some eye for books of value, but my sign on the front window says not just Used Books, but Used and Rare Books." He then gestured to the locked bookcases behind him. "I am sure you are aware of the more valuable tomes I have behind me. In point of fact, you made a purchase of one of these not too long ago. I suspect you know something about that author that I don't. Yet.

"However.…" He rose from his seat and waved for Wally to follow him. "I don't think you have seen my rarest room." He led Wally to a locked door in the back of the shop. Wally had always assumed that it was Thalman's office or storage area where he sorted new additions, maybe a sauna that no one else was supposed to enjoy. But, once the door was opened, he was astounded at the shelves filled with a collection of books that he had only dreamed about. Hemingway, Mark Twain, Bradbury, L. Frank Baum, Sinclair Lewis, Thomas Jefferson, Longfellow, Helen Keller were only in the first shelf he saw. He took a few steps in and said, "Wow. I assume these are first editions and some are signed?"

Thalman nodded. "These are all first or early editions, sometimes rare publishing houses with only a few printings. And many of them are signed."

"Wait." Wally stopped in front of one. "You have a copy of _We Cuss a Little_? Back here?"

Thalman shrugged. "It's signed. To me. You would be surprised how few of his are signed, as the author wasn't that popular when he first came out."

"I, um, I have met that author."

"Yes, so have I. He started writing too late in life." He turned, looking at the shelves in pride. "This is where I make my money, Mr. Wright. This room is open only for specific collectors and customers who ask for specific items. Just last week, I had someone ask for illustrated or early copies of _A Christmas Carol_ and anything related to _The Mutiny On The Bounty_. I sold him an 1846 edition of the Dickens classic and a first edition of _The Court-martial of the 'Bounty' Mutineers_, both very rare copies. Not too many people know of the non-fiction books relating to the Bounty Mutiny."

Wally looked straight at the bookdealer. "Mr. Thalman, I thought, actually I was hoping, that this is what you were doing. I could spend all day, really many days, just looking at all these, but right now, I need to ask you another question, regarding who you may have made some sales to about one and a half years ago, around that time." He held up his hand. "I'm sorry, you may have some sort of client confidentiality, and I'm not trying to violate that, but I am trying to confirm something that I think may have happened. With some rare books. It's really, I mean very important."

Thalman looked thoughtfully at him for a minute. "I'm not a lawyer or a doctor, but I do think my customers have some legitimate rights to their privacy. There are some purchases that certain city commissioners, say, may not want other people to know about, but they're not usually interested in rare or antique books. However, I don't think there was anything in what you're asking that should upset anyone. Let's go check my records." Wally followed Thalman out of the room as he locked the door behind them and led the way back to his front counter.

He pulled out a laptop from a locked drawer toward the bottom of his antique rolltop desk behind the counter. The computer looked almost as old as the desk, but apparently it still worked. Wally belatedly recognized that any computing devices older than two years looked ancient to him.

Thalman booted it up and selected an icon that opened to last year's sales. "A particular date?"

Wally shook his head. "I don't know the exact date, but somewhere in the late spring, I think. It would have been for a very large purchase. Really large. Somewhere between one hundred and fifty thousand, and two hundred thousand dollars worth." He looked at Thalman with a small smile. "I'm hoping."

Thalman raised his eyebrows and took a moment to respond. "Yes, I remember that request. It was more than unusual. It wasn't for specific works of literature. This customer had a certain amount of money he wanted to invest in books, as quickly as possible. He trusted me to select which ones would be worthwhile, and to be honest about the prices. I told him I needed a day or two to gather the ones that met his purchase price, and that I may have to contact some other dealers. Amazingly, he had the money to leave with me, even before receiving the books, and told me that someone else would be by to pick them up. I think he felt very uncomfortable carrying that amount of cash with him and was anxious to leave it somewhere. He told me the other man would be using the name Theodore Geisel, his favorite author." Thalman smiled, which looked natural even though Wally could not recall ever seeing him smile before. "I included two books signed by that author as a bonus, because of the size of the order."

He turned back to the laptop and scrolled down. "Here we go. This is a list of the books he purchased. To protect his privacy, I only have a code designating the buyer."

He saw a DG in front of the books. Did that stand for dog, or a reverse of God, since this money may have seemed to come from heaven to Thalman? Or was it combining Doctor and Geisel? It didn't matter, it was the books with their values that were important right now. "Is it possible, I know it's asking a lot, but is it possible to get a copy of this list?"

Thalman's smile disappeared and he looked around the shop for a moment, then sighed. "I guess these books and their suggested prices are all in the public domain. I'm not sure what you are going to do with the contents of this list. I know you can't afford to buy these."

Wally thought of what the customer probably looked like coming into the shop. "How did you know this buyer could afford them?"

"He had the money with him. I took it to the bank to confirm that it was real before he received any of the books. And to deposit it so that I didn't have to worry about carrying that amount with me." Thalman highlighted the list and clicked the print button. A noise came from behind them as the printer started up. When it was done, Thalman handed the paper to Wally.

"Andrew," reverting to the more informal, now that their business was completed, "as I said, you have respected my shop and my business, and have done your observations with circumspection. I appreciate that. You informed me that this information was 'really' important, but I have the feeling that you are not the one to whom it is vital. I am trusting my intuition, which is rarely wrong. I am believing in you as a person."

"Thank you, Mr. Thalman. That means a lot, coming from you."

"Please, you can now call me 'Sidney'. I believe we have shared much this evening."

Wally smiled. Now he knew why he was able to get away with calling Mr. Thalman by his first name six years in the future.

CHAPTER 47

Wally knocked on Cindy's door. After a moment, he knocked again. Still getting no response, he was tempted to knock just one more time, but instead he frowned and went to unlock his own door. He had information that he needed to share with her, and he needed to share it as soon as possible.

He set the list on his bed and pulled out his Laptop, anticipating a message to be waiting for him. He was not disappointed this time.

MyFate

Yes, yes, yes. You are on the right track. Your time is running short. You will need to confirm what you suspect and then decide what to do with that information. I know you will make the right decision at the right time.

The "right time", huh? Or should I say the "Wright" decision at the "Wright" time? Sometimes I kill myself. Just don't let someone else do it for you.

Wally kept clicking Return on his keyboard, but nothing more appeared. He stared at The Laptop in frustration. *Come on, you know what I'm supposed to do, just tell me.* But it didn't tell him, though he could have sworn it almost smiled.

He sat for a few moments, then slowly closed the computer. It was time to confirm what Mr. Thalman had told him. He was pretty sure he knew where the money was and he knew why no one had been able to find it. And why he was the one that had come back in time to do it.

Crossing the hall, he knocked on Cindy's door that one more time. Still no response. He went down the stairs and rapped on the door to the Weidenbach's apartment. His knuckles were getting sore and he wondered, not for the first time, why there were no doorbells on these apartments. After a minute he raised his hand to knock again when the door opened a crack, still on the chain. Just enough to see the eyes of one of the sisters looking at him fearfully. Since he had never seen Eleanora display any sort of apprehension at any time, he took a guess.

"Isadora? It's me, Drew Wright. Can I come in for a minute?"

She drew back her head and glanced behind her. Then she closed the door to undo the chain and opened it all the way. "Yes, you better come in." Then she silently mouthed something to him that looked like, "Don't say anything."

But, of course, he said something. "What?"

She briefly closed her eyes in seeming exasperation, then closed the door behind him and waved him into their living room.

"Where's ...," he started to say before he spied Cindy sitting on the couch with her eyes wide open and barely shaking her head. Moving only his eyes to the left, he saw Terry Miller sitting in what was normally Eleanora's seat with another man, a man known only to him as Sammy, standing behind him. Sammy was the man from The Book Look, the man with the striped dress shirt and the checked sports coat and the briefcase. The man that wasn't supposed to be in the bookshop. He finished his question, "... my ... book?" He mentally kicked himself for saying anything related to books, but it was the first word that had come to him. He forced himself to focus on who and what was in the room, and not on who and what wasn't.

Isadora looked puzzled, but Cindy quickly responded, "It's in, uh, my room. Thank you, it's been a big help for my project. I'll get it back to you after ..." She vaguely waved at Miller.

Miller smiled at him, which somehow didn't reassure Wally at all. "Take a seat, Dr. Wright. I know, I'm a little ahead of myself, but what the hell. We were just getting comfortable waiting until you got here."

Isadora sat next to Cindy on the couch, the seat that Wally had wanted, but he understood Isadora's decision for the nearness of someone she could trust. However, he did not want to be too close to Miller either and squeezed in next to Isadora, forcing her to squeeze even closer to Cindy, who squeezed into the sofa's arm and glared back at Wally.

He hadn't expected Miller to be here, so he said, "Officer Miller, I didn't expect to see you here." Isadora crossed her arms and said, "I didn't either."

Miller now smiled at her. "Mrs. Weidenbach, I believe you had put on the kettle for tea. Maybe the water is ready now? I would love some tea. How about you, Sammy?"

"Maybe if you put something stronger in it?" Sammy grunted.

This time everyone turned to look at Sammy and he grunted again. "Nah, I didn't think so. So, no thank you, Mrs. Weidenbach."

Isadora looked over at Cindy and rose. Cindy took the hint and also stood up. "I'll help you, Isadora. You'll need more hands to carry the cups."

As they left the room, Wally said, "I thought you were looking for a Mrs. Weisenbach?"

Miller laughed. Sammy chuckled too, but as if he didn't know what the joke was.

"Nope, you were right. It was Mrs. Weidenbach, all along. Mrs. Eleanora Weidenbach." He wagged a finger at Wally. "And you told me you didn't know your landlady's first name. I heard you call her 'Isadora' at the door."

Wally inwardly breathed a sigh of relief that he had chosen that name at that time. Outwardly he shrugged. "I've gotten to know her better since then. Cindy was on a first name basis with her, so I started using it too."

Miller whistled lowly. "I can understand why you wanted to know this Cindy better." He raised a hand to Sammy. "Dr., I mean, Mr. Wright, I don't think you've ever met Sammy Jessup, my associate." Wally bit the inside of his lip at the word "associate". "And, Sammy, this is Mr., not yet Dr., Drew Wright. He has one of the apartments upstairs, the one that was no longer available when I came looking. Isn't that right?"

"I, uh, have one of the apartments upstairs, yes. I have no idea when you tried to get one here." But an image of those boots at the front door immediately after he checked in flashed into his mind.

The women returned to the room, each carrying two cups of tea. Cindy handed one to Miller, while Isadora set one down on a coaster next to Wally. He knew better than to pick it up right away.

"Thank you." Miller took a sip. "Ow! That is hot! I do believe you are trying to boil me alive." He shifted it from one hand to another.

Sammy grunted, "I told you that you needed something else in it. To cool it if nothing else."

Miller stood up and came over to exchange teacups with Wally's. "I'm trading with you. I think someone's trying to pull a fast one on me." He sat down again and took another sip. "Jesus, this seems even hotter! I can't drink this." He put it down on the bare wood of the small table next to him.

"Hey." Sammy picked it up and set a coaster under it. "You can't put it on the wood like that. It'll scar it." Miller rolled his eyes, but Isadora smiled gratefully at Sammy.

Miller laced his fingers together and smiled. He nodded at Cindy. "Miss Connor, I believe it was, it wouldn't surprise me, since you are such good friends of both of these people, to find out that you are aware that Mrs. Isadora, here, has a twin sister. And that we, the police, are presently looking for her, in relation to both the murder of her husband and the theft of a significant amount of money. So, now that we are all here, I am going to ask you one more time. Where is Mrs. Eleanora Weidenbach?"

Out of habit, they all three said, "Who?"

It didn't work. Miller simply sat there, now with his elbows on the arms of the chair and tapping his fingers together. Since they honestly didn't know the answer to the question, both Wally and Cindy looked at Isadora. She stared at Miller, trying to smile sweetly, but not saying anything.

"Well?" His finger tapping stopped. Then he stopped smiling. Sammy put his hands in his pockets and started rocking back and forth. Miller was menacing enough for both of them.

Wally broke the silence first. "I don't know. I just got here." His voice was higher pitched than he wanted it to be. "I mean, I told you I never met her." Trying to prove he couldn't be intimidated, he picked up his tea and took a gulp. It was still hot enough that he had to close his eyes for a second, but he took his time setting the cup back down. Focusing on the center of the coaster.

It was Cindy's turn. "I don't know her either. I just know Isadora. We have become friends."

Isadora said, "Of course I know her. We grew up together. But I haven't seen her in over a year. Not since soon after our husbands were ..." She had trouble picking the right word to use. "... killed." Descriptively adequate. "She said she needed to disappear for awhile. From certain bad guys who were after her. I've told you all this before, several times. Now I assume she meant she was running from you."

Miller paused. "I told you, I'm with the police."

"But I'm not," Sammy grunted.

Miller turned to look at him and shook his head. Sammy shrugged. "I think they figured that out."

Miller faced the others and stretched his neck as if it had gotten stiff. "I think you're right. It might be time to be honest with you. Sammy is not with the police. And I cannot be responsible for what he may decide to do. He's his own man." Sammy looked puzzled like he didn't know what that was supposed to mean. He had probably never heard that phrase used about him before.

"I suggest that all of you take one last good look around this place before telling me that Eleanora is not here." Miller continued. "I know that she showed up here last year and has not been seen since. I think someone is very aware of just where she is right now." He glared pointedly at Isadora, but her courage had returned and she smiled right back. "Mrs. Isadora Weidenbach, why don't you just sit right there, while Miss Connor and Mr. Wright take that look around? Sammy, you just follow them and make sure they're looking in all the right places."

Wally leaned down, lifting the skirt of the couch and looked under there. "Nope, she's not here."

"Good start. I appreciate your thoroughness," Miller snorted. "Now look elsewhere."

Wally and Cindy stood up and moved to the hallway. He noticed the bookshelves were still full, but now was not the right time to take a closer inspection. "Cindy, why don't you take this bedroom and I'll take the next one?"

Sammy waved them both into the first room. "No, you two stay together, so I can keep an eye on both of you."

Cindy bent down to take a look under the bed, which had a little more space below it than the couch. Wally went to the closet and pulled it open, not expecting anything, but finding Eleanora crouching there with a finger to her lips. Turning his head slightly, he realized that Sammy's attention was still on Cindy bending over, and inwardly breathed a huge sigh of relief. "Nope, nothing here." He closed the door and went to look behind a dresser.

"What?" Sammy reluctantly brought his gaze up.

"I just said, I haven't found anything or anybody yet."

"Oh, okay." He turned back but Cindy had stood up by then. She said, "I don't think there's any place else to look in here."

Another door led to an attached bathroom. Wally gestured for Cindy to continue on. "I'll just take a quick look here. I'll meet you in the next room."

As Sammy watched Cindy walk further down the hall, Wally pulled back the shower curtain, just so he could say he looked everywhere.

"Oh. What …" Professor Askovarik was cowering at the far end of the tub. "… is my towel doing here?"

Askovarik pulled the towel from the bar and handed it to Wally. Wally almost said, "Thank you," but stopped himself in time. He took the towel and turned around, holding it up for Sammy to see. "I've been missing this."

Sammy's eyes narrowed as if wondering if he was also missing something, but he knew they weren't looking for a towel, so he merely shook his head.

They joined Cindy at the doorway to the next bedroom. The bed was unmade, and Cindy said quickly, "This must be where Isadora sleeps."

She again looked under the bed while Wally went to the closet. Half afraid somebody else was going to be behind the door, he slowly opened the door and was greatly relieved to find no one, though he didn't know who else would be left. This time, Sammy had taken a step over so he could also see in the closet.

"Huh," he grunted. "I'll never figure out why women need so many clothes. All the closets are so damn full." Wally recognized that these clothes exactly matched the apparel in the other closet, but didn't think that Sammy would realize that.

One more hallway bathroom, with no one behind curtain number two, then the kitchen. Wally was familiar with how little space there was behind the refrigerator, but pulled the door open to show Sammy that there was no room for anyone to hide. Cindy opened the pantry. "Whoa, a lot of curry. She must like her food spicy."

To Sammy, canned goods were canned goods, and he didn't see anything suspicious about there being about twice as much as would be expected for an elderly lady living alone.

They returned to the living room to find Isadora playing solitaire on a side table and cheating, while Miller impatiently drummed his fingers on his knees. He looked at Sammy.

"Nothing, uh, Officer Miller. We didn't find nothing."

Wally thought, *that actually means we did find something. At least I did.* But now was not the time to explain double negatives to the two men. Now was the time to stay perfectly quiet and not explain anything.

Miller stood up. "I think we're done for the moment, but I will be back. Mrs. Weidenbach, I know you're hiding Eleanora, and you probably know where the money is. I will return with a warrant to do a more thorough search of the entire property. Meanwhile, Sammy, as well as a few other, uh, associates, will be keeping an eye on the place, just in case Eleanora decides to return, you understand." He cracked his knuckles in what was supposed to be a meaningful manner, but the others didn't need any more meaning, mannered or not. "Sammy, let's go."

Isadora walked with them to the door. "Officer Miller, I believe that if you could have gotten a warrant to search this property, you would have already done so."

He glared at her, but left without another word. Sammy waved goodbye as he went through the doorway. She closed the door then collapsed against it in relief, sliding down to the floor.

CHAPTER 48

Cindy knelt next to Isadora sitting on the floor. "Are you okay?" The older lady nodded and reached a hand to be helped back up.

Wally hurried to the hallway, with the others slowly following. He pulled a piece of paper from his back pocket and went to the bookcases.

"Isadora, when did you get these books? Was it just over a year and half ago?"

She thought for a second. "That could be about right. Dieter came home with his car full one day, and said he'd gotten a good deal on them. He said he'd always wanted to read many of the classics, which was news to me. But, as a matter of fact, I don't ever recall him ever getting one out to read. He put these two cases together from some sort of a kit, and filled them up and that was it. I dust them every few months, but I've never really looked at them. I thought maybe I could have a yard sale and get a little money to pay Officer Miller. But what do they have to do with what just happened?"

"This is the money. These are all first editions and many of them are signed." He excitedly but gently pulled a few off the shelves. He had never held such valuable books in his hands before, and was almost afraid to even touch them.

"But they can't be worth that much. They're just books. Most of them you can get from the library, for goodness sake."

He held one up. "This is *The Call of the Wild* by Jack London, worth $27,000 to a collector. Here's a signed Hemingway *For Whom the Bell Tolls,* worth $45,000. Barrie's *Peter and Wendy,* the novelization of Peter Pan, worth $8,000. All together, this collection was valued at about $180,000 when Dieter bought it. It may be worth even more now." He pointed to one, not daring to touch it. "There's Frederick Douglass' *My Bondage and My Freedom.* $5000 if unsigned, but, if signed, almost priceless. His name is printed by hand in the front, but Thalman wasn't sure if it was a signature or not." He scanned through the list in his hand. "It appears to all be here. Wait a minute. There appears to be one missing. Erica Jong's *Fear of Flying*, personally inscribed to Phyllis Schlafley."

Isadora slightly reddened. "I was looking for something to read late one night. It's still sitting on my bed stand."

Wally straightened up. "This is your fortune. This is what happened to the money stolen from the gamblers. This ..." He gestured at the books. " ... is what they have been looking for. It's been right here all this time. Right under everybody's nose, or noses."

Isadora started to wobble, but Cindy held her up. "Oh, my. Oh, my. I was going to hold that yard sale this spring. Oh, my goodness. We never knew. I have to go sit down."

Eleanora suddenly appeared in the doorway to the bedroom where she had been hiding and whispered, "Have they gone?" She looked toward the front door. Isadora nodded and pointed to Wally, as Cindy took her to the living room. "Look at what Drew has found."

Over her shoulder, Cindy blurted, "Wait a minute. You were here all this time? Where were you hiding? We looked everywhere."

To Cindy, Wally said, "She was in the closet. Sammy was watching you and never checked what I was doing. I just closed the door again." To Eleanora, he tapped the top of one of the bookcases. "This is where the money is."

"The bookcases?" Eleanora looked puzzled. "I think you can get them fairly cheaply at BillMart."

"No, the books. Gus bought these books with the money he stole, and Dieter stored them here. Miller and Sammy were looking for cash or something they would recognize as valuable. They had no book sense." He chuckled at his own joke, but no one else noticed.

Eleanora just said, "Oh, so this is what all the ruckus has been about." She shook her head. "If we'd only known. Gus, what did you do?"

The two of them joined Cindy and Isadora in the front room. Cindy, sitting on the couch holding Isadora's hand, asked, "So, now what? Do we give them the books, or do we sell them and give them the money?"

Wally sat down on one of the chairs, but let Eleanora take the one Miller had been in. "No, there's more to it now than that. Dieter and Gus were murdered. Maybe the widows want it to be over by giving the bad guys the money?" This last was directed at the landladies, but they both vehemently shook their heads. "I suspected not." He shifted in his seat. "And there are real police looking for their killers."

He told them about his conversation with Derek Trueblood and Steve Getty. "This is one of the reasons I was coming over here to talk with you all. That and to look at the books. This list is from Thalman's Used and Rare Bookstore. He was the one who arranged the sale of these books to Gus. He couldn't tell me it was Gus, but here are the books. If needed, he'd probably be willing to tell the police."

He sat forward. "We now know that Miller is working directly with the gamblers, because you told me that Sammy Jessup was the bookie that Gus bet with. And, I think I know who is behind this, who is running the gambling operation. And who had Gus and Dieter killed. I need to let Derek and Steve know. This is the guy they've been looking for."

Wally stood up and went to the front door. He opened it gingerly and peered out. There was no one waiting in the hall. He turned back.

"Cindy?"

She now had her arm around Isadora. "I'm going to stay here with the sisters for a while. I think this has been pretty traumatic for them. And for me. Are you sure you have to go?"

"I need to talk with the cops as soon as possible. It's getting late, but since they need to study about as much as I do, I think they will make themselves available at this time of night. Be careful who you open this door to."

He closed the door behind him, but it reopened right away. The women looked up fearfully until Wally poked his head around the door. "By the way, you could probably tell Dr. Askovarik that he can come out now."

Eleanora jumped up and hurried to the bedroom. "Oh, my, I almost forgot Anton."

Cindy was startled. "You mean he's here too?"

"Yep. He was hiding behind the shower curtain. In his underwear. Cindy, you make a great distraction." He sighed and left again.

Eleanora returned. "Anton's getting dressed. But why was this towel in the middle of the hall?"

CHAPTER 49

Wally punched numbers into his cell phone as he walked across the dark campus to the student union. He tried not to pay attention to Sammy Jessup, following at a distance. Sammy was attempting to be discreet, but obviously was uncomfortable on a college campus, and, at this time of night, there were no crowds of students to hide behind, and the trees were spaced too far apart to be of much use.

"Derek? This is Wally Stephens, I mean Drew Wright?" He was forgetting who knew what about him. "I'll explain when I see you. I need to talk with you and Steve right away. Let's meet at the union in the dining room. I'm positive there are some Bradford peach cobblers still available." He listened for a second. "I'm sure Peggy will understand. After all, you've already been not telling her the truth for some time. Sorry, didn't mean to imply anything, it's been a very long and stressful day, but be there soon. Please."

There was only one Bradford bread pudding left, which meant it wasn't fresh, but, with enough Bradford vanilla sauce, was still edible. Wally was halfway through it when Derek and Steve came over to the table.

"Get something to eat." Wally told them. "I was followed here." He inclined his head slightly in the direction of Sammy sitting in the opposite corner. Steve yawned with a stretch and looked around in general at the room, but Derek merely nodded. "I want this to look like I'm just meeting fellow students for a late-night snack. The other side doesn't know you're cops, do they?"

Steve was already on his way to the ice cream dispenser. Derek this time shook his head. "Nah. But I did wonder what Sammy Jessup was doing here. We know he was Gus Weidenbach's bookie. But he doesn't know us. He really looks out of place at anything having to do with a college." He followed Steve.

Steve came back and dug into his chocolate sundae with hot fudge sauce and chocolate sprinkles. Wally looked at all that chocolate.

"What?" Steve asked between mouthfuls. "If I'm supposed to be eating something this late, I'm going to eat something worthwhile."

Derek appeared with an unrecognizable dish. "I thought we were all supposed to be getting the peach cobbler. Wouldn't have been my first choice, or second, but it was there. I think this is it." He sat down. "What do you have for us, Drew? It must be juicy if Sammy is on your trail."

Wally filled them in on what had just happened with the Weidenbach sisters. By the time he was done, Steve was finishing up his second sundae, but Derek had only poked at his cobbler for Sammy's benefit.

Wally wrapped up. "Now we know where the stolen money is, and I also know who is behind all of this, who must have ordered the killing of the brothers."

Derek smiled. "What stolen money?"

Wally looked surprised. "The money that Gus stole from the gamblers. I told you about it. What Miller has been looking for. What the brothers were killed for."

"No stolen money was ever reported to us." He winked at Wally. "We're just looking for the people who murdered Gus and Dieter Weidenbach. If Gus stole money from these gamblers, they never told us about it."

"Oh." Wally sat back. "Oh. Only Miller knew about that because he was hired by them to get it back. The gamblers weren't going to tell the real police that they had been robbed."

Steve wiped his mouth with a napkin and nodded. "You got it. Yeah, we always knew there was money involved somewhere, but that's not the crime we were investigating. As far as we know, that money belongs to the Weidenbachs, fair and square." He turned to Derek. "I think we got enough on Sammy to bring him in with these witnesses to his threats and intimidation. Maybe put a little pressure on him. I don't think he's used to pressure from this end. I suspect he'd fold like an accordion."

They both looked at him. Derek asked, "Fold like an accordion? Is that the language they use in Summerfield?"

"What? I'm just trying to get in the mood. If we're going to deal with gangsters, I gotta talk like a gangster."

Derek waved his hand for Steve to keep his seat. "Yeah, yeah. But wait a second. I think there are some other things we should know.

"Wally, first of all, is there anybody else that you know that might be involved? Like where this money was stolen from?"

"I think it was a bar. I'm not sure which one." Wally suddenly straightened up and murmured almost inaudibly, "Hold on, I think it was called Mattie D's. Oh, my, I should have seen that." Louder, he said, "I know the bartender must have been involved. And I bet his name is Tony."

Derek nodded. "Yeah, I know the place. And I think you're right about that bartender. And his name is Tony. George really, but he's called Tony." He tilted his head to the left, a habit he displayed when he wanted a real answer. "But now we need the real reason you're involved in all this and why you're pretending to be a student. On the phone you started to tell me that you were, Wally ... Stephens, was it?"

Wally grimaced and closed his eyes for a moment. He had known this was coming.

"My real name is Wally, Wallace, Stephens. I think I am here to save the Weidenbach sisters."

Derek was silent, but Steve blurted out, "You think? Did they hire you to protect them or something? Is that why you're in their rooming house?"

Wally smiled at the concept of his being hired to protect anyone, a bookstore manager who hadn't done anything physical since being the first one out in dodgeball in freshman gym class. "No, I wasn't hired by anyone, certainly not for protection." He ran his hand across his forehead.

"I'm from the, uh, future. From six years from now."

"What?" Steve obviously thought that was the craziest thing he had ever heard, but Derek merely raised his eyebrows. Out of the corner of his eye, Wally saw Sammy take his phone out of his pocket and hold it, as if he thought he should call someone about what was going on, but not knowing yet what he was going to say.

After a silent pause, filled with the kind of quiet that you can almost hear, Derek spoke. "If you're really from the future, then you already knew all of this and what's going to happen now."

Wally shook his head. "No, I didn't know any of this. It doesn't seem to work that way. I wish it did. I think that none of this happens, at least saving the Weidenbachs, until I came back to …." He licked his lips. "Since I know books, until I came back to find where the money went. I had no knowledge of anything to do with the Weidenbachs until I got here. As a matter of fact, I thought I was coming back to, uh, to, uh, … to find a girlfriend." He finished with a rush and shrugged.

Now Steve was stunned into speechlessness, but Derek merely asked, "Which one?"

Wally started to answer, but then realized he didn't know the answer to that question. Not any more.

Derek absentmindedly took a bite of the cobbler and chewed it without tasting. "There's a lot more questions that I have about what's going on with you. It's hard to swallow that you're from the future, and yet …. Here you are and I have no other explanation for what could, or could not be happening." He shook his head.

"Steve, I think now is the time to take Sammy in for questioning. Let's just act as if we're leaving. He's got a phone out and I don't want him making any calls right now."

Steve nodded and they got up to head for the door. Sammy watched them, still holding his phone until they neared the door. As far as he knew, they were just other students and there was nothing yet to report to anyone. He looked back at Wally, who still hadn't moved, but raised his hand and waved to him. When his attention returned to the door, there was no one there. A hand came down on his shoulder from behind and another one grabbed the phone from his hand.

"Hi, Sammy. We'd like to talk with you for a little while." He wasn't sure which hand that voice belonged to.

Wally walked back to his apartment, this time with no one following. At least not that he could tell. As he moved up the steps, he noticed a couple of figures across the street, who seemed to be looking behind him as if they expected someone else to appear, and being surprised to find no one.

Back in his room, he started up The Laptop.

MyFate

You're not quite done yet. You need to make one last observation, both to satisfy your own curiosity and to watch a bad guy get his just desserts, so to speak.

If you are reading this when I think you're reading it, then you have done well. If you are not in a position to be reading this, then I, personally, more personally than anyone else possible, am very sorry about that.

Picking up his phone, he made a couple of calls.

CHAPTER 50

First thing in the morning, immediately after its doors opened, Wally, with his computer bag slung over his shoulder, entered The Book Look. Matt Dubois seemed surprised to see him at that early time, but merely waved and said, "Hi, guy," going back to the sports section of his newspaper at the front counter. Wally walked back and took his usual seat, able to see most of the room, opening The Laptop as if to take his usual notes.

About ten minutes later, Derek entered, looking up at the top of the door as the four bells jangled. Dubois stood up straight and rubbed his hands.

"Hey, man, don't think I've seen you in here before. You looking for some excitement? I've got a good-sized thriller section, and I think there could be a cinnamon roll with your name on it at the back table."

Derek licked his lips at the thought of a cinnamon roll that was not a Bradford cinnamon roll. He said, "Thanks, I'm just going to look around for a bit, then I may take a bite of that roll."

Dubois nodded and went back to his paper. He looked at the courts section but, not seeing his name, turned to the comics. Derek wandered for a few minutes before heading in the general direction of Wally. He stopped just short of Wally and pulled out a book at random. The title was something to do with animal husbandry. He didn't even know what that meant and quickly stuck it back on the shelf, finally grabbing one called *Like Rabbits*. At least he knew what rabbits were, even if he didn't know what the title referred to.

Out of the corner of his mouth, he spoke softly to Wally, "Well, I'm here, just like you asked when you called. Steve is outside, ready to come in when it's time."

Wally continued to expectantly watch the front door. "Thanks. Hopefully it will just be a few minutes." An older woman entered, looked disappointed that the two young men were in front of the lurid Amish romance novels, and headed straight for the pastries.

Derek continued quietly. "We brought both Sammy and Tony in last night. We didn't arrest them, but held them for questioning and managed to keep them away from a phone. Can't do that much longer. They both have spilled what guts they had, and are willing to testify against their boss, so we have him now. They also both said that they were only supposed to scare the Weidenbach brothers, 'scare them to death' was the term they used, but that Miller was the one that took it literally and set fire to the place. They don't want to go down for murder. We've got men looking for Miller now." He turned to also look at the front door. "So, why am I waiting here at this time in the morning?"

Wally didn't move. "Any minute now."

The door opened and the bells tinkled, for some reason much more melodically than when Derek had come through. Lori Gibbons walked up to the front counter.

Dubois straightened up even straighter this time. "Well, good morning, sweetheart."

Lori stiffened. "I don't mean this to be offensive, but I don't appreciate being called that, especially by someone I don't even know."

The older woman was now standing nearby, perusing the new Henry Miller-like bestseller, and commented under her breath. "It doesn't bother me."

Dubois smiled with as much charm as he could put into it. "I apologize. That's just my way of talking. I don't mean anything by it. But I will choose my words more carefully from now on. What can I do for you?"

She placed a book on the counter. "I have recently come into possession of this book and was wondering if I could sell it. What could you give me for it?"

He picked it up. "*Through the Looking Glass*, huh? Looks like it's an older version." He opened it to the copyright page. "1935. I know there are much better editions out since then. And look, some one's written their name in it. Alice Hargreaves. A relative of yours?" He flipped through the pages. "I don't know who would buy this, but, okay, I'll give you twenty dollars, ah, it's got a nice jacket, I'll make it twenty-five dollars."

"Alice Hargreaves is the married name of Alice Liddell." Lori held out her hand and Dubois shrugged and gave it back.

"So?"

"That's the original Alice of *Alice in Wonderland*. This is the only edition she ever signed. She is who Charles Dodgson wrote the book for."

"It says the author is Lewis Carroll, but, alright, I'll give you forty dollars for it."

Wally nodded to Derek. "Go ahead, I just wanted to see if Matt Dubois, or Matty D, knew as little about books as I thought he did. That book is currently valued at about fifteen hundred."

Derek first detoured to pick up his cinnamon roll, then walked to the front counter, waving through the front window for Steve to come in. Lori picked up her book and moved back to where Wally was still sitting.

"Matthew Dubois, you are under arrest." Derek Trueblood set the half-eaten roll on the counter and pulled out a pair of handcuffs.

"For what?" Dubois was stunned. "For calling her 'sweetheart'?"

Wally was about to close The Laptop when it dinged.

Miller is still out there. Be careful. You only have a short time left within this time period. You must be sitting in your chair within one hour. Lori and Vern need to be with you.

CHAPTER 51

Lori read over his shoulder. "Your chair?"

"That's what carries me in time. Don't ask me how."

"In one hour? Then you'll be gone?"

"Yeah, I guess so," Wally responded without really thinking. His mind was stuck on "Miller is still out there." Derek had also said that there were men still looking for Miller.

"Drew, er, Wally, I hate to say it, but that's a big deal. After all the time you've been here, you're leaving right away?"

Wally closed his computer and packed it in his bag. "Lori, we need to get back to the Weidenbach sisters. I'm afraid Miller might go to them if he thinks the rest of the gamblers have been arrested. Finding the money or holding them hostage may be his best way of getting out of this."

She pointed at his bag. "Your program said that you also need both Vern and me. I don't know why you would need me there, but if you're leaving, then Miller is not really your concern anymore. Let the police get him. That's their job."

"You told me one time that maybe my destiny here was to think of someone else first. Not what I may want, but why someone else needed me here, in this time."

"Not exactly what I said."

"Well, something along those lines. I need to make sure they're okay before I go. I have to believe this is why I'm here."

As Dubois was being led through the front door, Wally spoke to the two student-cops. "You said you were still looking for Miller. I'm thinking he may be looking for me, or the widows. I need to get back to their rooming house."

Derek nodded. "We'll head over there as soon as we get this guy taken care of."

Dubois interrupted. "Terry Miller?" At their nods, he continued, "You better get him before he gets there. I'm not saying that I know what this is all about, but this Miller is not someone I'd want mad at me. He is one scary guy." He shuddered. "The scariest guy I ever met. He doesn't know where to stop." He shuddered again for emphasis.

Wally pushed past the other three men, with Lori at his heels. On the sidewalk, he handed her his computer bag. "I have to run. And it's been a long time since I have had to do that. You take my bag -- I can't run with it -- and go find Vern, then meet me at my apartment. That's where the chair is. Go." He took off running for ten steps, then stopped, turned around, and ran back past her. "It's that way."

Wally was right about not being a runner. Every once in a long while, he would tell himself that he was going to get up early in the morning, sometime between seven and eight, he wasn't going to be crazy about it, and go out running. Much less often than that, he would actually do it. His running consisted of something that sort of looked like running for about a block, then walking for the next three blocks, then sort of running for one more block, then back to walking. And so on until he had circled back to where he had started. By running in a planned loop, he figured he couldn't stop halfway and give up because he still had to finish the circle. At least that's what he figured.

He ran as fast as he could for as far as he could. He glanced back over his shoulder and realized that he could still see Lori watching him, so he pushed himself further until he was no longer in her sight. Though he stopped the running, he continued to walk fast. That he could do. He was trying hard not to think about what may be happening or what could still happen, he just knew he had to get there as quickly as possible. After another five minutes, he started running again, using this running and walking pattern all the way to across the street from the Weidenbach's house.

He leaned against a lamppost for a moment trying to catch his breath, deciding he wasn't going to be any good to anybody if he was so winded he could barely stand. He didn't see any of Dubois' men from last night standing guard outside. They must have either left on their own or been rounded up by the police.

Though he was still breathing heavily and could barely move, he could move barely, so he walked across the street and hauled himself by the railing up the steps.

No one was in the vestibule. Out of habit, he glanced at his mailbox, but realized that if there were any bills, they weren't going to get paid for another six years. He knocked on the door to the Weidenbachs' apartment.

After a minute, he heard a voice say, "There's no one here."

He didn't have enough breath yet to speak, so he just knocked again.

This time, a different voice, a male voice, asked, "Who is it?"

"It's me. It's Drew," he finally croaked out.

"It doesn't sound like you."

"Oh, for goodness sake, look through the spyhole in the door."

After another ten seconds, the door opened a crack, still on a chain, enough for an eye to peer through. "Oh, it is you, dear." It closed just long enough to pull the chain off, then opened again to reveal three of them standing there, the sisters and Dr. Askovarik, all still in their sleeping outfits.

"We needed to be sure." He was pretty sure this was from Isadora.

"Good, good. No one else has been here?"

"Nope." This time it was Eleanora, in a much briefer nightgown than Isadora. "We stayed up all night after Cindy left." She held up a bat. They each held a baseball bat, as if they knew how to use them. They had three baseball bats here? Wally passingly considered who played.

Askovarik straightened himself up as tall as he could get. "I stayed to protect them. They need a man at time like this." Eleanora grabbed his arm and leaned against his shoulder. He was wearing some sort of gym shorts and a t-shirt with words in a different language. *Sexy je ako sexy robi*. Wally wondered what "sexy" was supposed to mean in whatever language that was, but decided he was better off not knowing.

He leaned against the doorframe in relief.

"That's good." That's all he could say.

Isadora put her hand on his arm. "Are you alright, dear? You're out of breath. Did you go out for a run this morning? Maybe you're exercising too much."

Wally almost laughed. Working out "too much" was not his problem. "I wanted you to know that they've arrested Sammy and his boss, Matt Dubois, who owned The Book Look and Mattie D's, and some other guys who worked for him." He took another couple of breaths. "They're the ones who are behind the gambling and your husband's deaths."

"Oh, wonderful," said Isadora. "That's great," said Eleanora. "Is about time," said Askovarik.

"But." Wally held up a finger. "But don't open the door to anyone but me, Cindy, or the police yet. Terry Miller is still out there and I was afraid …." He looked at their smiling faces, not wanting to spoil the moment. "Never mind. The real police are on their way. Officers Derek Trueblood and Steve Getty. Make sure they show their IDs. They will have real ones. I'm just glad you're okay now."

He turned away from the door and took a step. Then he suddenly turned back. "I hate to keep pulling a Columbo on you. I may not see you again." Their faces fell. At least the women's did. Askovarik almost smiled more broadly. "My time here is almost up. I really can't explain it, but I may be leaving suddenly very soon. You can let the police or a few friends of mine in my room for a few days. Cindy will know who the friends are. I am glad I was able to be here for you."

"We are sorry to hear about your leaving, dear." Isadora said. "But what about Cindy? Is she going with you?"

"Oh my God, Cindy. I need to say goodbye to her." He ran to the stairs. As they closed the door behind him, he heard Askovarik ask, "I thought he was Mr. Trueblood?"

He took the stairs three at a time. In front of her door at the top he looked at his watch. About fifteen minutes to go. Just enough time to … to what? To say goodbye? Farewell? It was nice knowing you? He still couldn't tell her who he really was. He knew he was going to see her soon in his lifetime, but, for her, it will have been six years. And he couldn't promise her anything. He thought, maybe she will have gotten fat in that time. He had changed, maybe she will too. But he shook his head. In my mind, she won't have changed. Maybe it's just better if I suddenly disappear. I could be her mysterious dream man for six years ...

The door opened in front of him. It wasn't Cindy.

It was Terry Miller. Holding a gun. "Are you going to stand there all day? We've been waiting for you. Come in, come in."

Cindy was sitting on the couch. He went over to her and took her hand. "Are you alright? Did he hurt you?"

"Sit down and offer her comfort." Miller waved the gun. "It may be your last chance." He sat down opposite them and shook his head. "I figured it was going to be you. You just didn't fit."

Wally thought, everyone keeps saying that.

"You just didn't fit. You didn't make sense as a student, but you didn't make sense as anything else. You weren't a cop. I know cops and, after spending some time with you, I could tell that wasn't it. You seemed to be protecting the sisters, but why would you do that? Unless you were getting some of the money. So, you had to know where the money was. They had to show you there was money, had to prove it to you."

He pointed the gun at Cindy. Wally put his arm around her and pulled her into him. "This was your weakness." Miller lowered the barrel. "Sammy and Tony disappeared last night. No sign of them. It didn't take much to figure out that they were probably in custody. I guess we overstepped when we came here earlier in the evening. I thought I could still pass as police, but Sammy was a bit much. Shouldn't have brought him. Now it's every man for himself."

Wally recognized that Miller loved to hear himself speak. If he could keep him talking, Wally knew there were police on the way. He was listening hard, to see if he could hear a slight creak on the steps. About the third one from the top, he thought. Was that one? He listened hard and could have sworn he heard it that time.

Miller was still talking. Cindy was still shivering and he held her closer.

"I don't think it's here. I really don't. But I do think you have a good idea where that money is. And we are going to go find it now. If Sammy and Tony have been arrested, it's not going to take long for them to spill their guts. Neither one of them has much to start with." Wally was thinking, *do the bad guys really talk that way? Or do they get it from television?* "So, Dubois will be getting an official visit at any time. They're all weak and they'll confess to anything. But not me. I'm going to take the money and get out of here."

The gun came up again. "But I need you two to get it for me."

Wally made a decision and brought his hands up. He was running out of time. "Okay, okay. I can take you to it. You're right, the money is not here."

"Drew! No!" Cindy cried out.

He stood up and took a step. He had to get the gun aimed away from Cindy. "But she doesn't know where it is. I'll take you to it but only if we leave her here. That's my terms. Okay?"

Miller also stood up. "All I want is the money. I don't care what she does. But you and I are going to take a walk."

Miller backed to the door, keeping his gun trained on them. "We're going to move out real slow and easy. No cares in the world. Just the two of us." He reached down for the doorknob and pulled the door open behind him. "No funny business. I can always come back. Now come on – "

There was a very loud "THWANG!" and he fell to the floor as if he'd been shot. In the open doorway stood Lori holding The Laptop, now severely dented from Miller's head. Next to her with his fists up as if he really intended to punch somebody, was Vern Sheffield. Looking over their shoulders, mirroring Wally's own shocked expression, stood Dr. McElroy.

CHAPTER 52

Up the stairs behind them were the sounds of more creaking and pounding feet. Derek and Steve arrived at the top, and the others moved further out onto the landing to give them room. Wally stepped aside as Derek bent down to Miller's prostrate form, and Steve rushed to Cindy.

Lori reached into the room and pulled Wally into the hallway. "I hate to do this to you now, but you've only got a couple of minutes left. You have to get into your room, now."

He looked back at Cindy and saw her shaking her head as Steve asked her something. Then both Lori and Vern pulled him away.

"Thank you," he said to them as he got out his key to open his door. "You got here just in time. I knew somebody should be coming, but I didn't know if it would be you or the police first. But what's Dr. McElroy doing here?"

As they entered the room, Lori said, "It took me awhile to find Vern. He wouldn't answer his phone, but eventually I tracked him down. He and Dr. McElroy were sitting on a bench outside Burgett Hall, having some discussion about time. The impermanence or flexibility or instability or something like that, and it took me a minute to get them to stop talking and listen to me. When Vern finally understood and got up to come with me, the professor just got up and followed both of us. But he kept wanting to take us in a different direction until we had to explain everything to him. Well, maybe not everything, but at least tell him that you were from a different time period and that you had to leave immediately."

"He knows I'm from the future?"

"I knew something wasn't right about you, even if your name was Mr. Wright. You didn't fit in." McElroy interrupted and Wally rolled his eyes at that phrase repeated once more. "But now it makes sense. There was a reason you became my graduate assistant. Time. It's all about time."

"Right now, I don't have much of that time." His watch said three minutes to go. He went to an open suitcase on his bed and pulled out a box, handing it to Lori. "Inside is a Power of Attorney giving you access to my bank account and safety deposit box, and anything else you may need to do on my behalf. I got that done when MyFate said you needed to know everything. You will need the money to get Vern's institute going in order to get me back here, and to give me money to start my journey. Invest it in something, like rare books, or bet on the Cleveland Browns to win the Super Bowl. Not this year, but next year. With the Browns, it's always next year. I know you'll get good odds against that happening, but it does."

He turned to Vern. "Vern, there's also some papers for you. As much as I know about how this whole thing works, and what and when you have to do in six years to make sure it works. We know it will happen because, well, because here I am."

He took The Laptop from Lori and stepped in to give her a hug. "You have been the biggest help to me. Without you, none of this works out. I am so glad I met you. You have actually been the best part of this trip back in time. Seriously. I wish … I wish I could get to know you better. Thank you for everything.

"Now, hopefully, this program will tell me what to do right now." He sat down on the chair and tried to open the computer, but, after being used to render Miller unconscious, it was bent and jammed shut. "What the …? I don't know what I'm supposed to do to make the chair work." He tried to work his fingers under the edges, but nothing would move. "Anybody have a screwdriver or a pen or something to get in here?" McElroy handed him a pen, but the tip broke off. "Anything else?"

Vern got down on his knees in front of the chair and started to reach under towards the button.

"Don't touch that! I don't know how it works and I don't want you messing with it. If you break it, I may be stuck here. I was counting on the MyFate program to give me final directions."

"I'm so sorry." Lori put her hands to her mouth. "I had to hit that man with something and it was the only thing I had."

"No, no. You had to use it. You were right."

McElroy was watching his pocket watch. "Mr. Wright, I hate to point this out, but … you're late. It's a few minutes past your go time." He showed them the watch face.

They all stood in silence for a moment.

Wally sighed and lowered his head. "It looks like Miller may have finally been able to stop me by using his head."

Vern pointed to the chair. "It's still here. Maybe there's something else that's supposed to happen."

Wally's head snapped up. "Dr. McElroy, take another watch out of your pocket and look at it."

McElroy took a watch out of his right pocket and looked at it. "Now, you are nine minutes past your time."

"No, try your left pocket."

He checked that one. "Aha, you have one minute left."

Wally sat down on the chair. "Lori, hand me the suitcase. This morning I packed some things I thought I should take with me. Anything else still here, the three of you figure out what to do with it."

She reshuffled the stuff inside so she could close the suitcase and then she handed it to him. "Remember me."

"Oh, I will remember you. You can count on it."

She smiled. Vern reached under the chair before Wally, with his hands full, could stop him. "I think if I do this …" He pushed something.

An image of where he had first seen that smile flashed into Wally's mind as her face faded away.

CHAPTER 53

Only her face didn't fade away.

Lori was still smiling at him, only the face was slightly different somehow, maybe just a little more mature.

This time, the smile told him everything.

He looked into her eyes for a second and smiled back. Then he slowly looked around. There were the computers and the whirring machines and the flashing lights, and an older Vern in a white lab coat, slightly rocking on his feet.

"Wally, are you okay? Do you know where you are?" Her smile faded slightly. "Wally, say something."

He let his breath, which he didn't realize he had been holding, out, and said, "Hi." He mentally took stock of himself, lightly tensing some muscles and stretching his legs. He held out the suitcase for Vern to take. "I think I'm alright. But let me out of this damn chair before I go somewhere else again."

He stood up. "I am back. Everything looks the same."

"You were only gone a second, if that. We wouldn't have even known you were gone, except your clothes are different, and ..., and you look as if you've, uh, lived more. A little firmer set to your face. As if things have happened to you." She winked at him. "As we know they have?"

Vern coughed. "We, of course, knew that you were able to go back in time, because we were there with you. But," he grimaced. "But we didn't know if you would be able to make it back. Not until just now, when you reappeared. Whew." He wiped his brow and started to sit down on the chair. Both Lori and Wally said, "No!" and he caught himself in time and said, "Probably not a good idea to do that."

Wally looked at him. "You didn't know if I could come back?"

Vern shrugged. "We knew you disappeared from the rooming house six years ago, but we couldn't be sure where you had gone. This moment hadn't occurred yet. We were simply hoping and keeping our fingers crossed. However." He held up crossed fingers, then uncrossed them and continued holding up the index finger. "Speaking of traveling in time, I know there is something I need to do right now."

He reached under the chair and pushed the button. The chair disappeared. Completely and immediately. "Aha," he said. "It worked."

Wally was startled. "What the ...? Why did you do that?"

Lori touched his arm with her hand. "In order for the chair to be here when you first needed it, we had to send it back to when and where we were. So that we would have it here to set you in it five minutes ago. It's okay, we know where it is now. We got it."

Wally put his hands out. "That means I am now back to when and where I was when this started?"

Lori nodded. Vern said, "Yep."

"And nothing has changed?"

"You're still you, if that's what you mean. You still manage a bookshop, and you're not married. And you have a class reunion coming up."

"What about the Weidenbachs? And the bad guys? All of that? Did everything work out?"

"Yes. It did. The sisters are doing fine. Isadora still runs the rooming house. Eleanora is now married to Anton Askovarik. Happily. They live in a large stone mansion, bought with some of that rare book money. He has retired and is very excited about not having to deal with any more of those 'odd students'.

"As for the crooks. Sammy Jessup served his time and is now out on probation. He's actually working at Thalman's Bookstore and staying clean. He's keeping the accounts and reportedly doing a good job. Sidney Thalman is a big believer in second chances. Matt Dubois is still behind bars, but he's making the best of it. He has become a sort of social director for the entire prison, believe it or not."

Wally laughed. "I can see him doing that. He was always a friendly guy and wanting to keep everybody happy. To a certain extent, if you know what I mean." His laugh died away. "But what about Miller? He was the dangerous one."

Lori dropped her hand from his arm. "He's locked up for a long time. Everyone else immediately testified against him, even Dubois. But, after the conk on the head that I gave him, he changed. He was very meek during the trial and didn't even seem to remember some of what he had done. He never said anything about you, and, since you were gone, you were never referred to at any time. We won't be seeing him for a very long time."

Wally breathed a sigh of relief. "Good. That's a load off my mind." He went to sit down on a chair, but it wasn't there. Vern was in the only other one, a padded seat that had coasters, and he was gliding around the room, lifting his feet and doing circles. You could almost see his mind saying, "Whee."

"So now what? Where do I go now?"

"You go back to your life. I assume your job is still waiting for you tomorrow morning. And don't you have a class reunion coming up? Wasn't that the point of your journey?" Lori spoke quietly. "You can do whatever you want."

Vern stopped spinning. "How did your romance, um, sex, thing work out?"

Wally reddened slightly and tugged at his collar. "Well, yes, I did meet Cindy, as you know. But the relationship never got as far as the, um, sex, part, and the romance sort of got interrupted by all that stuff with the Weidenbach sisters. I don't think that idea of 'if I knew then what I know now', with the expectation of me being more mature and sophisticated, ever really had a chance to prove itself. Maybe it wasn't supposed to." He sighed. "I don't think life is supposed to work that way."

Lori clasped her hands in front of her. "Okay, but you'll still have a chance to get together with her at the reunion, won't you?'

Wally looked sheepishly at her. "I don't know what's going to happen at the reunion. I honestly have no idea how she's going to react to me, if she reacts to me at all. Maybe I'll just still be Wally and sort of look like someone she used to know. I don't know." He reached out and touched her hands. "But I do know I don't want to go there by myself. This is probably very awkward for you, but ... but you were with me throughout this whole experience. You were the very first person I met back there, at your sorority, and the very last face I saw when I left. Would you, ..., oh, no, I didn't think." He looked at Vern Sheffield, who winked back at him, which didn't really tell him anything. "Are you and Vern, um, are you together? I mean, I don't know, it's been six years, and maybe you, um, you know ... I'm not very good at reading these things ...."

She took his hands in hers. "You are stammering again. I thought you would be doing better by now. You know, Vern has had needs, and I have had needs."

"Oh." Wally's face fell.

Lori laughed. "But I have no idea how he has met his needs, and how I met my needs is absolutely no business of yours. We, Vern and I, are not in a personal relationship. It is purely business."

Wally breathed a sigh of relief. "Well then, would you, if you're not seriously involved with anyone else, I mean, and I will understand if you say 'no', but would you consider going to the reunion with me? Please? Pretty please?"

Lori was silent for a moment, what seemed to Wally like a terrifyingly long moment, but he had gotten used to waiting. Then she smiled.

"Alright. But I will consider it a date this time." She poked him in the chest. "And so will you."

Vern resumed spinning in his chair, with both his arms and legs thrown out. And "Whee!" came out very loudly.

CHAPTER 54

Wally was as nervous as he had ever been. Going out with Cindy had been sweating under the armpit nervous. This was that plus perspiration on the palms and behind the knees anxiety. Part of it, he knew, was because he was wearing a suit, something he preferred desperately not to do. But desperate times, such as attending this reunion, called for desperate measures, such as wearing a suit. However, another part of it was because he wanted to make a good impression on somebody tonight. As good an impression as it was possible to make.

He rang the doorbell for the second time. This time the door opened to reveal Lori in a very elegant, form-fitting black dress.

"Whoa. You look … beautiful."

"Thank you. Somebody has to make you look good at your reunion."

"You certainly do, you will, you … look amazing." He held up his arm and she took it for the short walk to his car parked at the front of the apartment building. He held the door open, just like the gentleman he was pretending to be, and she got in.

As he drove, he said, "I discovered the book you must have snuck into my suitcase just before I left the institute, the signed copy of *Through the Looking Glass and What Alice Found There*. I don't know when you did that. You were supposed to return it to the sisters."

"Both Isadora and Eleanora insisted that I give that to you. They had no sense of its real value, but they thought you should have something for all your troubles. Everything that you went through for them. Maybe it has even gone up in value since then."

"I appreciate it. That was very nice of them. They, and you, didn't have to do that." Wally said, and then thought, *but it's not like it was signed by Charles Dodgson himself. That would have been worth something.* "You know, I didn't really get the chance to ask how you have been doing, what your life has been like the last six years."

"I've been fine. Really. I took your advice and I bet the money from your bank account on the Cleveland Browns winning the Super Bowl. The next year, of course. As you said, always next year. One hundred to one odds. Everyone wanted to know how I knew. I told them I was just lucky, but, since you never told me any other sports outcomes, I didn't do any other betting. I know what it did to Gus Weidenbach. Maybe you could have let me in on who was going to be president in between. No one saw that coming."

"Would you have believed me?"

"No, I would never have believed that many people would have thought that he was a good idea. Or even an okay idea. Or even a 'what the hell' idea. And I don't think I would have felt good about those winnings anyway. It would have felt like dirty money somehow, like giving somebody money to buy the worst kind of drugs.

"I ended up investing it in Vern Sheffield's company, though you could have told me to invest it in Amazon or something. We fixed The Laptop and got the other machines for the lab. And the rest was the money you took back with you. Oh." Lori turned to him. "The MyFate program said it hoped we were able to get you on the chair in time. It knew it wasn't going to be able to help, that it would be incapacitated. We were just going to have to trust that it was going to work out." She shrugged. "Dr. McElroy is still at Bradford State. The rest of the staff there still thinks he's nuts, but he still gets together with Vern to talk about time travel and other time issues. Vern is the only one who knows that he has some valid points. Not all of them, but some."

"How, and when, did I write the MyFate program? Was it really me?"

She shook her head. "I don't know. I assumed you had been rewriting it as you went, after you knew what to write. But you couldn't have done that for the last message, could you?"

It was his turn to shake his head. "I wasn't writing any of it, not unless I was writing in my sleep. I guess we'll never know." He took a deep breath. "And I guess there's no more time travel. If the chair is caught in a loop between now and six years ago. No one can use it again."

"No, we'll never see that chair again."

"You didn't say what you have been doing."

"Oh, I'm a school psychologist. I went on to get my Master's degree, and I'm working in the Summerfield school system. I wanted to use those psych classes for something. After all, it turned out that those were the most important classes I took at BSU."

Wally pulled into the parking lot of the Lincoln County Banquet Rooms, host to the reunion dinner. He sat for a moment, just staring at the building, thinking that this was what the last few months had been building to. This evening was why he had gone back in time and had gone through everything. After all that, he wasn't sure he was ready for whatever was going to happen next.

When she realized Wally wasn't coming around to open her door, Lori pushed it open herself and got out. She went around to his side of the car and opened his door. "Come on. Tonight isn't going away. The parking lot is already two thirds full and I'm sure you want to get a good seat."

He sighed and got out. "Yeah, you're right. That's why we should go in. To make sure we get a good seat."

Just inside the front door, Maria (Sharper) Carpenter, as her nametag informed everyone, sat behind a table set with piles of reunion programs and alphabetically arranged nametags.

"Hi, glad you could be here …" She looked from Wally to Lori, then back again. "Wally Stephens, right?"

"Yeah, right. Good of you to recognize me."

"Oh, I recognize everybody. That's why I got to be the chairwoman of the reunion organization committee." She handed him his own personal nametag, labeling him for the rest of the evening as "Wallace

Stephens". He groaned. In high school, no one had known that was his real full name. She turned to Lori. "But you, give me a minute, I'll get it."

Wally interrupted. "Oh, she didn't go here. This is my, my date. Lori Gibbons. I called in to get her on the list."

"Oh, yes, here we are." Maria handed Lori a nametag outlined in red. Wally's was outlined in blue and yellow, the school colors. "The red means she's here as a guest, not an alumnus. So other graduates don't think they're supposed to know you. And keep trying to guess which math class you were in with them."

"Thank you." Lori peeled off the back and stuck it high on her chest. "I'll wear it with pride."

They walked further into the large open area, neither one actively looking for a good seat yet. The bar and the appetizers table drew their immediate attention.

As they waited in line to order their drinks, Wally paged through his program, stopping at the page labeled, "Those No Longer With Us, Bless Their Hearts." Fortunately, there were only four names. One had died in an automobile accident while they were still in school, and two others he knew about, but the fourth absolutely stunned him.

"Oh, no, I didn't know Jeremy Lane had passed on. I just had lunch with him a couple of months ago. And he had a couple of little kids."

"I know." A voice came from behind him in line. "And they haven't gotten much bigger."

Wally whirled around. "Jeremy! What the …? You're supposed to be dead!" He pointed at the program.

"Tell me about it. Maria said the same thing when I came in. Then she was totally astonished when she also found a nametag for me among the living. She kept saying that the nametag must be a mistake, not the notice in the program." They shook hands. It was the first time Wally had ever shaken hands with a dead man.

"This is the first time I've ever shaken hands with a dead man."

"Well, don't make a habit of it. Wally, you remember Beth." The slim brunette standing next to Jeremy took Wally's hand and said, "I'm alive, anyway."

Wally introduced Lori. "This is Lori Gibbons. Lori, Beth and the late Jeremy Lane. Beth used to sit in front of me in English class. Jeremy used to sit wherever and whenever he could."

Beth added, "Wally would look over my shoulder and try to copy from my vocabulary tests."

Wally's mouth twisted. "Not a good idea. It turned out she was worse in English than I was. My grades went down."

They were now at the head of the line. Wally ordered beer, first checking to make sure it wasn't a Bradford Beer, and Lori asked for a half orange juice, half ginger ale. She turned to him and shrugged. "I picked it up from Peggy."

"So, how long have you two known each other?" Jeremy asked. "Wally has never mentioned you before. And I am sure I would have remembered."

"Six years," Lori answered, at the same time as Wally said, "A couple of months."

Both Jeremy and Beth raised their eyebrows.

"Um," Wally started, but Lori finished. "We met six years ago, but we reconnected just a couple of months ago."

Jeremy took a sip from his drink of unknown mixture. "Wally, you always did have an eye for the best-looking female in the room." Beth elbowed him in the side, but he tried to ignore the pain. "Besides Beth, I mean. I remember the crush you had on Cindy Connor." He put his hand to the side of his mouth and spoke, sotto voce, to Lori. "She was the daydream of every heterosexual male in our class. And some of the girls too."

Lori took Wally's hand and squeezed it very, very tightly. "I know. She and I have met."

Jeremy raised his eyebrows again. "Really?"

Beth touched Lori's arm. "Why don't we go find a table? Before they fill up. I think there are a few left."

Wally agreed, as much to change the subject and to get his hand free as anything else. "Yes, we said when we first came in, that we wanted to find a good seat. That was the first thing we were going to do. Before or after we had gotten a drink. And maybe an appetizer."

They found an unclaimed table, at least as far as they could tell, and set their drinks down. However, before they could seat themselves down next to the drinks, Beth pulled Lori aside. "I could also use something to nosh on from that appetizers table. And it doesn't look like they're going to be ready to serve dinner anytime soon. Let's go get something and you can fill me in on whatever attracted you to 'Wallace' there." She laughed at finally discovering his full real name.

"Well, first of all, I didn't know his real name was Wallace," Lori said as they moved away.

Jeremy took a swallow from his glass. "So, anything exciting happen in the last couple of months? You heard that I died, right? Beth is going to insist that we hang on to this program now. Just so she can say that dead people don't get to make the big decisions in this household."

Wally took a moment to consider how to respond. "Nothing as exciting as that. Nope, nothing significant has happened. Same old, same old. You know how it is. Still working at the bookstore. But I did recently find a couple of books worth something." He was about to start into a slightly amended *Through the Looking Glass* story when they were interrupted by a commotion near the bar.

Two men were arguing and looked like they were ready to become physical.

"That was my idea and you know it!"

"That was not your idea! Your ideas are always shit, and you know it!"

Jeremy took another sip. "Looks like Josh Smith and Josh Jones got started drinking a little bit earlier than usual."

"Oh, yeah." Wally took his own sip, or swig since it was a beer. "Weren't they best friends in high school?" And in college, as an image of them in the Irrelevant Practicum class came to mind. Funny that he hadn't paid any attention to them as former classmates then.

"Still are." Jeremy set his glass down. "After school they both went to work for Josh's dad at the Do-It-Again jigsaw puzzle factory. They're in the Concept Department together. Have you ever heard of The Couples Board for doing puzzles?"

"Shitty shit!" Another volley came across the room.

"Shitty shit full of shit!" The reply was just as linguistically articulate.

Wally laughed. "I do remember they were not the best at verbally expressing themselves. A lot of 'Oh yeahs' and 'You toos'." He looked back at Jeremy. "Of course I know the Couples Boards. We used to carry them at the shop. If I recall, they were hot for a while, then kind of faded out, though it's still around. It was two boards propped up at an angle against the backs of each other, hooked at the top, with magnetized puzzle pieces, so that couples could each work on the same puzzle but on their own side on their own board. Playing together, but not fighting over the same pieces."

"Yep. Seemed to be a good idea at first. Even Beth and I did it for awhile." He picked his glass back up, looked at it, and set it back down again. "But it became too competitive. Who was going to get done with what part first and 'Why did you start there, you dummy?' And, if you had pieces out to work on, some of them would still get mixed up with the ones belonging to your partner. I guess there are some couples who can make it fun and some who can't."

The two Josh's were now hugging. "I love you, man." "I love you, too, man." "It was both our shitty idea." "Yeah, man, shitty together."

Jeremy chuckled. "Didn't take long for them to get to the melancholy phase. They always get there, sooner or later."

Wally was recalling a similar altercation at a party, fairly recently in his time-out past, but an eon ago in this life. He seemed to remember drinks being thrown at some point. He smiled at the thought.

The women returned with heaping plates, and another young woman carrying two plates, one filled with deviled eggs, and the other laden with bacon-wrapped shrimp. She sat down and said "Hi, Drew." She then looked closer at his nametag. "Wallace?"

It took him only a moment to place her. "Peggy? You, you're not giggling. You were always giggling. And it's Wally, not Wallace, please."

"And you're apparently not Drew anymore. Your nametag says 'Wallace'. We've both changed." She tilted her head. "But you look exactly the same. Same haircut, same body build, same posture. Same everything." She looked quizzically at Lori.

Wally wasn't done being startled. "You're not in my class. No offense intended, but what are you doing here? Are you dating someone from the class?" He then noticed the ring on her finger. "Married to someone?" He leaned in to peer at her nametag. "You're now, Peggy … Trueblood?"

"Yes, Derek and I are married. Have been for four years."

"But he's not in my class, either."

"No, he's working security here for a little extra money. He thought you might be here and that it would be fun to surprise you. But he didn't tell me you would have a different name."

Wally looked around the room and spotted Derek standing near an exit door, trying hard not to look too formally official, but official enough to keep problems from happening. A little bit older, and a little bit heavier, but still the Derek Trueblood from Bradford State. He glanced over and waved at Wally.

Jeremy interrupted. "I want to know about this 'Drew' thing. Did you have another life that we never knew about?"

Peggy had her mouth full of deviled egg, and Lori hurriedly answered for her. "Peggy was my college roommate. When I first met Wally, for some reason, I thought his name was Drew, I don't remember why, and that's how I introduced him to Peggy. I still call him that sometimes, sort of a pet nickname."

Derek had worked his way over to the table. "Mr. Stephens, now, I presume?"

Wally stood up. "Yes, but please, Wally, not Wallace." They shook hands. "Derek and Peggy Trueblood, this is Beth and the late Jeremy Lane. Jeremy dated a Penny in our freshman year, but that relationship was doomed from the start."

"Oh, yes." Derek shook their hands. "I heard about the mix-up in the death listings. I'm surprised it wasn't Wally here. I haven't seen him in six years. I thought he might be gone for good."

"And I never expected to ever see you again," Wally said. "But I am glad that you are here. Really. This means a lot to me." He stepped over to Derek and put his arms out to hug him. "I'm just surprised to see you here, of all places."

Derek hugged him back. "I'll get a chance to come back and eat with you later." He kissed Peggy on the cheek. "So, save me a seat. But right now, there's still a lot of people coming in and I need to keep an eye out. After all, that's what I'm getting paid for." He moved back to the door where he had been standing.

"I didn't get a hug," Jeremy complained.

"Hey, I wasn't going to hug a dead man. You're lucky I even touched you. Yuck." Wally nodded toward Derek. "I guess it has been six years. He was a good friend in graduate school."

"Graduate school? When did you go to graduate school? I never knew about that." Jeremy laughed. "You really did have a secret life."

"Oh, it was only briefly. Didn't really work out. That's where I first met Lori."

"And me," Peggy blurted out. She was now nibbling one of the few remaining shrimp. "Don't forget about me."

"And Peggy."

Beth asked, "What were you studying? I don't remember you having a driving passion to become something in particular, like a doctor or a lawyer. You always figured that a bachelor's degree was enough to get wherever you wanted to go."

"Psychology." Wally looked into Lori's eyes. "It didn't take with me. But Lori is a psychologist. A school psychologist. In Summerfield."

"Oh, maybe you know our son's teacher. He's in kindergarten."

Beth and Lori started talking about school activities and Wally let his eyes wander the room. He was pretty sure Cindy was going to be here. After all, she had been the shining star of high school life. The queen of it all. In his mind, everything had buzzed around her. If she was here, everything should still be focused in her direction. Like an irresistible magnet. Maybe she had moved on from her high school circles, though. Maybe she had continued to soar higher in the heavens. And high school was just a blip in her rearview mirror. Maybe she ....

There she was, across the room, talking with only two other women from their class. They were familiar to him, but he couldn't even recall their names. Not from this distance anyway. There was no magical halo around her, like there would have been in the romantic comedy movies.

She was just another former classmate, talking with other former classmates.

She had not gotten fat.

She had not gotten wrinkles.

She had no gray in her hair.

She was stunning in a slim red dress that seemed made just for her. Maybe it had been, he didn't know. His clothes were all from the comfortable, on sale again, marked down again, rack. But she was no longer the pretty girl from high school and college. She was a full-blown beautiful woman.

Jeremy muttered, "I see you found Cindy."

Lori turned around to look and her shoulders sagged slightly.

"Yes, Jeremy," Wally said, "but as you pointed out earlier, I am already with the most beautiful woman in the room right now." Since she couldn't reach Wally, Beth punched Jeremy in the shoulder again. "Except for Beth, of course." Lori tilted her head at him, as if what he had said was more meaningful than she had expected. Their eyes met for a moment, and both of them smiled at the sudden realization.

He looked back at Cindy and found her staring at him. Glaring at him. Not as in "I am so happy to see you", but as in "what the hell are you doing here?" Uh-oh. She excused herself from her small group and made her way in the direction of their table.

As she was approaching, Wally turned to Lori and grabbed her hand. "Please believe this. I am here with you and I want to be here with you. I don't want to be anywhere else. Please believe me that I want to continue to be with you."

Before Lori could respond, Cindy was at the table.

CHAPTER 55

"Wally." Cindy's voice was low with an edge to it, a little icier than Wally would have hoped. "So, you're not Drew."

"Uh-oh," said Jeremy out loud. To his wife, he whispered, "I should really have had a secret life and used a different name when I was younger." She punched him in the shoulder, much harder than she had hit before. Much, much harder.

"Hi, Cindy." Wally's voice was higher than he wanted it to be, almost cracking out of his upper range. With effort, he managed to lower it. "How are you doing? Long time, no see?"

"Long time, no see," she agreed, but her voice was even colder this time. "What have you been doing?"

"Hi, Cindy," Lori interrupted, trying to draw attention away from Wally.

Cindy turned to her and her voice thawed slightly. "Hi, Lori." She even smiled a little. "I am glad to see you. I still like you." There was an emphasis on the "you".

Beth took Jeremy by the arm. "Let's go find something else to eat."

He glanced at her plate. "But you're still half full. And this is getting interesting. Could be the best part of the night." His eyes were begging her to let him stay.

Now Beth's voice was filled with steel. "Let's go find something else to eat. Now."

Jeremy knew when not to argue anymore and got up. "Bye, Cindy. See you later." But Cindy's attention was focused elsewhere.

Lori also stood up and slapped Peggy on the shoulder. "Come on, get some more deviled eggs before they're all gone."

Peggy had been finishing her last shrimp, oblivious to the tension at the table. But the mention of more deviled eggs got her attention. "And I'm all out of shrimp, too."

As they left, Cindy dropped into an empty seat.

"So." The "so" was drawn out over several seconds. "Who are you? You can't be Drew. You look exactly as he did the last time I saw him. I mean exactly. And nobody can stay exactly the same for six years. You do look like an older Wally. And that's why Drew always reminded me of you. He looked like an older version of you."

"Well ...." Wally started and then stopped. Completely. This was not the reaction of his dreams. A completely understandable reaction from Cindy, of course, but not the one of his dreams.

Cindy turned to follow Lori walking away. "But Drew was the one that knew Lori. Not Wally Stephens from Summerfield High. Wallace Stephens, I guess. So, once again, who are you?"

"Would you believe I have a slightly older cousin named Drew, who people say could be my identical twin?"

"Do you?" The glare was becoming glarier.

"No." He took a deep breath, and tried to start again. "And I really wouldn't try to pull that one over on you. Not after what we went through.

"I'm ... Wally. From high school. But, for a while, ... I was Drew." He licked his lips. His mouth had become awfully dry.

She tilted her head. "You had better explain." Her voice had returned to ice. "I am listening."

His saliva was completely gone. He licked his lips again. "You're not going to believe this, heh, heh." He tried to laugh, but it came out as an uncomfortable gargle.

"Try me."

"I went back in time." Her eyes widened, but she hadn't chewed his head off. Yet. "I went back in time to ...." He didn't think telling her that he went back in time to, um, have, um, sex with her was a smart thing to say. At least right now. "I apparently went back in time to save the Weidenbach sisters." That's how it ended up anyway so that at least was true.

Her face softened. Slightly. "But what, how, I mean, huh?"

He finally sat up a little straighter on his seat. "Do you remember that wooden chair in my apartment?"

"Yeah, the one you told me never to sit in?"

"That's the one. I can't explain it -- no one can, so don't ask me how it works -- but I sat in that chair and someone pushed a button underneath, and I went back in time. To when you met me at Bradford State."

She was becoming more intrigued, and, more importantly, less angry-looking. "A chair. And you said someone pushed a ... button. Who was that someone? Lori? One of the Weidenbachs?"

"No, no, I met her at Bradford, just like I ran into you. Do you remember Vern Sheffield?'

"Do you mean that sort of weaselly guy, from class? The one who kept getting degrees and didn't want to go out into the real world? That Vern Sheffield?"

Wally nodded. "That Vern Sheffield. Dr. Vernon Sheffield, now, as a matter of fact. He's the one that had the chair."

"A chair." She shook her head. "I'm not saying that I buy all this, though it does sort of make a cock-eyed sense, of a purely bizarre fashion, but why did he pick you? You, of all people?"

"Because, six years ago, I told him to." Wally spread his hands. "Since I was the one that had been there, I was the one that he had to find to send back."

"You." She shook her head again, but it wasn't helping to clear anything up. "You didn't know anything about the sisters till I told you. You thought it was just one wacky landlady."

"I didn't know till then. I guess I just had to meet up with you to find out about them. And that turned out to be the real reason I was back there."

"Is that the only reason you 'had to meet up' with me? Just to find out why you were back in time?" She sat back and crossed her arms. "I.... I really liked you. And I thought you really liked me. You were still shy and awkward and not what I thought I was looking for. But you were nice, and I trusted you. And you rescued me from that Officer Miller. I was falling for you. You jerk."

Wally heaved a deep, deep sigh. His original idea had worked. But it was not working out. He didn't say anything.

Cindy asked, "So what did you think you were going back for?"

Wally looked around the room until his eyes fell on Lori at the appetizers table. "It wasn't like I was going back in time to do anything dramatic or earth-saving, like fight dinosaurs or aliens, or fight dinosaurs and aliens. It was purely selfish. I wanted to change my life, to change what I would be at this reunion." He recalled a conversation with Dr. McElroy. "I needed a time-out from my life to discover where I was going and what I was going to be, and what I really wanted out of life. A pause before going on with everything. Going back six years was my time-out."

Cindy followed his gaze. "Did Lori know? About you going back in time? And everything? You didn't tell me, you told her. She was the one that pulled you out of my room that day, at the end."

He nodded. "I had a program on my laptop that sometimes told me what I needed to do. It told me to tell her, and then later, Vern. She was the one who had to get me back to my own time and to meet me back here. She had to help get Vern ready to send me back in the first place. The program told me to tell her." He was starting to feel miserable again. "And that I couldn't tell you."

"You just left." Now she didn't look angry, just sad. Very sad. "You left and didn't say good-bye or anything. All of a sudden you weren't there anymore. And I couldn't find you. Anywhere. The sisters said you had told them you were leaving, but you didn't tell me."

"That's why I came to your room that day." Now he was pleading for some recognition of the relationship they had started to develop. "To tell you I was going. My program said I had to leave by a certain time. But Miller was there, and things sort of went to hell. And Lori knew that I had to leave right away, at that moment, or I would never get back, to be here now."

"Would it have been so bad, to have gotten stuck at that time? Maybe we could have been together, to have made a life together?"

This time Wally took a deep breath in. "Believe me, that would have been a dream life for me.' And out. "But I had a different life that I had already lived for the next six years. My life was already being lived. I can only change from this point on."

Cindy sat back. "Wow. That is some story, one that you could have been practicing for a long time." Wally scratched at the table. "But." He scratched with both hands. "But. It does explain everything. You did completely disappear. I even went to try to find you, as Wally. I saw you at a distance in a mall, but you still seemed almost as dorky as high school, and you definitely weren't Drew, so I didn't approach you." She smiled, for the first time in a long time. A genuine smile. "I assume that none of this would have made any sense to you at that time. And, if I had talked to you, you would have thought I was nuts."

Wally wanted to say that he would never have thought she was nuts, but, yeah, he probably would have thought her story was crazy, and would have slowly backed away from her. And he may never have then wanted to go back in time to see her. "It was probably a good idea not to have talked to me then."

Lori was coming back to the table alone -- Peggy was probably still counting shrimp -- and she stopped ten feet away. She looked in, waiting for some sort of signal, whether it was safe to return or if she should still stay out of range, to make sure she didn't get hit by any stray missiles.

Cindy noticed her and waved for her to come in and sit down.

Noting that the tablecloth was not as blood-soaked as she expected, Lori asked, "Are you guys okay?"

Wally shrugged, but Cindy said, "Lori, Wally just told me a fantastic story about what he was doing six years ago. I have one question for you. Is it true?"

Lori looked at Wally and he nodded. "If he told you about going back in time as a graduate assistant named Drew Wright, and then having to leave abruptly, then that is true. If he told you something about fighting dragons and aliens, then I don't know anything about it."

"Dinosaurs," they both corrected her.

"Dinosaurs? Then I definitely don't know anything about that."

Cindy closed her eyes and shook her head. "Someday, the three of us are going to have to sit down for a whole day, and you are going to have to tell me everything about what went on. And I mean everything."

She opened her eyes again. "Wally -- it feels funny to call you 'Wally' when you're sitting here looking like Drew -- Wally, I have moved on with my life." She looked across the room to where Derek was talking with someone who first just looked familiar to Wally, before he suddenly recognized him.

"Steve? Steve Getty? He wasn't in our class either. What is he doing here?"

Cindy smiled a bigger smile than she had yet displayed. "Steve is my plus-one. He and I are engaged." She leaned across and took Wally's hand. Their first contact in what Wally was going to have to think of as six years. "He was there. After everything that happened. When you weren't. When you were gone."

Wally recalled looking back for the last time and seeing Steve sitting next to her, talking with her. Providing comfort. Finding out how she was feeling and how she was coping. Steve had been there for her and Drew hadn't.

He smiled at Cindy. "I'm glad. Steve's one of the good guys. I'm happy for you. I mean it."

Cindy stood up and turned to Lori. "I'm happy you're here with Drew, I mean, Wally. Wallace." She rolled her eyes and chuckled. "I never knew that. Take care of him. He's basically also a good guy and you're good together. You're right together."

Lori got up and they hugged. Cindy left, crossing the room to join Derek and Steve.

Lori sat back down and tentatively asked Wally, "Is your heart broken?"

Wally met her look with a smile of what surprised him was relief. "No. No, it is not. I'm, I'm more saddened that I disappointed her so long ago. She did mean a lot to me and I'm deeply sorry she was hurt. But she never meant as much to me, both then and now, as someone else. So no, my heart is not broken."

He looked into her eyes. "Not unless, you tell me that you never want to have anything to do with me."

She took his hands in hers. "I am not a rebound girlfriend. I want to know that this is because you want to be with me, not because your true love has dumped you."

He squeezed her hands back. "I want to be with you. I have ever since I first saw your smile, but now I can feel more joy in it, because I won't feel I owe it to Cindy to be with her. I just thought that being with her was supposed to happen, but I know that this is where I really want to be."

Peggy came back to the table with a glass of something and a plate full of something else. "They were out of eggs and shrimp. So got something that looks like, like, I don't know what it looks like, but I took a bite there and it was pretty good, and, …, oh, am I interrupting something? A moment, maybe?"

Jeremy and Beth came up right behind her.

"Is it alright to come back? I see Cindy has gone and you're still breathing. Or should I notify Maria to add a name to the 'No Longer With Us' part of the program? You've got to tell me what is going on between you two." Beth punched Jeremy several times, really hard. "Oh, oh, I guess Cindy is no longer the topic of discussion."

EPILOGUE

Doctor Vernon Sheffield walked through his lab, whistling a happy tune, something about meeting you at the fishing hole, reminiscent of the same ringtone he had on his phone for at least the last six years. He punched a button on one of the machines, briefly looked at the message that came up, and clapped his hands happily. He pulled another lever that blared a horn and threw confetti out of the top of the machine.

"Great, great. I've been saving that for quite a while. It's about time for a celebration."

He danced a little jig to the side door and entered the back room, the room that Wally had never seen. He returned, carrying a wooden chair, remarkably similar to one that used to sit in the middle of the lab.

"Hah." Sheffield was used to talking out loud to himself, particularly when Lori wasn't here, but, to be honest, her presence hadn't always stopped him either. He set the new chair down where the other one had been.

"Did everybody think I have been wasting the last six years, not doing anything, when I had a perfectly good model to work from?" He took a rag from his back pocket and began polishing the seat. "Now. Aha, the question is not now, but when.

"When?"

ABOUT THE AUTHOR

After writing reports as a school psychologist for 42 years, Kevin Creager pursued a second career in writing what he wants to write. His first book, *We Cuss a Little: The Life and Times of a School Psychologist*, humorously, but honestly tells stories about his career. The second book, *The Body on the Roof*, is a small-town mystery relating the efforts of the local police to solve the death of a local teacher.

NOTE FROM THE AUTHOR

Word-of-mouth is crucial for any author to succeed. If you enjoyed
Time Out!, please leave a review online—anywhere you are able. Even
if it's just a sentence or two. It would make all the difference and
would be very much appreciated.

Thanks!
Kevin Creager